FAST
AND
FASTIDIOUS

FAST
AND
FASTIDIOUS

A NOVEL

R.M. CALDWELL

HARPER PERENNIAL

NEW YORK • LONDON • TORONTO • SYDNEY • NEW DELHI • AUCKLAND

HARPER ● PERENNIAL

hc.com

Originally published in Australia and New Zealand in 2026 by Moa Press.

FIRST U.S. EDITION

Designed by Jamie Lynn Kerner

Title page and text break art © Getty Images

Library of Congress Cataloging-in-Publication Data has been applied for.

ISBN 978-0-06-347707-0 (pbk.)

Printed in the United States of America

26 27 28 29 30 LBC 5 4 3 2 1

FAST
AND
FASTIDIOUS

PROLOGUE

"YOU'VE LOST, LUCY. PUT THE GUN DOWN AND YOU MIGHT GET OUT OF this alive."

He was lying. Even she could read that as plain as day.

But what other choice was there?

Even if she jumped, the road would likely kill her at this pace, let alone the rocks below.

There was no answer. There was no time.

She lowered the rifle to her side.

CHAPTER 1

WHILE IT MAY FOREVER BE DEBATED WHETHER THERE IS AN OBJECtively correct way in which things should be done, Miss Lucy Elliot held firmly in the belief that there was. That she was born to a good family, both in heritage and fortune, no doubt fostered this sentiment. Lucy strove to be a paragon of proper and precise behavior—in every way she could achieve.

Had this attitude manifested itself merely in social graces, she might have spared her parents a good deal of apprehension, but it reached into all areas of her life, even those where no rules previously existed. Her slippers had to be one-third of the way down from the head of the left side of her bed (an optimal position for rising), eggs poached for an exact duration (for optimum texture), and cards held fanned in an angle no greater than 120 degrees (to best facilitate open play). She eschewed lace handkerchiefs (impractical) yet insisted on always carrying a linen one (versatile). Her parents might have cheerfully dismissed these requirements as childhood whimsy had not Lucy continued to back them with earnestness and well-supported facts.

Her meticulous nature extended to the mechanical world. For instance, it was not enough to know how to *play* the pianoforte—Lucy frustrated her music tutor by being vastly more interested in the internal workings of the instrument than in the artistic subtleties of playing.

While Andrew and Alice Elliot found their youngest daughter's behaviors concerning, she placated them with her otherwise good-hearted and thoughtful nature. She was polite and pleasant on all occasions but for those where her internal ordering conflicted with the arbitrary rules of society.

This was exemplified in a tale that her mother delighted in retelling, despite her father blushing beetroot if it resurfaced at social occasions. At the age of ten, Lucy Elliot was presented with a gift from her wealthy aunt. It was an ornately crafted replica of a coach carriage, complete with crossbar and spring suspension. While her aunt was concerned that the lack of horses might be upsetting to a ten-year-old, Lucy was thrilled by the gift and thanked her aunt with excessive enthusiasm. She was left to play while the adults conversed. When they next looked in on Lucy, it was to discover—to the utmost dismay of her aunt—that the floor of the conservatory was now laid out with row upon row of neatly dismantled coach pieces.

"I just wanted to see how it worked," a tearful Lucy tried to explain as she was sent to her room by her father.

Whether it was fierce determination to complete her task, or youthful indignation, Lucy waited until the adults were walking the grounds to defy her confinement and descend to the conservatory once more. Upon their return, the adults discovered Lucy sitting proudly with the coach perfectly reassembled.

"You've put it back exactly like it was," her aunt had exclaimed with surprise and more than a hint of pride.

"Not exactly," Lucy corrected her. "Now the suspension works properly."

This was by no means an uncommon occurrence in Atherton Manor in Lucy's youth. Her parents had hoped her quirks might soften with age, but now, at twenty, Lucy was as upright and proper a daughter as any manor estate might hope to produce. So firm was her sense of propriety, in fact, that her parents despaired of ever finding a suitor to meet her exacting and esoteric nature. She was highly intelligent yet displayed a focus that excluded all else; kindhearted yet earnest to the point of discourtesy; and expert in the theory of social rules yet ill at ease in their practice. Presented with the contradiction that was Miss Lucy Elliot, there was much speculation as to what manner of fortune she would find.

Thus, few who knew her could imagine that she might be found, sometime after midnight on a full moon, covertly reentering Atherton Manor well after those within were fast asleep. Nonetheless, there she would be, squeezing through a ground-level window into a dimly lit kitchen in a most improper manner.

What, they might wonder, had so altered the scrupulousness of Miss Elliot?

The answer was simplicity itself to those who knew it yet quite alien to those who did not.

Lucy Elliot had found the Night Races.

CHAPTER 2

THAT THERE HAD ALWAYS BEEN RACING IN SOME SHAPE OR FORM WAS not in doubt. The ancient Romans were known for chariot races in the Circus Maximus and even now the Rome spring carnival ended with horse races through the streets. Though only a little older than Lucy herself, the annual races of the Oaks, Saint Leger, and the Epsom Derby were well on their way to becoming institutions.

Night Racing was different. Its origins were fiercely debated, but no definitive conclusion had been reached. Among higher society (at least those within who acknowledged its existence), it was considered distasteful and its invention placed squarely on the shoulders of someone else. The English blamed it on the Welsh, the Welsh on the Irish, the Irish on the Scottish, and the Scottish on the English. Some labeled the whole thing a creation of that uncultured, fledgling nation, the United States of America.

There was equal variation of opinion among those who were enthusiasts of the races, though from the opposite position, each insisting it was *their* nation that originated it and not another.

Irrespective of its lineage, there was a purity of essence to the affair. Two coaches at a time would race each other around a strip of road. The first across the line was victorious. All manner of other rules and variations might be agreed upon by those racing, but the key points were set in stone.

Like the hours in which they took place, the Night Races were a thing of shadows. Meetings were arranged and spread by word of mouth. A code of honor and secrecy covered all those involved.

It was not written law or codified doctrine, more a collective understanding. To those involved, the ways of Night Racing were every bit as sacred as the laws of the empire.

That a young lady as proper as Lucy Elliot should not only find herself in such a world but also indeed find a home there, was a proposition that might confound a sound thinker. Lucy herself had pondered over this seemingly unexpected element of her nature.

Her introduction into the racing world had come by accident. One evening, some months after her eighteenth birthday, she had suffered from a restless night, as she was wont to do in the event of a full moon. It had been an unusually hot summer in England, and Essex, swept by winds from the Continent, was no exception. She threw off her bedsheets and minutes later was strolling in the gardens of Atherton. It was there, illuminated only by moonlight, she saw a group of four or five exiting the north wing and heading across the field. There was a muted but excited chatter among the group, three men and two women together in what struck Lucy as a scandalously casual fashion. In the still night she could make out the familiar and distinctive Irish lilt of Molly, a maid attached to the kitchen. Lucy found herself torn. It would be proper to wake the appropriate staff and give chase to these absconding servants. And yet, if there was a good reason for their going and no ill intent meant, it would be most improper to ruin several reputations and careers over a misunderstanding. She therefore contrived to follow them herself to ascertain the precise nature of their activities and to take appropriate action once she had obtained a fuller perspective.

After half a mile of pursuit, all the way certain she would be spotted in the open fields, Lucy trailed the mysterious party to a walking path through Broaks Woods. First her ears, and then her eyes, picked up signs that the group was heading toward a much larger gathering. Whatever her imagination conjured (for even the most rational of minds cannot resist invention when walking on a moonlit night), Lucy was wholly unprepared for the sight that met her as she came upon a roadway clearing.

Dozens of people, both men and women, stood in groups, chatting and laughing, illuminated by torches and lanterns. It took a moment for her to realize that the five coaches, each of a unique style and construction, were not merely the vessels used to transport the masses there but were also, in fact, the purpose for the gathering itself. Each coach was on display, wheels and horses being discussed in technical terms, paint and fluting admired, owners and riders boasting of their speeds. Lucy had seen many a coach and carriage, but these were something different. The quality and decoration of a coach for transport might represent wealth and standing, yet here the coach itself was the subject of praise, an artwork to be appreciated—and used. She could tell by the health and stature of the horses, and the sturdy-looking reins and axles, that these coaches were not built solely for decoration.

They were built for speed. For handling. For racing.

As she stood, still taking in the spectacle, she saw several faces she knew. Mr. and Mrs. Easton, a wealthy merchant couple from across the river. Mr. Jacobs, a store owner from Halstead. And more than a few servants who seemed familiar from visits to other houses. Molly was chatting excitedly with a group of other young women, one of whom appeared to Lucy to be impossibly similar to Anne Mayhew, the daughter of Lord Mayhew. It was quite inconceivable they should be conversing in so casual a manner. But before Lucy could contemplate this further, a voice came from her left.

"Are you here for the races, love?" came a strong Scottish lilt.

She turned to see a man, roughly dressed in breeches and a filthy shirt but topped with a cheerful smile and shocking red hair.

For a moment the question hung in the wind, and Lucy was suddenly aware of the importance of her reply. Somehow a restless moonlit night had led to a turning point in her heretofore ordered and neatly prescribed existence. And yet even as she considered the ramifications and the propriety, she knew there could be only one answer.

"Yes," she had replied. "Yes, I am."

CHAPTER 3

SOME TWO YEARS AFTER THIS PECULIAR DEBUT, LUCY WAS ONCE AGAIN walking through the moonlight toward the forest. Now, however, she was a far cry from the curious and naive young woman who had gone exploring against her better nature. In the time since, she had become a steadfast regular, an aficionado, as the suave Spaniard Dante Torres had once quipped. While the comment had made her blush at the time, she could scarce deny its accuracy. She seldom missed the Night Races, and even then only because of uncontrollable events, such as a family visit to relatives in the north or the untimely contracting of an autumn fever. The seasons also played their role, and in recent years the winter months had been unfavorably frosty, causing the races to be suspended for intolerable months.

Lucy had never paid much attention to the lunar phases, abstracted as they were from the practical calendar, but now she was acutely aware of its wane and wax in the sky. The Night Races were always held at the full moon, the English lanes ghostly but visible to the racers and spectators alike.

The frosts of winter had departed, but there was still a chill in the air that night. Lucy pulled her coat tight around her as she walked along the path. Molly's wool cape, with several patches visible even in moonlight, seemed barely sufficient to repel the night, but the Irish girl was of hardy stock.

"I heard Dante and his crew are back," she offered casually.

"I do wonder where they spend their winter," Lucy mused.

"Spain, I suppose."

"Torres is an exile, Molly. And Spain is under the rule of Napoleon."

"Oh," the girl replied, and was silent for a time as they walked.

Lucy still pondered her curious connection with Molly. It was only occasionally they would encounter each other in the house and pass with a formal nod. The Night Faces were a different world, and those worlds were not to entwine. The whole district—for all Lucy knew, the whole country—was populated by a strange group of friends, acquaintances, and rivals who were aliens to one another for all but one night a month. There was a kind of magic to that, augmented by the moonlight, though a sensible woman like Lucy dismissed the notion of magic as anything but artistic license. Yet her friendship with a woman close to her age and so vastly below her station certainly felt like an impossibility in the natural order.

It was only on certain issues that Lucy was reminded of their disparate stations. Molly's work kept her busy, and she scarcely had time for reading newspapers and learning about the world. Though, in fairness, Lucy's father was discomfited by Lucy's fascination with studying the periodicals.

"I don't know why you read those things, Lucy," he'd protested. "The nature of trade policies with France is hardly the type of conversation that will acquire you a husband."

"I have no intention of conversing in such a manner," she had replied. "But it can hardly be a disadvantage to know what fashions and styles might be influenced by a decline in textiles and fabrics. Or how the mobilization of troops might affect the regiments' attendance at balls. Or indeed how these new carriage designs might improve our travel time on visits."

Andrew Elliot had sighed and shaken his head as he always did when he had resigned himself to defeat, or when he ended a disagreement with his daughter, though in practice these two situations amounted to one and the same.

"It will be good to see Dante and his crew race again." Lucy broke the silence between her and Molly, hoping her earlier correction had not offended.

"It will." Molly nodded keenly, able to brush off curt comments as easy as the cold. "I wonder if Ulcha will be on messenger again."

In the Night Races, each coach seated two competitors: one the driver, responsible for controlling the horses, and the other the messenger, watching the lanes and the other coach, calling the turns and anything the driver might have missed. Dante Torres was a driver. Ulcha was his messenger.

Lucy could understand why her friend found the messenger fascinating. Even in the world of Night Racing, seeing a woman racing seemed improper to Lucy, but then Dante's entire entourage was as motley a crew as seemed possible.

Just as that thought crossed her mind, Lucy Elliot walked into the race clearing, and the very group she had been imagining stood assembled before her in the lantern light.

CHAPTER 4

THERE WERE FOUR COACHES ASSEMBLED IN THE CLEARING, SUGGEST-
ing two races for the evening. Two of them Lucy did not recognize—
probably out-of-district coaches come to test themselves. Such
wayfaring was not uncommon, especially among those from
districts where the authorities were less forgiving of such noc-
turnal activities. The solid, smartly trimmed coach apart from
the others was that of Lord Rathbone. In the Night Races all were
equal, but the nobleman never could shake the air of superiority
that clung about his well-dressed form. His coach was expensive,
the best that money could buy, with a team working busily on the
wheels and tending the horses. Rathbone enjoyed the speed of
the chase as well as any racer, but many also believed that, for all
he loved a challenge, he loved himself just a little more.

The fourth coach belonged to Dante Torres. What it lacked
in grace and elegance, it exceeded in efficiency and power. Every
curve and join, every bolt and connection served a purpose. It was
a coach stripped back to the very essence of what a coach should
be. Yet it could not be called rough or haphazard. A great deal of
time and care had gone into crafting the machine and keeping it
in top condition. Lucy could see not a single chip or flake in the
paneling, nor a tear in the canvas. It was not by chance that Torres
had seldom been defeated in the time he had raced.

As Molly walked ahead, eager to observe the newcomers,
Lucy took time to examine Torres's coach for changes. Though no
stranger to mechanical design upon her introduction to the Night
Races, the intervening years had been filled with a desire not

merely to observe the races but also to understand them. Nuts and bolts, wheels and axles, timber and iron. Lucy could tell someone a great deal about any coach just by observing it from a distance. She could tell them even more if she was permitted close inspection. Given the opportunity, she would tell them about it well past their level of interest in the subject.

"Dual-balanced suspension springs," came the thickly continental voice from behind her.

Lucy stood from her crouch and turned to face Dante Torres. He was a man of conflicting impressions, bearing both the physique and dress of a workman, and the self-confidence and integrity of a noble. His hair was short and dark, his mustache and beard trimmed to a fine point. Though the British weather had tried its hardest, he still retained a faint shade of the tanned skin that came from his homeland across the channel. When he spoke, his voice suggested neither kindness nor contempt, merely a cool practicality. Though his exile was known, no investigation had offered any further intelligence about his past; however, it was murmured among the other racers that Torres was a man whom the heat of passion and the winters of the world had forged into hard steel.

Lucy rose to what she knew was a challenge. "Dual springs will lose you speed on hard turns."

"Not if you can counter with acceleration," he replied, inscrutable.

"You'd risk losing control."

"Control is one of the many things that I do not lose."

"Is this what you were working on over winter?"

"Among other things," he replied, nodding politely and moving away.

How and where Torres and his team spent their winter months were a mystery to racers and observers alike. While other faces were familiar in the daytime world, Torres and his people were like fairies, appearing once a month under the full moon, then disappearing back to their secret groves. Lucy suspected it was no incidental thing that the group was seen this way. It was an image they cultivated, an edge of mystery that made them that bit more infamous among fellow racers.

She watched as Torres crossed to a log where Ulcha was sitting quietly. It was said the young woman was Irish, likely another reason why Molly was drawn to her. Perhaps it was through her that Molly imagined herself in a coach seat, speeding down a moonlit lane. While Lucy had certainly entertained thoughts of such a ride herself, she found Dante's messenger more unsettling than intriguing. She kept her black hair unfashionably short and, more troubling, never spoke a single word among the crowds. Only when racing was she seen to speak to her driver and, even then, only rarely, choosing most often to simply watch the lanes, her uncanny night vision spotting even the smallest of hazards.

No words were spoken between them, but Ulcha and Torres exchanged a glance as he sat beside her.

"Did you see the detailing?" asked a deep, familiar voice.

Lucy turned and looked up to the smiling face of the man known to most as Hercules. Of all Torres's team he was the most given to conversation and the most pleasant in demeanor. He was also the least like anyone Lucy had encountered outside the world of the races, or in many ways, within them.

"He is La'a Maomao," the tall man said. "'God of the winds.'"

Lucy let the strange syllables and sounds assemble themselves in her mind.

"La-ah-mo-mo?" she offered back.

He shrugged and smiled. "Close enough."

If Torres was an exile from his homeland, his teammate was a world away. His long journey led back to London, then years on a whaling ship, then back to his homeland in the heart of the Pacific. Unlike Torres, the weather had not paled his skin, a shade that even a sun-soaked Spaniard could not hope to match. Despite the equalizing nature of the Night Races, many still viewed him as a savage and steered clear of him, not least because of his size.

But Lucy knew that it was those large hands that were responsible for the finely carved and shaped wood on Torres's coach. It was the one piece of artistic flair in the otherwise practical machine, an oddity that Lucy could not ignore.

"How was winter, Hekeelee?" she asked, careful with her pronunciation.

"Cold. Far too cold. No wonder you people have such big houses. And you're getting better at that. Hekili."

"Hekili," Lucy repeated diligently. "Doesn't it bother you that people don't use your real name?"

"Not really," he said. "I reckon it's better to be called Hercules than to have to listen to you lot tripping all over my name every day, don't you?"

Lucy began to earnestly consider this conundrum but was distracted as yet another smiling face moved into view.

CHAPTER 5

While it is commonly acknowledged that humankind has an ingrained prejudice against those they consider different to themselves, nothing gets quite so under a person's skin as to see another who sharply reflects their own traits, like a mirror in too harsh a light. In form and philosophy there would be few individuals on earth more similar than the fastidious Lucy Elliot and the technical Elsa Reinhardt.

True, they were not so alike in appearance. The most obvious difference was the pair of glasses that rested delicately on the bridge of the Swiss woman's nose. This accessory, and several other differences in style, had been points of consternation for Lucy, and she had regularly explained to others that, while they shared similarities, there was absolutely no mistaking one for another.

Yet their height and stature were such that each woman's garments would almost perfectly fit the other, in form if not in fashion. But Lucy tended toward lighter shades of dress, adjusting to the fashion of the time, currently a sleek tan cloak; Elsa, toward deeper, darker colors, usually in the form of a long coat. Both had a similar shade of dark brown hair, though Lucy had taken pains to detail to Molly that her own hair tinted gold under lamplight while Elsa's tinted red. Furthermore, a gold tint to hair was better highlighted by a braided chignon, which Lucy insisted on, whereas a red tint was better accentuated by a simple bun, which the Swiss woman stubbornly refused. Instead she maintained a long single braid halfway down her back, which swayed defiantly as she walked, every flick an affront to the cultured sensibilities of Lucy Elliot.

With such deliberate provocation to navigate, Lucy kept their conversation focused on the technical.

"I see you installed a dual-spring system," Lucy opened politely.

"A slight modification. It will improve control on uneven ground," Elsa replied, her accent faint and her English frustratingly flawless.

"You must be anxious to see how it races for the first time."

"Not at all. I have, obviously, tested it thoroughly."

"But testing is not racing."

"True." The woman's eyes narrowed behind her glasses. "In honesty, I am more at home in testing than racing."

"Dante says he can keep speed on hard turns."

"I am confident he can. At least until I can compensate for the suspension."

"Well," Lucy suggested, "a dampener mechanism controlled by the angle of the front axle could lessen the spring time. Obviously."

"Yes." The eyeglasses quivered slightly. "I do hope you enjoy the races, Fräulein Elliot."

"I believe I shall, Miss Reinhardt."

Lucy allowed herself a very faint smile that disappeared, almost immediately, as the woman walked away, her braid swaying scornfully.

CHAPTER 6

THE FIRST RACE HAD BEEN AN UNINSPIRING AFFAIR. THERE HAD BEEN some hope that the visiting coach would offer a novel challenge, but it was outpaced by Lord Rathbone. To the untrained eye it seemed a given from the start, with Rathbone pulling away from the moment the flag fell. But Lucy Elliot was possessed of sharp vision, astute knowledge, and a fine pair of repurposed opera glasses. Rathbone excelled on the straights, but the heavier vehicle lagged on the curves, allowing the other coach to gain ground. In the end it was two factors that resulted in victory: the superior breed of horses in Rathbone's possession and his willingness to drive them harder than most riders would dare. Lucy watched with some sympathy as the groom took charge of the pair, walking them to cool them down. She might even have risen to mild anger at their treatment had not Rathbone and the groom clearly exchanged words, with His Lordship nodding in understanding, patting the white horse's mane in appreciation.

"Do you think the second race will be closer?" Molly asked, faint disappointment in her tone.

"It is difficult to tell with a new racer." Lucy replied. "They seem to have stronger horses than Torres. Their driver looks sharp—I'd suggest a former racer by his size. But I don't think they'll win."

"Why?" Molly asked, fascinated by Lucy's ability to assess the field.

"Their messenger. He didn't watch the first race. He's not observant."

"Is that enough to make a difference?"

"Quite often, Molly, that is everything."

Despite her confidence in her analytical skills, Lucy did feel a pang of doubt as the race began. The visitors pulled away strongly at the start and, on the first corner, Elsa's new spring system did exactly as Lucy had predicted, turning comfortably but losing speed. Dashing through the moonlight, the coaches drew apart on the second straight.

However, in the Night Races, the only lead that mattered was the one at the finish line. As the second corner flew by, there was a collective muttering among the spectators, the lead suddenly shrinking by a seemingly impossible amount.

"Acceleration on the hard curves," Lucy whispered to herself, marveling at Torres's driving ability as, even through her glasses, she could see no loss of control.

On the third turn the distance was shortened to less than a coach length, though the gain was not quite so much as the previous one. With only one tight turn left, it seemed Torres couldn't possibly make up the distance.

"He's not going to make it," Molly gasped in disappointment, her affection for Torres and Ulcha notable in her voice.

"You cunning Spaniard," Lucy muttered under her breath.

Lucy Elliot was perhaps, with the exception of Dante Torres and his team, the only one who saw it coming. Certainly the driver and the messenger of the visiting coach did not.

As they rounded the final curve, the lead coach slowed slightly to keep its balance. As it did, there was a flash of motion, Torres and his coach overtaking them altogether. The straight run to the finishing line was on, and, while the stronger horses pulled nearer, there was no question as to the outcome.

Torres crossed the line a full two seconds before his competitor, amid cheers rising up from the crowd.

"How did he gain so much ground all of a sudden?" Molly wondered aloud. "It was like magic."

"It was, of sorts," Lucy replied. "Like the kind Oliver St. Martin is fond of with his cards. The first corner was a feint. Torres gave up ground deliberately, testing how well the coach cornered. Then on the second corner he accelerated into the turn, building that large gain. But on the third, he held back, just enough to put him close to the lead without seeming a threat. A sharp messenger would have spotted it. When they rounded the last corner, they didn't think to try a blocking maneuver. Torres pushed hard and swung right in front of them. From there it was a matter of holding ground, which he knew he could do."

As she finished her explanation, Lucy took stock of Molly's expression. The servant girl was often impressed at Lucy's analysis, but something in her stunned look was markedly out of sorts. Following the girl's gaze, Lucy looked back over her shoulder, catching sight of Torres and Ulcha nearby, listening intently to her detailed explanation.

A thin smile grew on Torres's lips, and he tilted his head with an almost imperceptible nod before turning away. Ulcha's gaze lingered longer. Lucy could not help but meet it, and an inexplicable, and therefore greatly uncomfortable, shiver ran down her spine.

The girl raised a finger to her brow, then pointed to Lucy and turned to follow her driver.

Not a word had been spoken, but the message was quite clear. *I'm watching you.*

The group from Atherton chatted softly on their way home, aware that the still night would carry their voices far. Molly engaged in conversation with an older groundsman, leaving Lucy to her thoughts, a circumstance she rather preferred, running over the races and tactics in her head. Doing so took her mind off the disconcerting impression that the messenger's gaze had left on her. Lucy was someone who preferred to be the observer rather than the subject, and while she had cultivated a connection with some of Torres's companions, she was a little uneasy about them having an interest in her.

As they approached the grounds, the chatter became whispers, the group knowing that their clandestine outing would have harsh consequences were it to be discovered. They came and went via the servants' entrance at one end of the house, away from the main sleeping quarters. It was a simple matter of leaving it unlocked, well after everyone had gone to bed, then securing it again upon return. It was a method that had never failed them until that evening.

Upon reaching for the handle, Jackson, Mr. Elliot's dresser, gripped and pulled, only to find it jammed. He tried again with more force, but it became evident that the door resisted opening. For whatever reason, one of the staff had noticed the door unlocked and, thinking it an oversight, helpfully locked it. Helpful to all but those now assembled outside in the night. Another mode of entry would need to be sought.

Lucy was already theorizing. As the person with the highest status in the group, a lady of the house, she would be best positioned to knock upon a door and contrive an explanation to her absence with the least repercussions. She would accrue some suspicion for such behavior, but an excuse would not be beyond remedy. She was about to speak when the cook, Mrs. Harris, quietly announced a solution.

From Lucy's earliest memory, Mrs. Harris had been an old woman, and in the intervening years she seemed not to have aged a day. She ran the kitchen in a soft but strict manner such that there was scarcely ever a need for reprimands. The mere thought of being on the receiving end of her tenderly announced disappointment was more than enough to keep the kitchen staff focused on the task at hand.

They would use, the cook announced, the elves' entrance. Despite the fantastical name, it was of a most nondescript nature—a small window at ground level in the kitchen. The tradition was said to have come from slipping food out to children on holidays. This had carried over to every kitchen she had ever worked in, and she had brought it to Atherton. This evening it would not be for elves but for race watchers.

As they discussed who was best to enter, Lucy realized the proximity to the house had reestablished their social order and that despite being the slimmest and spryest among them, no one even mentioned the possibility of Miss Elliot being the one to do it. But under the circumstances, she felt that practicality ruled.

"I shall enter," she stated plainly. And that was that.

So it was that Miss Lucy Elliot of Atherton found herself wriggling through a small window in the dead of night to climb off a kitchen table, circle back to the servants' door, and unlock it for their entry. She did so in fear that, should she fall or make a noise that attracted attention, it would defy any reasonable explanation.

By good fortune and natural dexterity she was able to shimmy through and descend to the floor with neither incident nor damage to her dress. Likewise, her walk through the corridors, shoes in hand, was swift and silent. The door opened, the servants entered, nodding in thanks, each going their own way in silence, the order of Atherton restored.

With rays of moonlight guiding her, Lucy drifted through the halls to her room, only feeling a wave of fatigue after she had closed the door gently behind her. She wondered briefly as to whether it was possible to illicitly enter one's own home. Before she could adequately resolve this, sleep had already taken her.

But not far from the quiet walls of Atherton, far worse crimes than the covert deeds of Lucy Elliot were taking place.

CHAPTER 7

ᒪONG AFTER THE CLEARING HAD FALLEN DARK AND SILENT, AND LONG after Lucy was slumbering peacefully in her bed, a coach rumbled down an empty lane. The moon had nearly set, the lanterns casting a narrow band of light on the path ahead. Unlike the slick vehicles from earlier that night, this was a bulky affair, built for steadiness rather than speed. The special-dispatch courier ran only on request and came with security as demanded. This evening the coach carried five men.

Jeremiah West held the reins in his weathered hands that had been shaped by a life on the road. There was not a county in the British Isles he'd not ridden through. While the heyday of highwaymen were well in the past, he still recalled a few poor attempts from his younger years. On evenings when drink and merriment caught up with him, he'd tell the tale of the young fool who stood in the middle of the road with pistol raised and the wild surprise in his eyes when Jeremiah West ran him down without a moment's pause. Not a tale of bravery, but he was a practical man.

For some reason this memory stirred in his mind as he rode and he gripped the reins a little tighter. *The driver watches the road*, he told himself. *Let others fret about such risks.*

Others, like the twitchy youth sitting next to him, who gripped the coach gun tightly as if it were the only thing keeping him on board. Not the trigger though; Jeremiah would have chewed him out over that kind of carelessness. Two guards stood at rear posts, their upright posture their only defense from sleep in the face of the black night and steady rolling roads.

The fifth man was secure inside the coach, the passenger with his cargo.

Jeremiah did not ask. He'd carried enough passengers to recognize a lawyer and a strongbox. He'd made a guess at some inheritance, and once that had satisfied him, he put the idea from his mind.

When the bell rang, Jeremiah neither paused nor turned. "Boy," he said simply.

Eager to please, or perhaps just itching for a change of posture, the boy rose and looked back to the guards who had triggered the signal.

"A coach, sir. Some way off. I can see white horses."

Jeremiah ran over the map inside his head. There were plenty of lanes that joined and divided on the path. Nothing too odd there.

"Went off a side lane, sir."

Jeremiah nodded, though he doubted the boy could see the motion.

The boy sat down, resuming his tense pose. Nervous. But disciplined, Jeremiah noticed. Nothing worse than a chatty passenger.

The bell rang again. This time the boy took initiative and stood.

When no reply came, Jeremiah shouted for a report.

"The coach, sir. It's back. Closing in."

"How far?"

"Two lengths."

"Two lengths?" Jeremiah called out angrily.

Impossible. No coach could have gained such ground so quickly. There was no shortcut that might permit it.

"Horses?"

"Two, sir. Light, trimmed carriage, but—"

"Driver? Messenger?"

The boy did not reply, so Jeremiah repeated. "Who is the driver, and is there a messenger?"

"Yes, sir. Two . . . dressed in b-b-black," the boy stammered. "They're getting closer."

Jeremiah focused on his reins, anticipating what would come next. The warning shot rang out and he held tightly for any panic from his horses.

None came. They were experienced coach horses, well-trodden on this route. They likely knew it even better than Jeremiah himself.

"Still coming, sir," the boy noted.

Jeremiah nodded. It was a shame. The guards would follow protocol and shoot one of the horses next. But special-dispatch couriers were authorized not to take any risks.

Ahead of them a familiar copse of trees rose up in the last of the moonlight. Only another twenty minutes to the port from their location.

Whether it was sharp eyes or years of instinct, Jeremiah never had the chance to tell. He spoke the instant the thought crossed his mind.

"Get down, boy!"

The boy ducked on command, and a whistling noise sped over their heads. There was a gunshot, a scream, and two dull thuds.

A rope between the trees. *Such a damn simple trick*, Jeremiah cursed. But it hadn't been close enough to catch him or the coach. Just the two guards standing ready to fire, facing the other way.

Exactly as protocol required.

For the first time in many years Jeremiah felt a chill run through him. Robbers who knew their path and their tactics. And twenty minutes from the nearest port.

Jeremiah cursed again and worked the reins. Speed was all he could offer now.

"Gun at the ready, boy. Tap warning to the passenger."

Inside the locked coach, their passenger had already heard the gunshots, already heard the scream from above. There was no doubt in his mind that the strongbox at his side was the target. He drew his pistol, checked its powder, ready for what might come next.

He heard loud cursing, felt a jolt as the coach lurched around a corner. A moment later he was thrown back onto the seat, fortunate that his pistol did not go off. A loud gunshot rang out from the front, then another. He heard the cry of a younger voice, then a third shot.

For a moment there was only the sound of horses again, and he relaxed slightly, hopeful the danger had been outrun. Then the sound of galloping hooves became a trot, and then finally complete silence as the coach came to a full stop.

The coach had only one door, bolted from the inside.

He gripped his pistol, steadied it, aimed at the door, and waited.

It was shortly after five when the coach finally rode into port, twenty minutes behind schedule. The guards yelled out wildly and remained in a panic until dressed down by their sergeant, a man of cool wits and little imagination. He questioned them tersely and looked over the coach.

Jeremiah's idle thought had indeed been correct. The four horses had known their way to port with no driver. There was no sign of a struggle or anything being forced or damaged. Nor was there any sign of the five men who had left with it.

"Send a messenger to London immediately," the sergeant ordered the men. "Tell them it's happened again."

CHAPTER 8

IF THERE WAS ONE GAP IN THE PROPRIETY OF LUCY ELLIOT, THEN ONE would expect it to appear in that most common of relationships: sisterly irascibility.

The Elliot sisters were fond of each other, but of altogether different dispositions, which caused much of their friction. Mornings were one of the occasions that provided the siblings the greatest cause to vex each other, equaled only by the opportunities of afternoon, evening, and night. Lucy rose at the appropriate time of 7:00 a.m., regardless of the season, her one variation to this being the mornings after the Night Races, when she often overslept. Her sister, on the other hand, was entirely flexible with her hours and, though the season was fast moving toward the early dawns of summer, remained clinging to her winter patterns as tightly as she did to her bedcovers.

"Breakfast is getting cold," Lucy stated with no preamble.

"Good," came the petulant reply. "It's a hot morning."

"It is only hot because the sun is up and you remain huddled under eiderdowns."

"I'm comfortable."

"You just said you were hot."

Her sister pulled back the covers and yawned. "Fixed," she replied, and curled back into her pillow.

Deciding that further rational discussion was futile, Lucy took what she saw as a perfectly logical course of action, lifting a pillow from the sideboard and tossing it at her sister's exposed head.

There was a grunt followed by a flurry of motion. Lucy discovered herself flat against the wall and holding the pillow she had just flung. Densely packed goose down proved to be an effective missile when hurled with sufficient force. Once again Lucy had been caught off guard by the fact that "sufficient force" was very definitely on her sister's list of talents.

Though only a year older, Margaret Elliot loomed over her sister and mother and just edged out her father's six-foot height as the tallest of the Elliots. She had always been a tall, thin child, but as she reached into adulthood she grew out as well as up, her parents initially fearful some illness might be to blame and that she might grow perpetually. Instead she settled in to her current frame, built like a fearsome farmwife and cursed to a life of customized dress fittings.

The Elliots were grateful that the extremes of their daughters had confined themselves to a single area: Lucy in her fastidious behaviors, and Margaret in her appearance. In other aspects of life Margaret was a mild, dutiful daughter, doing her best to fit what was expected of her. She lacked the natural dexterity for needlework and the pianoforte but worked at both diligently. She had a solid background in French and Italian and could sing well in both of them. In recent years she had overcome the clumsiness of her rapid growth and acquitted herself well at dances, though she could do little to placate the awkwardness of the partners she overtopped.

Of all the clashes of words and opinions that she and her sister had engaged in over the years, her size was the one area exempt from Lucy's critiques, through her own discernment rather than any agreed-upon limits.

I cannot imagine a circumstance where any civil person should begrudge my being five feet and four inches, Lucy once reasoned to herself. *And Margaret is no more responsible for her height than I am for mine.*

Besides, there was no shortage of other things for them to conflict on.

"Mother has news she wishes to discuss," Lucy explained. "Will you please get dressed, Margaret?"

"Meg," groaned the voice from the bed as her sister rose slowly.

Lucy briefly resisted the urge to rise to the bait and then failed utterly. "Meg is the name of a servant or a farmwife."

"A name is no more than a descriptor, Lucy. I am the same person whether I am called Meg or Margaret."

"You will not be perceived as the same person," Lucy replied, acutely aware of the importance of social perceptions and persistently trying to overcome her weakness at them.

"But in that case, wouldn't interaction adjust the perception of the person I'm talking to? We may shape how the name is perceived as much as the name shapes our perception."

"You are delving into philosophy again," Lucy protested. For Lucy, to divert an argument into philosophy was the last refuge of the intellectual scoundrel.

"Well, David Hume does go into some depth on the concept of words, ideas, and meaning."

The scale of Margaret's reading interests was of almost indecent breadth. While she would never claim to be highly knowledgeable in any field, there was scarcely a topic on which she could not be found to have some foundation. It made arguing with her both irresistible and infuriating. Lucy's knowledge was a tall, rock-solid island. Margaret's was a vast, scattered archipelago. Any attempt to push her into the sea and she would skip merrily away.

"I am quite certain," Lucy retorted, already spinning on her heels, "that no Meg I have ever met has read David Hume!"

It had not been her finest summation.

"Wait. What does Mother want to talk about?" Margaret asked.

"There is a new occupant at Elsworth Manor," Lucy replied curtly. "And we have been invited to a ball."

CHAPTER 9

For as long as Lucy Elliot could remember, Elsworth Manor had been empty. Not abandoned, for there was a groundsman in residence and a couple who lived as caretakers—the Marbrooks. Mrs. Marbrook had formerly been a nurse to the Elliot sisters, and Lucy had twice visited, so the grounds were not wholly mysterious to her. The main manor itself had seen only brief spells of residence in the past few decades, visited infrequently by Lord Harrow, an elderly gentleman who came to the country for his health but did little other than sit and read in the conservatory.

A new resident in the area was always a point of interest to the neighborhood, and the addition of Elsworth Manor to the equation had heightened conjecture. The society of the district liked nothing so much as novelty, so long as it was safe, local, and familiar. With the opportunity to see and explore the manor for the first time in decades, the ball invitation made for a high level of excitement throughout the district, accompanied by an equal escalation of gossip.

Lucy Elliot was a firm believer in entering any given situation with the maximum possible information at the ready. In short order she found herself with the knowledge of those expected to attend, the dresses they were likely to wear, and the coaches they would travel in. The order of dance she'd failed to secure, but the quartet that had been employed was one she was familiar with, and she was confident she would not be surprised.

The one point of consternation for her—a single but important consternation—was the dearth of any information regarding their host-to-be.

"Captain James Dashwood," her father said when the topic was broached. "An army man. He has been overseas in Africa, but his father has fallen ill and he's come to assess some of his holdings. It seems he shall be staying for a while and wants to acquaint himself with local people."

Lucy nodded politely. "I know all this, Father. Everyone knows this. It has been about the district for a week. But what do we know *of* him? Of his character? Of his circumstances? I feel as if the gentleman is deliberately keeping himself a mystery."

"And yet he invites us all to a ball at his residence. A mysterious man indeed."

"It's true that does conflict somewhat with any such suspicions."

"I believe that was one of Father's annual attempts at sarcasm, Lucy," her sister added.

Margaret had been sitting quietly, working on the dress she intended to wear for the ball. While the town dressmaker did much-appreciated work for the eldest Elliot sister, at times she felt the need to add additional safeguards. Mrs. Calloway's needlework could not be faulted in her accommodation of Margaret's frame, but she retained a blind spot about the forces held therein.

"I know one thing about him," Margaret noted as she finished a stitch. "He rides very well."

"And how do you know that?" Lucy asked.

"I saw him in Halstead this morning when I was buying thread. A gentleman rode past, tipping his hat to the grocer as he went."

"What manner of man was he?"

"I could make out little of him from where I stood. He wore a blue coat. Not a military uniform, though in an odd way he seemed to wear it like one."

"And you noted how he rode?"

"Yes. Well."

"That is frustratingly vague, Margaret. Many people ride well. I ride well."

"You ride tolerably, Lucy," her sister replied.

"I ride *well*," she insisted. Lucy had always taken her riding lessons to heart, learning the right way to sit, to act, to react, to mount and dismount. She was studious and precise in her equestrian activities. If only the horses were as observant of the rules, she should have no trouble at all.

"I meant," Margaret went on, "that he seemed exceptionally at ease in the saddle. There was something about the air of confidence that struck me. As if the saddle fitted him better than the coat. In any case, I asked the grocer who he was, and I was informed that he was Captain Dashwood, arranging food for the ball."

"In person?" their father interjected in surprise.

"So it would seem."

Lucy added this to the list of character traits she was compiling on the newcomer. Some of this intelligence had been provided through Sarah Mayhew of Luxton House, which was near Elsworth. Dashwood had brought with him a footman, a maid, and a cook, but no other staff. Sarah speculated (speculation was of less value to Lucy, but not without some merit) that this meant he was planning on only a short stay, while Lucy's mother believed more staff would arrive later. Lucy, with an absence of further information, wondered if they might both be wrong and that Captain Dashwood approached life in an unorthodox fashion.

"Unorthodox" was a word that gave Lucy cause to shudder. There was a right way and a wrong way of doing things, she firmly believed. The possibility that there might be *other* ways was something she didn't like to consider.

"It seems to me he is trying to make a good impression." Andrew Elliot diverted Lucy from her unpleasant line of thought. "And that he wants everything to be in order for the ball."

"Perhaps he has heard of the fiasco of the Mayhew assembly," Lucy mused. "That was certainly something to avoid." She glanced across the room to see Margaret blush before she was able to turn back to her dress. "My apologies, Margaret. I did not intend to bring up embarrassing memories."

Margaret did not reply but instead buried herself in her work. Among the various disasters of the Mayhews' first and last assembly, the most personal had been an incident during the first dance of the night in which Margaret's shoulders had been overtly hostile to her dress seams, forcing her to keep her arms close to her sides for the remainder of the evening, unable to dance or play pianoforte, both of which she had been most looking forward to.

"Well, so long as he doesn't have dogs . . ." their father noted.

The sisters chuckled lightly. Margaret's awkward accident had been overshadowed by other events, chiefly the pursuit of one of Lady Ambrose's dogs by one of the Mayhews' hounds, an aggressive chase that ended with the smaller animal plunging into a tureen of pumpkin soup. The dog was salvageable, whereas the soup (and half the supper) was not. That the attendees were subjected to an unseasonable hailstorm as they awaited the coaches meant they returned home cold, wet, and hungry, but with Margaret's unfortunate apparel accident largely forgotten.

Lucy dearly hoped this ball would have no such disasters. But in the back of her mind she felt an almost alien feeling, which most would call instinct but which she preferred to dismiss as foolishness.

Though she had never seen the man, there was something off about Captain James Dashwood. As her personality dictated, Lucy was determined to find out what.

CHAPTER 10

ELSWORTH MANOR WAS A CHARMING HOUSE ON MODEST GROUNDS surrounded by farmland. As it was not on any major thoroughfare and seldom inhabited, it made little sense to have expansive gardens and rather it was dotted with various copses, and beyond them fields and orchards tended by local farmers. Lucy noted as their coach approached that the existing gardens, while simple, had been well tended recently to bring them up to the required standard for hosting a social event.

The interior was well lit and cheerful, but not overly decorated. There was still a faint scent in the air of dust and absence, one that even the light aroma of cleaning and candles could not fully disguise. Lucy, who often found such events initially overwhelming, was grateful for the simplicity of it all.

There were already many familiar faces assembled as the Elliots entered. While decorum suggested introductions, Lucy instead found a quiet corner where she could process the surroundings in her own time. Turning down the voices of the crowd to a tolerable level was a skill Lucy had been forced to develop over time. Her debut some years prior had been a thoroughly unpleasant affair that still on occasion arose in her nightmares.

While she had been to a handful of larger gatherings before that event, such as the wedding of a cousin or a Christmas spent with family friends, that first ball was on quite a different scale. In the preparation she had been excited, being especially particular about her dress and her hair, gathering a list of guests and food and dances. As she always liked to be, she'd entered the ball

as prepared as possible. But the practical experience was something no level of foreknowledge could prepare her for.

There was talking. More talking than she had ever encountered
in a single place. Dozens of voices were speaking, each drawing her
attention, but each crossed with so many others that to focus on any
one was like trying to focus on a single drop in a waterfall. There
were footsteps, laughter, the distant sound of a string quartet. . . .
A young man had endeavored to talk to her, but she was unable to
make out his words, let alone form any in reply with so many others
drowning her out. Drowning. That was what she imagined it felt
like; inundated by so many other voices, so much information, that
even the inside of her head could not be heard.

It had been too noisy. And too hot. And, if anything, the
crowds insisted on getting louder and louder, each new piece of
chatter or laughter causing her hand to twitch of its own accord.
The only way to silence them, she'd concluded urgently, would be
to take one of the candlesticks and shatter the large mirror on the
wall beside her. She had almost started reaching for it before a
hand had seized hers and dragged her with irresistible force.

She'd found herself on a patio. It was dark, it was cold, it was
unknown, but the noise of the ballroom was muted by distance.
The distance gave her the space to think, to reason, to hear her
thoughts, her pounding heart. Just enough distance that she
could focus on something else.

The first thing that came to mind was to name the types of
coach, which she began to list in reverse alphabetical order.

"Underwood, Thornbrook, Rawleigh, Pemberley Cross,
Norfolk . . ."

By the time she'd reached Carrington she could feel her
breath returning to normal, her heart swift but calming. She'd
realized her eyes were closed and decided to open them.

Margaret stood before her, calm and compassionate.

"Too much talk," Lucy had explained, still gathering her
thoughts.

"We'll go to the sewing room. Nobody visits the sewing room during a ball. Once the dancing starts, people talk less."

And indeed they had. Lucy had enjoyed the dancing. And the meal. And the dresses. She did not enjoy the conversation, but she had managed, though she did visit the sewing room more than once.

When she had returned home from London, she'd done what she always had. She'd planned. There would be more balls, more occasions, more chatter. She would need to prepare herself.

Now, her mind settled, Lucy's thoughts returned to Elsworth Manor. Only when she felt she was ready did she rise and prepare to move among the guests. Lucy was not a natural mingler. Rather it was something she had forced herself to develop through time and observation. There were proper ways to do things, pleasantries to exchange and unwritten rules to follow.

Unwritten rules frustrated Lucy, and she converted them into written rules as best she could, as evidenced by a large notebook in her chest of drawers. Some she deemed reasonable. Some she deemed unreasonable but necessary: Civilized society had chosen a specific order to lay out cutlery; the fact that it was not smallest to largest was something she would suffer in silence. Where her instincts failed her, she propped herself up with this encyclopedic knowledge of etiquette and a sprinkling of topics that could be dropped into appropriate exchanges.

She had just disengaged from a conversation on the most appropriate time to start wearing summer hats (the third week of June), when she was intercepted by the smiling face of George St. Martin.

"Miss Elliot. A pleasure to see you here."

"As it is to see you. Are you well?"

"I am. Though I am pleased to see the end of winter. One prefers to get out of the house more often."

She nodded in polite agreement.

George was the eldest son of Sir Walter St. Martin, a well-respected statesman. George had inherited all the charisma that had made his father a success but less of his ambition. He was a tall, handsome, and charming man, a fine dancer and a fair hand at cards. Their two families socialized regularly, and at first his affable demeanor had been a great comfort to Lucy, who found his mood easy to interpret where those of others were more obtuse. But over time she found him less charming, for his blithe happiness was always on display, and he seemed to drift through life too carelessly for Lucy's tastes.

"Did you see the cherry trees coming in?" he asked after it became clear she was not responding further. "They shall bloom later than usual this year, I think."

"It was a long winter," she replied. "How is your father?"

"Back and forth between London all the time. Something to do with some affair happening in Europe."

"The war?" she suggested helpfully.

"Hmm. Yes. Probably something like that. I wonder if our host knows anything about it. But no, he was in Africa, I hear."

"The war affects Africa," she replied, immediately worrying her tone might have been too sharp.

Fortunately, her lack of eloquence was surpassed by his lack of acuity.

"Really? Well, he must be glad to be home from it, then."

"I have not had the pleasure of meeting him yet. Are you able to point him out?"

"Dashwood? Oh, yes, that's him there over by the mantel-piece."

Even with George pointing it took her a moment. There were three gentlemen happily chatting together. One she recognized as Ford Mayhew, Sarah's older brother. One was an older gentleman she recognized but did not know well. Thus, by process of elimination, the third man must be Captain James Dashwood.

He was handsome in a slightly rough way, his face a shade darker than the other men, suggesting his time spent in warmer climes. His hair, coat, and boots all conformed to the fashion of the season in a way Lucy found sadly uncriginal. There was, of course, a very narrow conformity that must be followed in style, but a host should endeavor to define himself in at least some way. A broader stock perhaps, or a stronger color. He bore a smile at least, a jolly one in reaction to the conversation she could not hear.

"Shall I introduce you?" George offered.

"Perhaps later. Thank you."

"Then I shall take my leave. Would you permit me to add my name to your dance card, Miss Elliot?"

She smiled. "That would be most pleasant."

George might not make for scintillating conversation, but he carried his dancing feet as lightly as he did his burdens.

Left alone, her attention returned to Mr. Dashwood. Perhaps he was more fetching than her first assessment, though it was clear he was a conventional gentleman.

Almost studiously so, she thought.

Lucy felt a rare sensation, a prickling along the nape of her neck, an uncertainty and excitement she had felt only once or twice. Felt in those moments at the Night Races where the outcome hung uncertainly between seconds.

"Almost studiously so," she repeated aloud.

But perhaps there was no "almost." His laughter was authentic. So too seemed his conversation. There, he appeared to have none of the shortcomings Lucy realized in herself. His coat was well tailored to his lean frame, but he seemed ill at ease with it, as though he preferred a looser cut. He held his glass in his left hand, while his right rested by his side, moving back and forth, with fingers tapping his thigh.

And he watched the room. Not obviously, but rather in quick glimpses, checking faces, taking stock.

"He is not what he seems."

She might have started in surprise, but the words were so close to her thoughts that at first Lucy did not notice they came from behind her.

"Mr. St. Martin." She nodded in greeting as she turned.

"Miss Elliot."

Oliver St. Martin shared little of his older brother's charm, but there was a certain presence that his physique lent him. He stood a head taller than George but was of notably lighter build and a considerably darker disposition. George was a bush in full summer bloom while Oliver was an autumn tree thin of leaves. Yet, in a way, Lucy held him in higher regard than his amicable brother. He was certainly taciturn, but always polite and never bitter that his father's favor and fortunes were placed upon his older sibling. And where his brother was often oblivious, Oliver was shrewd, a trait Lucy could not help but admire.

"Why do you say such a thing of our host?" Lucy asked.

"Why do you think it?" he countered with a thin smile.

"His manner is too studied," Lucy said. "His eyes are ever watching people's faces."

"Not merely their faces—their positions."

Lucy followed this intimation and found it to be quite true. Every so often Dashwood would scan the room as if mapping it out in his head.

"How extraordinary," she exclaimed. "I am at a loss to explain it."

"Exits," Oliver replied. "He is watching the exits. The instincts of a soldier, Miss Elliot."

She was about to ask how he discerned this, but he merely nodded politely and drifted out among the other guests, his head bobbing above his contemporaries like a buoy on the ocean.

Observing the exits, she wondered. *For threats coming in? Or for the shortest route out?*

CHAPTER 11

LUCY WANDERED THE ROOM WITH THE HOPE THAT THE CONTENTS might give her some better clue as to the nature of the new occupant, but as yet, Elsworth had not been decorated with anything more than modest furnishings. It was a charming and intimate space. While some of the larger estates were sprawling affairs, Elsworth had been constructed with an efficiency of size and flow that appealed to her practical mind. Were she to build a house to her specifications, it might well be a fine starting point. It was the perfect venue for an early-spring gathering, where the collection of torches and bodies kept at bay the cooler evening air without overheating those in attendance.

Likewise, Lucy approved of the meal—simple local fare, but well prepared and more than enough to meet the appetites of those in attendance. Again it reflected the tone of Captain Dashwood, eager to please his new neighbors but not given to unnecessary extravagance.

If there was one excess of the event, it was in the dances, the number of which was greater than at any ball Lucy had ever attended. It was well indeed that the food had been filling, for the effort of participating in every dance exceeded the endurance of every man and woman present, save Captain Dashwood himself, who insisted on remaining on the floor with an indefatigable vigor.

After a cautious testing of her dress in the first dance, Margaret had concluded her additional stitching sufficient and danced several numbers, twice with Oliver St. Martin. Such a repetition of partners would usually be cause for rumors of a match, but, constrained as they were to the limitations of her height, a certain leeway had been tacitly granted to the pair by district society.

Lucy danced first with Ford Mayhew, whom she always found a sufficient partner, though often a little off-rhythm. She then danced with George St. Martin, who could have been an excellent dancer rather than merely a good one, were it not for his habit of being more spontaneous than timing allowed.

It was not until the end of the evening that Captain Dashwood approached Lucy and requested a dance. She eyed him for perhaps a moment too long before replying in the affirmative. Her feet were weary, but she could not resist her desire to discover more about the man. If he noted her hesitation, he certainly was polite enough to make no mention of it.

There was a roughness to his hands that surprised her, from the grip of reins perhaps. Margaret had mentioned that he rode well. Yet his touch was light, almost cautious, as if gauging hers. And warm, though perhaps she was confusing the warmth for her own.

You shall have to say something presently. She cut into her thoughts. *And it must be a topic other than the texture of his hand.*

"You approve of Elsworth Manor?" he stated, relieving her anxious obligation.

"It is a fine residence. Do you plan on staying long?"

"Alas, that is not wholly in my hands. I am here at the behest of my father."

"I have heard he has been ill of late. Has he improved?"

"I fear his decline is a steady one. He was a bachelor until late in life, and he is not getting any younger."

"No one is getting younger. That's how time works."

"Quite true." He laughed. "He still has his wits but can no longer travel."

"But you can, I understand. I have heard tell you've recently returned from Africa?"

"Sierra Leone. A small place—"

"On the western coast," Lucy finished.

"Indeed." He nodded. "Have you traveled, Miss Elliot?"

"Only as far as Edinburgh, when I was fifteen. My mother had distant family there."

"How did you find it?"

"It was on the main road."

He smiled, and she breathed a sigh of relief that her humor had landed.

"Was there much opportunity for dancing in Sierra Leone?" Lucy asked.

"Alas, no. My time was often in less-elegant engagements."

"Take care with that word, Captain. There are many young women in the district in search of an eligible gentleman."

"Why do you assume that I am?"

"Eligible?"

"A gentleman." He smiled again.

In that moment, in that look, Lucy was assured she had been quite right, that there was something beneath the mask of conformity he wore so well.

"I can only speak for myself, Captain, but I should be most disappointed if you were not."

"Eligible or a gentleman?"

It was her turn to be enigmatic, as the dance circle moved on and she left him with a demure expression that belied the pounding in her chest.

When next she encountered Captain Dashwood, the dancing had concluded, her pulse had settled, and the conversation had been reviewed half a dozen times in her head. She found herself on the edge of a collective discussion about continental delicacies.

"Frustrating, I say," George St. Martin complained. "I've developed a taste over the years for Belgian hot chocolate, but now you can't get your hands on the stuff for love nor money."

"Textiles are in equally short supply. Though it is something of a boon for the local industry," Lucy noted.

"I can't wait for the whole mess to be over," George continued. "How is Napoleon doing? Surely he can't hold out much longer?"

There was an uneasy pause, and Lucy noted a flare in the eye of their host, as if the ignorance of the man was a personal affront.

"He controls most of Europe," Lucy said evenly.

"Ah. Well. I dare say we'll be able to push him back again, right, Captain?"

"I hope so," he replied, his voice cool. "For if we do not, I dare say it will only be a matter of time before he makes his way here. Whereupon I suspect your lack of chocolates shall be the least of your inconveniences."

Again there was a silence, this time more deliberate.

Captain Dashwood straightened up, visibly collecting himself. "My apologies, Miss Elliot. This is meant to be an evening of merriment. I shall take my leave to see what remains of supper. The dancing was more of an effort than a march." He bowed and smiled, the latter more forced than the former.

As he headed away, George shook his head. "I seem to have hit a nerve there. Good of him to apologize to me."

Lucy smiled but did not correct him that, in truth, Dashwood had apologized to her.

Rough hands but a light touch, she recalled.

Soon after, the men retired for brandy and cards, leaving the women to discuss the events of the evening. Margaret was pleased with how the night had turned out, extolling the virtues of both the dancing and the food.

"I was quite impressed. More than one assembly has been catered with food too rich or too sparse to be sustaining. I suspect Captain Dashwood has something of an army pragmatist in him. And he danced with you, Lucy, which was nice."

"He danced with almost everyone," Lucy said, dismissing the

comment humbly. "There were certainly enough numbers. I hope the musicians were well recompensed."

"He didn't dance with *everyone*." Margaret laughed. "He seemed quite selective."

"What do you mean?"

"Oh, I don't know. He wasn't just asking anybody is what I mean."

As talk moved on to a different topic, with Margaret explaining her dress alterations to Sarah Mayhew, Lucy turned her thoughts inward, glancing at her dance card to refresh her memory. For the second time that evening she felt a certain chill of revelation toward her host. Dashwood's dance partners had been varied across the evening, and it had seemed to her out of politeness or casual interest.

He had danced with Lucy, but not Margaret.

He had danced with Sarah, but not her sister, Anne.

In Lucy's mind she filled in his dance card, checking off names. It became clear that over the course of the evening he had danced exactly once with a lady from every household in attendance.

There were innocent explanations for this, of course, the most likely being a desire to familiarize and ingratiate himself with as many people in the district as he could. Not unheard of for a man new to the area, and a bachelor at that.

But perhaps, as he had intimated, not a gentleman.

The intention of the dancing might well have been innocent, but the process was studied, which was what drew Lucy's curiosity. *Studied.* That had been the word she had used earlier in the evening, but it no longer seemed to quite fit.

She sat in silence for some time before she found the word she wanted to describe his actions.

Tactical.

CHAPTER 12

ALL AGREED THAT THE BALL AT ELSWORTH HAD BEEN A FINE SUCCESS. The affable nature of Captain Dashwood was often at the front of discussion, with more than a few young ladies, and several more mothers, fancying future marriage prospects.

Lucy was unconvinced that Captain Dashwood had such intentions in either of the modes in which she perceived him. The charming-socialite version of him had a blithe and impermanent nature that did not lend itself to settling down just yet, and it quite vexed Lucy to see her fellow ladies pin their hopes on an intemperate man. And in considering his other mode, the one operating beneath the surface, she suspected it led to the same risky end. If indeed he had some ulterior purpose for being here, then it was quite likely that once his objective had been achieved, he would not stay.

Thus Lucy resolved to give no further thought to the curious Captain Dashwood, other than to try to deduce more of his character through memory, analysis, and supposition. As a purely intellectual exercise, of course.

Several days later, the three Elliot women found themselves at the large estate of St. Martins Hall. Mrs. Elliot and Sir Walter shared a niche interest in the practice of preserving fruit and vegetables. It was merely a hobby for Mrs. Elliot, but more an obsession for Sir Walter, who had converted a large vault in his cellar to the task of creating and storing preserves, with bell peppers being his latest passion.

"It is curious to have one's two main interests at such odds with each other," said Sir Walter. "The markets are such volatile and urgent things, always changing and short-focused. But preserves are quite the opposite. Patient and long-lasting. There is something very calming about a fine jar of raspberry jam."

"I am more inclined to plum myself," Alice Elliot offered.

"Plum. Then I must show you my latest sampling—a blend of Shropshire prune and Saint Martin, which I am fond of for reasons of vanity."

The elders departed, leaving their four offspring collected on the patio. It was a warm spring day, and the shade of a large awning was most welcome as they chatted, eventually deciding to play cards.

"It often makes me wonder what people think of our father," George spoke idly. "A politician, a businessman, a knight of the realm, and yet fussing around with his jam jars like an old maid."

"I daresay we all have our follies," Margaret said.

Oliver nodded in agreement before speaking. "In any case, I think it quite likely that his position allows him to veer into interests unavailable to those of lesser standing." He said this without glancing up from his cards. When he played at such games he tended to loom with something of a praying mantis in his form.

"Do you really think so?" Margaret asked.

"I do. A poor obsessive will be called a madman. A rich obsessive will be called eccentric."

"Come now, Oliver," said George. "It is unfair to call our father a madman, however frustrating we find his behavior."

"I said no such thing. Nor did I denote frustration. Merely that station and privilege are accompanied by acceptance. I for one am delighted he has such a productive hobby. His lemon honey is as rare a delicacy as I have ever tasted."

"Productive in short perhaps. I sometimes wish he had quite as much passion for business as he does for jam." George sighed.

As this conversation unfolded, Lucy shifted her attention

back and forth from the words to her cards. She was disinclined to partner games as they often brought with them a greater level of uncertainty than she liked. But as there were four of them, it seemed it was decided such a game should be played, and lots were drawn to decide partners. Lucy and George were paired against Margaret and Oliver. It was not her preference. George was a fine-enough card player, but he was also frivolous and selfish in how he played. He seemed to completely overlook her cues, and though one or the other of them often won a hand, as a pair they tended to score lower than their opponents. Margaret and Oliver, on the other hand, were more cautious players, neither of them of excelling skill but still rather steady and complementary.

On more than one occasion Lucy had considered that her sister and Oliver St. Martin might make a match for more than merely their height, an aspect she considered too shallow to value greatly. They were affable to each other, respectful, and clearly enjoyed the other's company.

Sadly there were two unassailable obstacles to such an outcome.

The St. Martins were of a higher station than the Elliots, not that such a pairing would be unthinkable but certainly enough to create pause for thought. The second obstacle was of a more complicated nature. As the two Elliot heirs, Lucy and Margaret stood to inherit a comfortable lifestyle, though by no means an opulent one. But Oliver St. Martin was in a far-less-enviable position. Through a longstanding precedent of the St. Martin lineage, the eldest would inherit the entirety of the estate. Any other sibling was to receive an endowment, but the sum had been set as fixed law three generations before, without thought of inflation. It was known that Oliver had followed his father into the markets but, as in cards, his conservative speculation would lead to slow growth. If he played those cards right, he would never be poor, but the lifestyle he now lived would not last forever. Thus he was at once a man of too high a station and too poor in prospects to make a match with Margaret Elliot, however well suited her sister might sometimes think them to be.

The proper path is seldom a fair one, Lucy thought. As if to demonstrate this, George played a card that turned their certain victory into a certain defeat, and Lucy threw down her jack of spades in frustration.

Upon completion of the hand, Oliver drew the cards together and began shuffling, cards dancing between his nimble fingers.

"I swear, Brother, did I not trust your character and that of Miss Elliot, I should suspect you of cheating." George chuckled.

Oliver laughed in response. "Nonsense. If we were cheating, Lucy should surely have noticed it by now."

Lucy blushed slightly but was gratified by the compliment of her observational abilities.

"Besides, my brother, I should not know where to start on such a scheme," Oliver continued.

"Why you should devise some manner of communication beneath the table, of course. You both have legs long enough for it."

"Spoken like a man at ease with the length of his limbs," Oliver retorted. "The space beneath the table is no safe haven to those of us of the lofty persuasion. It is in fact a place of particular peril. One sits folded in such a way that one's knees go this way or one's hips go that. To pass messages beneath this table would be akin to writing and exchanging notes on horseback."

Having completed his shuffle he placed the deck on the table, inviting his brother to cut, then shuffled swiftly one more time, placing the deck in the center. "In any case, Brother, whyever should I cheat at cards by communicating in code with my partner when there are much simpler ways to show you the fool?" He flipped the top card of the deck.

George stared down in amazement at the smiling joker.

There was a momentary pause before George burst into laughter. "Oliver, you never cease to amaze me. I should like to see you play against Captain Dashwood some time."

The sudden introduction of Captain Dashwood into the conversation startled Lucy, who had staved off thinking about him for well over an hour.

"Why do you say that?" Margaret asked.

"Father has certain connections," the older St. Martin explained. "Suffice to say he asked around about our neighbor and found out why he's here."

"To assess his father's holdings, is he not?" Lucy countered with a certainty to her voice that was not matched by her inner suspicions. She was unsure why she should defend the man so earnestly and wondered if she might be frustrated that she was about to be told the answer to a riddle before she could figure it out for herself.

"He is not," George went on. "Though it really is his father's land, his reason for being here is quite a different matter."

"A cover story?" Oliver chuckled dubiously. "Like some manner of Gothic novel?"

"Nothing quite so grand. The fellow is a gambler. Apparently quite a good one. But you're only a good gambler until you're not. He got himself into debt and trouble, and his father had to pull some strings to cover it all up. Now he is lying low for a while."

"How mortifying," Margaret exclaimed. "And he seemed like such a charming gentleman."

Lucy silently agreed, feeling a sense of disappointment heavier than she had expected. She shook off the thought, reminding herself that placing expectations on the character of the newcomer was exactly what she had so recently criticized in others.

"Well, he is not what he seems." George shrugged. "I'd be wary of him. Once a gambler, always a gambler. Now, Oliver, how about a real shuffle? I'll be watching this time."

"Well, in that case, I won't cheat this time."

The Elliot sisters and Oliver all laughed in unison, a joke that George failed to understand as he had been the only person at the table whom his brother had not just tapped with his feet.

CHAPTER 13

WHILE THE SOCIAL CALENDAR ROLLED ALONG STEADILY, THERE WAS another calendar in parallel with it. With the disappointing revelation of the mystery of Captain Dashwood, Lucy turned her thoughts to the next full moon. Spring was well in bloom, the nights becoming warmer and shorter. Warm enough that, by the time she reached the clearing, Lucy almost felt her coat was too much. Molly had come down with a light spring cold and had been convinced by wiser heads that she should stay in. Thus Lucy had walked the path in silence that evening, wondering what excitement the night ahead might hold.

Three coaches had assembled by the time Lucy arrived. Torres and his crew, Lord Rathbone, and a sleek-looking coach attended by a group of roughly dressed men she did not recognize. She wondered, from their appearance and furtive behavior, if they might be on the fringes of the law, but at the Night Races such questions were not to be asked aloud.

"Southeast coasters," came the continental accent that could only belong to Dante Torres.

Lucy turned and nodded a welcome to him.

"Built for speed on the seaside routes," he added.

"But not for durability," she mused.

The coach was finely tuned but had clearly seen better days. The wheels were new, but the frame and axles looked weathered. If it had seen serious coastal use, there would also be greater rust to contend with.

"They've come out to the country in search of easy marks,"

Dante noted with a leery eye. Torres was a man who took in every-thing but gave away little.

"How can you be so sure?"

"Because that's what we do." He smiled.

"I trust the new moon was been well spent for you?" Wherever Torres and his friends had been, she doubted it involved a life of balls and dressmaking.

"We get by, Miss Elliot. We get by." He bowed and took his leave, neither offended nor surprised by her fishing remark.

Her thoughts were interrupted by the sound of hooves ap-proaching, along with the rattle of wheels. A fourth coach rode into the clearing, drawn by gleaming chestnut horses, calm and disciplined. The coach itself was a surprisingly common affair, with little custom work to be seen. Like the coasters, this model had seen much use but had been better tended, with parts re-placed as needed. It was a coach built for utility as much as speed; one that might easily be seen on any road in the Empire. She was in the midst of assessing the wheels and trying to determine what manner of road they were best suited for, when the driver dis-mounted, seeming to pause as if waiting for her attention.

Once she finally turned that attention to him, there was no mistaking Captain James Dashwood.

Lucy's first reaction was to feel her sensibility offended. For a gentleman who was a part of her social circle to show up at the Night Races felt like an invasion of her privacy. This feeling was an absurd notion, she would readily admit; the Night Races no more belonged to her than they did to any other. Yet somehow it felt to her improper, and impropriety vexed Lucy in a way few things did.

Her inner thoughts delayed her from turning away until the opportunity for stealthy retreat was well past.

"Miss Elliot. What a surprise to see you here. Though I sup-pose one never knows who might turn up at the Night Races."

"You are familiar with the Night Races?"

"Oh, yes. I myself am not a regular, but I enjoy the escapism of it from time to time. It is nice to put one's profession into practice recreationally."

"Your profession?" she asked, realizing that beyond his rank and posting, she had given little thought to what the captain actually did in the army.

"Cavalry. Messenger division."

Her opinion of him, already on unsteady ground, lost another wheel. "Messenger? You're an army . . . mail carrier?"

"Ha. I suppose one might see it like that. But most mail carriers don't work under cannon fire. I do hope your Night Races don't run under cannon rules."

"Cannon rules!" she exclaimed.

"That was a joke." He smiled calmly. "Though every region has its own rules for this kind of thing. What can you tell me of them?"

Obliged through politeness and her attention to detail, Lucy realized she was likely the best person to explain things. She found herself expounding the local rules, of which she had gained a firm grasp over the years.

Dashwood swiftly revealed himself to be no fool on the subject, occasionally clarifying local slang but engaging heartily on the subject in a manner that Lucy seldom got to enjoy. She was on cordial terms with Torres and his team, but they were hardly the most conventional of people. Torres was terse and studiously enigmatic, Hercules was less interested in the technical side of racing, and Ulcha was functionally mute. Lucy could likely have conversed with Elsa Reinhardt had not their characters ground against each other like a downhill coach with locked axles and possibly no wheels. For Lucy to freely engage on the topic of coaches and racing with someone both as knowledgeable and interested as herself was the rarest of pleasures. So engaged were they in conversation that only the preamble to the first race broke their focus.

Lord Rathbone and Dante Torres had agreed on a large wager, and there was excitement around the clearing as it was commonly agreed that the two had the finest coaches in the district. Rathbone and his messenger were already in place, his horses fresh and ready to go. With a careful pace, Hercules led Torres's horses and coach to the starting line, seeming to give the animals even more attention than usual. Ulcha sat in silence, her eyes closed as they always were before the start of a race. Lucy had once believed it might be some kind of meditation; her current theory was that it was more about adapting her eyes to the dark road that awaited her. She was strange girl but, like the rest of the team, she fitted into her role with precision.

Once the racers and the crowd were assembled, there was a brief pause, silent anticipation falling over the clearing.

The starter sounded, and the race began.

Torres was the first to gain the lead, his deft horsemanship weaving him into an advantage. Both coaches were large, meaning less margin for error as they moved side by side, hoofbeats racing into the night.

Torres was pushing forward hard, with a pace he seldom used this early in a race. Despite their speed, he was forced to slow slightly on the corners, the dual-spring axle system still in place. Rathbone used this to gain ground on his rival, his coach steadier on the turns.

Lucy took a moment to glance to the side to the sight of Captain Dashwood tracking the action through a sturdy spyglass. There was a faint glimmer of excitement on his face among his stern concentration. He observed the race with an analytical eye, the way a scout might scan across the field of battle. This was no mere race to be enjoyed. This was reconnaissance. Lucy wondered whether her features might display such an expression when she was engaged with a race, assessing and contemplating every shift and turn.

"He's driving his horses damn hard," Dashwood noted. "He'll be overtaken in the last stretch."

"I don't believe he shall," she replied with a confident pride.

"You think so? Care to wager?"

Her mind shot back to the card game at St. Martins Hall, and the tale of the downfall that had forced the man homeward under false pretenses.

"It is not proper to wager on a race already underway," she offered politely. She almost left it there, but something prompted her to push further. "And I have heard that you are not always the safest man to wager with."

"Have you indeed? Why not a forfeit, then? No coin need change hand."

"Very well. If I am correct . . . then you owe me a ride in your coach."

"I am quite certain that can be arranged."

"And if you are correct, Captain Dashwood?" asked Lucy, uncertain what to expect.

"Then you must tell me who informed you of my proclivity for playing fate and fortune."

This suggestion caught her quite off guard. However, as she considered it, she saw no real harm in it. She was confident of her success and willing to pay the price of failure.

"Agreed."

Without another word, they returned their attention to the race. As Dashwood had anticipated, Rathbone had drawn closer with each turn; the last arc left Torres with the slimmest of margins. They were now in the final straight, a race to the line and a battle of nerves. By most measures, Rathbone should have been able to gain the lead, and there seemed little doubt he was moving up on Torres. From their observation point in the clearing, at their angle, it was difficult to say which of the moonlit coaches was closer. Only when they finally crossed the line, the horses slowing and the coaches rolling to a gradual stop, was it clear that Torres had held off his competitor by the slimmest of margins.

As the lord's grooms took the horses, and Hercules and Ulcha took away theirs, a hearty laugh escaped from Rathbone, his cheeks flushed as he gradually relinquished his grip on the reins. His excitement seemed a world away from Torres and his collected swagger, though there was a matching smile on both their faces. The two men dismounted, faced each other, and shook hands. Rathbone passed over a purse, the sum within likely meaning little to him but much to Torres and his team. Lucy wondered if they lived on the proceeds of racing. It was hard to imagine any of them making a living in other work.

"It seems," said Dashwood, "you have me at a disadvantage."

"It would indeed." She smiled.

"What is your secret?"

"A somewhat unfair one," she explained. "Local knowledge that you could not possibly have possessed. Last month Lord Rathbone overworked his horses. He took this on board from his groom. Torres knew this and played into it. He raced hard at the start, knowing that on the final stretch His Lordship would be unlikely to repeat overtaxing them."

"Noli equum praetercurrere, sed hominem."

"Race not the horse, but the man?"

"A saying. Your Señor Torres is quite a canny driver."

"He is. I sometimes wonder if we are graced with the finest race team in the isles."

"Certainly the most curious. Quite the motley crew he has assembled. But there is no denying talent." Dashwood seemed to contemplate something as he watched Torres heading back toward his team. He abruptly stepped forward, intercepting Torres as he walked. "Well raced, sir. You have a remarkable ease at the reins."

"Thank you. You must be Captain Dashwood."

"It seems my reputation precedes me."

"A man of your history comes to the county and racers talk."

Lucy wondered what Torres meant by this exchange.

"Stories tend to be exaggerated," said Dashwood.

"Stories like the emergency orders at the Battle of Roliça."

Dashwood stiffened slightly, then resumed his smile. "That story would, of course, be a classified military matter."

"Of course." Torres returned the smile slyly. "You know the best thing about the Night Races? They have their own rules of standing. A racer is a racer, no matter what. The only wagers that matter are the ones you honor here."

The intimation was clear enough. Torres knew about the gambling and hinted at a good deal more. But there was an earnest respect in his words.

"Thank you, señor. I quite agree that the skills of a racer should be commended by moonlight though they may be condemned beneath the chandelier. Some of the most impressive feats will never be written in the history books." Dashwood paused, letting the moment hang before following up. "Such as the flight of Lisbon perhaps?"

This time it was the turn of Torres to tense. It seemed he was not the only one with sources of intelligence.

"Good racing," the Spaniard answered, cooler than before. "If you make it past the start line." With an enigmatic smile he bowed his head, then glided away.

CHAPTER 14

I'M NOT QUITE SURE WHAT HE MEANT BY THAT," DASHWOOD SAID AS HE stepped back to Lucy. If he held any concern that she had overheard their conversation he did not show it. "I certainly do hope to race and, so far as I know, I have come prepared, horses, coach, and all."

Lucy nodded. Everything seemed to be in order with his ride. "Who is your messenger?" she asked.

"I prefer to ride without. I am more accustomed to solo travel."

"Then we have easily unraveled the mystery of Señor Torres's statement. Local rules insist a messenger accompany all drivers. My apologies. I thought the rule so ubiquitous that I neglected to mention it."

"I see. That is unfortunate. Had I known, I should have brought Jim, my footman. But it would be unforgivable to wait another month and leave these . . . fine gentlemen without an opponent."

"Perhaps you can find a messenger from the spectators?"

"I am quite certain I can. And assuage myself of a debt in the process."

"I do not follow."

"You wished for a ride on my coach, Miss Elliot. Would you be offended if it was a ride at speed?"

"Do you mock me?" Lucy replied after an uncomfortably long pause.

"That is in no way my intention. I am in need of a messenger, and you have demonstrated yourself to be as knowledgeable and sharp-eyed as any driver could wish for, with local experience in addition."

"You yourself will admit there is a vast distance between observing a speeding coach and racing one."

"I admit this freely. But I also believe that the best way to cross a vast distance is by coach ride."

Eye contact had always left Lucy uneasy, yet now she found she could not look away.

She wanted to ride. That she would not deny to herself. But the mystery of Captain Dashwood still left her uncertain.

She held his steady gaze, trying—against her nature—to read his feelings. Charm, absolutely. Confidence, certainly. And yet . . .

Just there. For a moment. A flicker of doubt. Of uncertainty as strong as hers.

He needs me, she realized. *And he is worried I may not choose to help.*

For all the masks he wore, this was one truth in him she saw with utter clarity.

She let out the breath she had been unaware of holding. "Very well, Captain Dashwood, I accept your proposal."

"I do believe you cautioned me about such language, Miss Elliot."

"Then let me say that I place my fate in your hands."

His eyes darkened almost imperceptibly. "And mine in yours." Dashwood gave a polite nod, strode confidently to the group of southeast coasters, exchanged polite but terse words, shook hands, then returned to Lucy.

"The race is agreed upon."

"The wager?" she asked, thinking of it only for the first time. She was certain there had been a change in his humor and felt frustration that she could not read his intent.

"Wheels," he replied casually.

"Wheels?" she exclaimed. "You have wagered your coach against theirs?"

"They're driving a Pemberley Cross. Fast, but not built for the country. And it's their first time racing in the district."

"It's *your* first time racing in the district," she countered. "And mine!"

"Fear not, Miss Elliot. I am confident in both our talents. One cannot always plan for every challenge before it appears."

"But one can try!" she said, aware that there was more agitation in her voice than she wished to present publicly. The composed mood she had briefly felt following their exchange was rapidly being replaced once more with anxiety.

Yet there was no changing of circumstances now. Dashwood was already climbing into the driver's seat, offering her a hand. She took it, stepping up to sit alongside him.

The seat was of solid construction, though well worn by time and the elements. She ran her hand along the railing, her fingers finding a small hole, which she traced with curiosity.

"Musket fire," Dashwood offered as he casually took up the reins.

She nodded without a word. The world of war was as alien to her domestic life as the races. Beyond the news and occasional shortages of certain delicacies, it seldom made an impression on her day-to-day life. For a man like Captain Dashwood, it seemed the impression it made could be swift, literal, and fatal.

He smiled. "We shall see little of it tonight, I hope." Urging the horses on, he turned them gently, drawing them up to the starting line. He glanced over at the other coach, nodding courteously to their rivals. They replied in kind, but with no pretense of elegance. They were harder men than often showed up to the Night Races, men who were here for money rather than glory.

"The first turn is sharper than it looks," Lucy said quietly. "Take it with caution."

Dashwood nodded, gripping the reins.

Lucy closed her eyes, focusing, trying to still the beating of her heart and, far worse, the clutter of her thoughts.

"Underwood, Thornbrook, Rawleigh, Pemberley Cross, Norfolk," she whispered to herself. As she opened her eyes, she saw the starter moving into position, checking the riders.

And the race began.

Lucy gripped the railing firmly as Dashwood urged the horses to start, the acceleration pressing her back into the seat. She had galloped on horseback before, but this was something quite different. Here, control was entirely out of her hands.

No. Not entirely, she scolded herself. As thrilling as her position might be, she had a vital role to play.

She scouted the moonlit road before them, the southern coach in her peripheral vision. The horses of each coach had a similar acceleration, though their lighter competition was faintly drawing ahead. Lucy marveled at how much more there was to take in from her position. The view of the ever-changing ground, the growl of the wheels, the scent of the night air mingled with dust, horses, and oranges.

Quite out of season, she pondered before she realized it came from the cologne of her driver. *Lucy, now is not the time to focus on orange-scented cologne. And something else. Lavender. Left turn ahead!*

"Left turn ahead!" she called out over the noise.

Dashwood gave a faint nod, his eyes not moving from the road. Lucy stole a glance at his expression, focused and alert with just a hint of joy. The thrill of the race.

He eased back on the reins as they entered the turn, following her earlier advice. The other cart, underestimating the angle, tilted off-balance and only a quick counterweight maneuver by the messenger brought them back under control. The delay was enough for Dashwood to take the lead, increasing their pace once more as they edged into a long slow curve.

Lucy alternated between looking forward and back, between the road and their pursuers. The ride was far rougher than she was accustomed to, but remarkably steady given the speed at which they were moving.

So this is night racing, she thought. It was like riding a silver ribbon between order and chaos. She was appalled and delighted.

"Hold course. They're gaining," she called to the captain. "We don't want them ahead of us before the next turn. We can take it faster this time."

Dashwood nodded again, shaking the reins, the horses speeding up. Despite this, they were still losing their advantage due to their heavier weight. The two coaches ended up rounding the corner side by side.

At Lucy's advice Dashwood had maintained speed, but the southeast coasters had learned from the earlier turn, again off-balance, but corrected by the messenger leaning out, bringing the wheels back down. The bold move paid off, with the visitors now in the lead, slowly beginning to draw away as the road became a long straight bordered by thickets.

"Hold close," said Lucy. "We may be able to take them on the next turn if they try that move again."

He nodded, steady at the reins.

Lucy let herself sink into the world around her, trying to think of some tactic that might give them an advantage to re-take the lead. The world began to shrink, leaving only the racers and the road; the scent of leather reins gripped tight, of horses sweating as they galloped, orange—no—something else. Oil in the whirring axles. Hot oil. Hotter than it should be?

Below the hooves and the wheels, she focused on a sound, a metal grinding, faint but sharp. And not on their coach. Her eyes darted to the others, pulling gradually away from them. It was almost impossible to see in the moonlight, but Lucy was familiar with the Pemberley Cross. She had studied the design for days after she had insisted on purchasing a technical manual in a bookshop, much to the chagrin of her mother. She could envision every part of it in her mind, linking it to the sound she could now hear.

The front axle joint was grinding in a way that it should not.

That it *could* not. The sharp overbalancing maneuvers must have knocked a link pin loose. Without it . . .

"*Hard stop left!*" Lucy shouted before the sentence could even complete in her thoughts.

Had Captain Dashwood been a driver of another profession then he might have hesitated, but he recognized the urgency of order by instinct. He tugged back at the reins, commanding the horses to slow as quickly as their pace allowed.

Not a second too soon, as the events Lucy had predicted unfolded in precisely the way the forces of physics dictated.

Unsupported by the link pin, the joint had pressed against the inner connection to the wheel, grinding down steadily. Once it was too worn to hold firm, it broke away, jamming into the left axle. The wheel locked firm, causing the coach to veer sharply with greater force than the axle could support. At full speed, the front left of the coach crashed into the ground, the rear vaulting upward, flying into the air as if tossed by an invisible giant. For a moment it seemed to hang there. Then it came down with a splintering crunch, directly where Lucy and Dashwood would have been, if not for her sharp senses and his quick reactions.

Amid the disaster, there was a merciful absence of critical injury. At the first sudden loss of integrity, the automatic release bolt had triggered on the front hitch, the horses speeding ahead of the crash, terrified but well away from the impact. The messenger had been thrown to the ground, but on his side rather than headfirst. He had rolled many times, his coat torn and ripped, skin covered in scrapes, nose and lips bleeding. But his low profile meant that the entire coach had flipped over him without contact.

The driver was even more fortunate given his position on the other side of the coach. As it flipped, he was catapulted up and over, high into the air and off the road before landing in a tangle of bushes and thorns. It eventually took the efforts of several men with knives to cut him loose, but aside from pricks and scratches head to toe, he was remarkably unharmed by his unexpected aerial journey.

Dashwood, who had first helped the messenger, then the driver, as others arrived to lend aid, returned to his coach. He seemed well at ease, as if in practical action he could drop whatever air he felt compelled to show otherwise.

"Are you all right, Miss Elliot?"

"Yes. Thank you . . . You are bleeding."

Guided by her gaze, he lifted his hand to his chin. "Just a bramble. Hardly the worst I've suffered."

His dismissal was in vain, Lucy's handkerchief already pressed to the thin red line.

"And what would be the worst?" she asked, assessing his jaw with all the clinical detachment she could manage.

"Shaving cut."

A lie. They both knew it.

"It was not how I imagined my first race," she said.

"I could not have asked for a better messenger. Few would have spotted that fault on their coach, and fewer still would have seen what was coming."

"And few would have stopped so swiftly."

He smiled, and she felt the motion beneath her handkerchief. She realized with a start how close they were standing. Too close to be quite proper, and she quickly withdrew her hand. Avoiding his eyes, she folded the handkerchief and tucked it away.

"Your coach is ruined," she said abruptly.

"Not at all," he replied, confused. "A hard stop, but it can handle worse than this, I'm sure."

"Not this one. That one." She pointed to the wreckage that was just barely discernible as a vehicle.

"That is—"

"Your coach," she corrected him before he finished. "You wagered for wheels. In the result of a crash, the surviving coach is the winner."

"District rules?"

"District rules."

CHAPTER 15

THE MOOD BACK AT THE CLEARING WAS A CURIOUS MIX OF SOBRIETY and excitement. Crashes on this scale were a rarity in the district, where greater rules and decorum were in place in comparison to some wilder regions. Lucy had heard tales of races on the back-streets of London without respect for life, limb, or property. No serious harm had befallen the team, and yet at the same time the crash had been spectacular, and everyone felt something of a shared thrill at the risks that came with the Night Races.

All pitched in to help with the recovery effort, so the moon hadn't moved far in the sky when the last of the scrap had been loaded into the cart of Mr. Kelly, the town blacksmith. If ever one wished to locate the nearest Night Race in a foreign district, the local smith was always the best place to start. Either through repairs or acquisitions of scrap, they were usually involved.

For the more technically minded, there was also the opportunity to analyze the cause of the crash.

"Front-left axle failure?" Elsa Reinhardt asked, confident in her assumption.

Lucy nodded. "A lock pin came loose."

"A flaw I believed to have been corrected in the Pemberley Cross."

"Only those made in the past three years. I suspect they hadn't upgraded their coach in quite some time."

"A shame. The Pemberley Cross is an excellent starting point for customization."

"Forgive my rudeness," Dashwood interjected. "Captain James Dashwood." He bowed courteously.

"Elsa Reinhardt," she responded in kind. "I must commend your driving, Captain. A coach like yours is not easy to manage. British Army, I believe?"

Lucy felt a prick of irritation as Elsa smiled—smiled!—at Dashwood.

"Former." He nodded. "With the war on they've been replacing and upgrading them rapidly. This one was put out to pasture, but I purchased it for my own use. Now, your vehicle, on the other hand, is far from common stock. I do not recognize its make."

"Custom-built." Reinhardt preened.

"That cannot be cheap."

"No."

As Lucy felt her temper rising inexplicably, Torres approached, eyes darting over Dashwood again. For Dante Torres, every moment seemed like a race, checking for dangers, scouting for advantages.

"Trying to get our technical secrets, Captain?"

"Merely interested. An enthusiast of the Night Races must be as invested in the coach as the driver."

"A shame you didn't get a full race on your first night in the district."

"There will be others, I'm sure."

"Some people would say it was bad luck not to cross the line on your first time out." Again there was a challenging tone from Torres, more daring than mocking.

"I'm not a superstitious man." Dashwood smiled. "But if that is your concern, it is one that can easily be rectified."

It was rare to see Torres caught off guard, but even Lucy picked up on it.

"Are you challenging me, señor?"

"My horses only ran half a circuit, but yours are more rested. I believe it would be a fair race."

"No," Torres replied inscrutably.

"No?"

"It wouldn't be a fair race. The horses might be evenly matched, but we have the better coach, the better driver, and the better messenger."

"If you really think so, then it would certainly be worth your while to accept, wouldn't it?" Dashwood didn't break eye contact.

Torres held firm, his curiosity piqued. "What stakes?"

"Wheels."

"I already have a coach," said Torres.

"Wheels and reins, then."

Lucy and Elsa exchanged a glance. It was rare indeed for a racer to wager both coach and horses.

A confident smile grew below Torres's finely maintained mustache. "Then I must accept. I'll let the organizers know."

Torres and Elsa walked off, leaving Dashwood and a visibly flustered Lucy.

"Are you all right?" Dashwood asked.

"I am," she replied, though with muted enthusiasm.

"I apologize if I was presumptive. A crash can shake your confidence."

"There is no hesitation in my being your messenger once again, Captain Dashwood."

"Yet there is hesitation?"

"Had I not been previously informed of your imprudence with gambling, I should now be given to form such an opinion of my own accord."

"I do not bet when I believe I cannot win."

"No gambler does."

"Nor do I wager that which I cannot afford to lose."

"How, then, did you come to be at Elsworth?"

"Through misfortune entirely not of my own making," he replied with a firm tone. It was clear he would follow this topic no further.

Masks behind masks, Lucy thought.

"Very well, then." She nodded begrudgingly. "Let us check over our ride." She turned and crossed to the vehicle, leaving Dashwood to follow.

The army coach seemed unharmed by the emergency stop. There was certainly some wear and tear, but Lucy ascertained that there was no risk of structural failure.

"The suspension is a little soft for country lanes, Captain Dashwood."

"Still tuned for West Africa," he explained.

She wondered how many roads the coach had traveled, and in how many countries. The wood kept record of its history through scars. She pondered idly whether Captain Dashwood had similar.

More than a shaving cut, I am sure.

Before she could follow the thought further, he arrived with the horses, the captain impressively calm given the incident earlier.

Almost, Lucy thought, as if he had intended to race again all along.

The racers were called, the crowds excited by the addition to an already thrilling evening. Third races were uncommon in the district, where it was unlikely that six coaches would turn up on one night. For a racer to ride twice in one night was equally rare, taxing as it was on the horses.

As they approached the start line, Lucy looked across to Ulcha, whose eyes were closed with an eerie calm. If Napoleon's army charged suddenly out of the darkness, Lucy wondered if that haunted expression would change even a fraction. She turned her attention ahead once more, focusing on her role.

Torres nodded to them, and Dashwood replied in kind.

There was a wave of quiet anticipation.

Then Lucy's second race began.

Both coaches came to the start line quick but steady. Lucy knew Torres would have a strategy for the race, but until it presented itself the wisest approach was simply to race to the best of their abilities. Dashwood was more familiar with the course now, and his focus was on the road and the reins. Lucy allowed her eyes to drift over the road ahead, briefly feeling a ripple of disorientation.

"The moon is in a different position," she murmured softly. "Different shadows."

The coaches built up speed, but neither was driving the horses hard, aware they had all been taxed earlier in the evening. She glanced over at the other coach, spotting Ulcha signaling and Torres nodding his head faintly.

There was a plan. But what was it?

Don't race the coach. Race the man.

"He expects us to slow on the first corner. But you know the track this time," she said.

Dashwood nodded, gripping the reins as they approached the turn. Lucy held the railing, ready for the sharp forces, leaning to one side to counterbalance better.

This time, instead of slowing, Dashwood took the corner at a steady speed. Torres tried to overtake, but his coach's suspension slowed him just enough that he fell slightly behind as they entered the slow curve.

Lucy glanced to her side. Not only was she racing, but she was now ahead of Dante Torres. For a moment she was lost in the thrill of it, the uncertainty of the night pressing against her. This was most unlike her. But then, who was she really? Surely her parents could not imagine that their daughter was out at midnight racing a coach beside a man she had met only a few weeks earlier. If the Night Races were another world, was there another Lucy?

She shook herself from her philosophizing. There was a race to be run. The road was clear and colorless as they sped forward, making the next turn. Torres drove his horses faster, bringing them in line with his challengers, then drawing slightly farther ahead.

"He cannot hold this pace," Lucy reasoned. "What is he planning?"

Suddenly he sped on even farther, seeming to accelerate out of nowhere. It took her a moment to realize Dashwood had slowed. Torres had timed his charge perfectly to emulate the positions at this stage of the previous race, just where the crash had occurred. Out of instinct, Dashwood had slowed ever so slightly, allowing Torres to pull ahead. Sure enough, now that they were back on even ground, Torres eased his speed slightly, maintaining a steady lead.

"He is quite the racer," Dashwood noted with a mix of admiration and frustration.

"He is."

They were now on a section of road that Torres had raced many times, while Dashwood was heading into uncharted territory. Lucy eyed their path with a heightened awareness, knowing that her spotting was vital on a novel trail.

Torres maneuvered fluidly over the terrain, but Lucy's sharper wits and Dashwood's quick reflexes meant they held pace without losing further ground.

"Another hard turn ahead," she advised.

"Like the first?"

"Almost identical."

"Excellent."

Lucy was unsure what he had planned, but she held on tightly. Whatever was coming, she expected turbulence.

Dashwood urged on the horse, gaining some ground so that the two coaches were side by side as they entered the bend. Gripping the reins, he turned them into the same overtaking maneuver that had given them the lead on the first corner. This time Torres was ready for it, moving in sharply to cut off their path.

But the instant Torres began to change direction, Dashwood slowed and turned back to the straight. To avoid collision, Torres had to veer off the edge of the lane, momentum throwing him off course. With expert skill, Torres steadied the coach and drew them back to the straight line. But it was too late. Dashwood had gained the lead in a shallow curve. The double bluff had put them back in front. Lucy marveled at her driver, who, with only a few moments' notice, had crafted a trap that had drawn in a skilled racer.

The two coaches sped along the curve at a steady pace. How long had they been racing? Surely the end could not be far. And yet Lucy knew there was one more turn to come. Time itself had seemed to slow again.

She caught a glimpse of Ulcha whispering something to Torres. Lucy stared ahead, trying to scout whatever it was the Irish girl had seen.

"Pheasants!" she exclaimed.

The birds flapped up in a flurry, catching Dashwood by surprise and causing him to slow slightly. Torres used the moment to draw alongside them.

The birds that were now flying off into the night, flustered but unharmed, had been spotted by Ulcha well before Lucy had seen them, even forewarned. Lucy might have quick wits, but the vision of the Irish girl was almost supernatural.

All Lucy could do now was focus and think. The two coaches were level, and the final turn was ahead. Would Torres use the same tactic or would he try something else?

"Even turn ahead. Driver's call." She put her fate in the hands of her companion. Lucy knew that reading other people was one of her greatest weaknesses. It seemed to be one of Dashwood's strengths. She held tight, unsure what to expect as the coaches neared the turn.

Dashwood drew them in a tight but steady curve. Torres did the same. Neither driver tried to pull a trick, and neither wished to fall for one. Instead they came into the final stretch neck and neck.

The road was clear, but Lucy kept her focus, lest anything unexpected appear.

Like the rest of the race, the section drew out longer than she thought possible. Dashwood gripped the reins, fixed forward. Torres did the same. No more tricks now, just a hard rush to the finish line.

Then, almost imperceptibly at first, Torres began to draw ahead.

"He's outpacing us!"

"I know," Dashwood replied.

There was a tone in his voice Lucy had not heard before. Doubt. Resignation. His features were difficult to read, but she felt there was a decision being made beneath the surface, a difficult one. He let out a low, steady breath.

Torres's lead began to grow. It was not a huge lead, likely to be uncertain to the spectators until the two coaches crossed the line.

But the result was indisputable. Torres was in front by half a horse length. He had won his second victory of the night.

Dashwood brought his coach to a gradual halt. Before them the horses were panting heavily, the exertion from one and a half races weighing upon them.

"Well," Dashwood said eventually, "you seem to have experienced your first win and your first loss on the same evening, Miss Elliot."

She nodded, running over the race in her mind.

As if reading her thoughts, Dashwood interjected into them. "Do not dwell on what you might have done differently, only let it be experience for what you might do next time. It is possible to do all one can with one's abilities and yet fail."

She sighed and nodded. For a blithe and reckless man, he had hidden depths. But wise as it was, the advice to not overthink things was certainly not her nature.

He descended from the coach, helping her down and bowing as Torres approached. "Señor Torres. I am honored to have lost so closely to a racer such as yourself."

"The honor is mine."

The two men shook hands firmly.

"Might I request water for your horses?" Dashwood asked.

"Already tended to." Torres pointed to where Ulcha and Hercules were looking after the puffed creatures.

"I meant your horses here." Dashwood nodded toward the coach he had just descended.

"Ha. I suppose they are in fact now my horses. Elsa, please bring some water."

"They are fine animals. Army horses. Demanding to care for but obedient and fearless."

"By my honor, they will be well looked after."

"Do you wish to take the reins now?"

"No. Elsworth Manor, correct?"

"Indeed."

"Give your messenger a ride home. We'll collect our winnings in the morning." Torres bowed and left the two in silence for a moment.

Dashwood broke it with a faint chuckle. "He was wrong about one thing."

"Which was?" she asked curiously.

"It was a fair match. It all came down to the horses."

"The horses . . ." she considered. "That was what you were deciding on in the final stretch. To drive the horses harder—"

"Or to lose." He nodded. "I know the horses. Army horses are bred and trained to do as they're commanded no matter what. They'd have won us the race, but it might have broken them."

"But you lost them anyway. What is the difference?"

"I lost them. The world did not. That is the difference."

"You are . . . quite right." She nodded, blushing slightly at having overlooked it.

"Sacrifice is sometimes necessary. But not tonight."

I am undecided whether he is a gentleman, she mused. *But I feel assured that he is a good man.* As she watched him, another thought occurred, more practical than personal.

"Torres was not wrong." She smiled.

"How so?" he asked.

"It was a fine choice not to harm them. But it was your choice to race—one he baited you into, knowing his horses could outpace yours where needed."

Dashwood nodded then laughed. "Perhaps you are right, Miss Elliot."

"I endeavor always to be so."

"A fine but impossible aspiration."

"Why impossible? Because we are flawed human beings?"

"Impossible because one cannot know all possible outcomes beforehand. There are circumstances, on the spur of the moment, where one must wager on the outcome to the best of one's knowledge. It may therefore be the case that the outcome itself may be right but the decision cannot be called correct."

"Midnight is too late for philosophy, Captain Dashwood."

"By the turn of the clock it is only the first hour of the day." He smiled.

"The first hour of the day is also too late for philosophy. If you wish to take it further, I suggest you converse with my sister."

"Is that an invitation to Atherton, Miss Elliot?"

She tensed slightly. "This is the Night Races, sir. It does not overlap with daytime hours. It would be inappropriate to invite to my house a man whom I had met but once."

He looked at her curiously. "Then all that remains is for me to drive you home."

A slow moonlit ride alone with a mysterious man beckoned.

That, I think, might be more dangerous than any race, she thought.

"I am grateful for your consideration. But to dance three times in one night with the same gentleman would be unseemly."

He nodded in amusement.

"It has been a remarkable evening. But there is moon enough left for me to safely walk home with the others. Good night, Captain Dashwood."

"Good night, Miss Elliot."

She curtsied, he bowed, and they parted ways into the night.

CHAPTER 16

"ARE YOU QUITE SURE YOU ARE NOT ILL?" ALICE ELLIOT ASKED FOR THE third time that morning.

"Really, Mother," Margaret replied. "You know how she often finds it difficult to sleep during the full moon."

Lucy chewed slowly on her mouthful of scone, unable to reply.

"You never had such difficulties as a child, Lucy. As I recall you set your own bedtime at age eight."

Lucy sipped her tea. "I have not been a child for some time, Mother. And Meg is quite right. Moonlight keeps me awake," she explained, technically truthful. Having risen late she was consuming a simple breakfast, which was now causing more contention than she had hoped.

"Do you still intend to walk to town?"

Their mother's question coincided with another mouthful of scone.

"We do," Margaret noted. "We hope to see what is new in the shops, and I think our odds are good that the market shall not close before noon on a spring day."

"I simply hope it is not something that becomes a habit for you both." Alice tutted. "Tardiness can influence impressions and have a strong impact on a young woman's fortunes."

"Is there a particular gentleman to whom you might be alluding? If he falls short of Lucy's precise conditions, I promise I shall offer him my full consideration."

"Captain Dashwood of course." Her mother laughed lightly at the good-humored offer.

Lucy resisted the reflex to splutter her tea.

"There has been a good deal of speculation by the local ladies of late as to the eligibility of Captain Dashwood and whose daughter might best suit him," their mother went on. "Most likely that is what put the thought in my head."

"But not Mr. Dashwood himself?"

"It is a peculiar thing, Meg. The captain certainly comes from a good family, as Elsworth is one of several of their properties, making him likely heir to a good fortune. And yet we cannot be sure of this. Has he brothers? Is there an inheritance, or is he merely here in his father's stead for now? None of the local regiment have heard of him, so he must have been posted far afield. Others are free to speculate and even court him if they are so bold, but there is a good deal more I wish to know about Captain Dashwood before I should contemplate his being a son-in-law."

"There are times, Mother, though infrequent, where I can see where aspects of Lucy originated."

Alice smiled at the notion, then continued. "Now Mr. St. Martin, on the other hand—there is an eligible bachelor who might make a mother proud."

Lucy helped herself to another scone. She was no longer hungry, but eating was proving an effective means of avoiding the conversation.

"George? I think you mistake him, Mother. He's a fine gentleman but a simple one. Lucy's sharp wits would be ill-suited to his shallowness, and his shallowness makes him ill-suited for me."

"You do yourself wrong, Margaret."

"If I am more pretty, it is only because there is more of me to be pretty. It is something a woman cannot disguise, Mother. With discipline she may hide her moods, with costume her proportions, with makeup her complexion, but height offers no such concealment. I do not begrudge how nature made me, but if I am to marry it will be to a man who will meet me at my level no matter the difference in our stature."

"You do me proud, Daughter. You both do. Frustrated on occasion, but proud. Unless, of course, Lucy partakes of yet another scone, at which point I shall have no choice but to disown her for gluttony."

Margaret smiled. "A harsh decision, Mother, but most fair."

CHAPTER 17

ᴴᴱʀ ᴛᴇᴀ ꜰɪɴɪꜱʜᴇᴅ ᴀɴᴅ ʜᴇʀ ᴘᴏꜱɪᴛɪᴏɴ ɪɴ ᴛʜᴇ ᴇʟʟɪᴏᴛ ꜰᴀᴍɪʟʏ ꜱᴇ-cure, Lucy set off on foot with her sister toward Halstead town. As a market town there was usually something of interest to be found for bright young women like the Elliot sisters.

"It occurs to me, Lucy, that if you were to move your room to the other side of the house, the moon would not trouble you nearly so much."

"A sensible suggestion. However, the change would trouble me enormously. I have had my room as long as I can remember, and I am well settled there. Any benefit to avoiding the moonlight would certainly be outweighed by the downside of this disturbance."

"I had not considered that. You are certainly a creature of habit. A place for everything and everything in its place. I cannot help but wonder if the greatest adaptation you might have in being married might lie not in your companion but in relocation to a new abode."

"And that is an aspect I shall admit that I have not considered." Lucy frowned. "It is, I think, a most difficult balance to determine between what is correct and what is merely familiar. I believe one should forgive any quirks of architecture, as they can only be blamed on the occupants of the time. There is little to be gained in holding grudges against the draftsmen of previous centuries. Objectively, then, it should be the case that a building should not be a consideration in respect to matrimony."

"Only to the extent of practical concerns," said Margaret. "I am fortunate that the current taste is for high ceilings. I daresay I should not endure long in a home with low beams."

"That would entail a marriage to a short man of limited means. I should imagine such a match to be quite impractical."

"How so? We have known several tall men to marry short women."

"But a tall man may lift a short woman to kiss her."

"I daresay I should be quite able to lift a small man."

"Now that would certainly be inappropriate in company."

"It need not be done in company."

"And now we are veering into a topic I shall speak not further on." Lucy flushed, though she blamed it more on the sun than the topic. It was a warm spring day, and while much of the path was shaded, there were patches where their hats were welcome protection from the glaring midday sun.

"Mother seemed focused on marriage options again this morning," Margaret mused.

"It is to be expected. We are certainly well into marriageable age, and the absence of any firm offers of courtship must be of concern to our parents."

"Not a total absence. There was Master Krippingworth."

"Oh, dear. That was something of a fiasco," Lucy sighed.

The Krippingworth family had spent a summer in the district some years prior, both parents social and confident creatures, and their son and daughter quite the opposite. Perhaps having been unable to grow in the shadow of their elders, they were perfectly affable but without much direction of their own.

Lucy had at first been very pleased with Ben Krippingworth. He was a slightly plain fellow, but had a pleasant smile and a fine form at dancing. Their first conversation had been an engaging one, and Lucy felt an amiable similarity with the young man as they broached topics of interest. Over the following weeks, however, the charm began to wear off. Lucy, sharp as she was, came to identify familiar patterns in their conversations. He was well-read and eloquent in any discussion, but never initiated a topic of his own accord. No matter the subject, he seemed to agree with her. She discovered, for example, that he knew a great deal about the history of roads in Britain, yet for all his knowledge he seemed to have no opinion about them.

"Had I wished," Lucy pondered aloud as they walked, "I daresay I could have shaped him into precisely the man I imagined. But in the end I would have been a wife with an idea of a husband and little more."

Lucy had begun to discourage his attentions, and any potential future melted away without obvious discomfort for either party. In the end he married Olivia Coleridge, a kindhearted but somewhat empty-headed heiress who bred roses. By all accounts it was a very happy marriage. On occasion Lucy imagined the couple, sitting by the fireplace in contented silence, external and internal.

Lost in thought and conversation as they were, the Elliot sisters failed to consider what section of path they were on—one that veered closely to the farm owned by Mr. and Mrs. Birkenshire. They were a wonderfully friendly couple with several children of equally pleasant disposition. That the animals they kept were of a polar opposite nature perplexed the higher classes of the district. Their chickens would go broody in local hedges, their horses were obstinate, their sheep were as ornery as goats, and their goats were even worse.

It was one such billy goat that the Elliot sisters now found blocking their way. It appeared to have staked a claim to a section of path where a narrow bridge crossed a stream.

"Go on. Shoo!" said Lucy, with a tone that might have struck aside any member of the spring assembly but had little effect on the irritated farm animal. If anything, her words seemed to make it more determined, stomping the ground fiercely and letting out a threatening bleat.

Bleats, Lucy thought, *should not be threatening.*

"This reminds me," Margaret said, "of that story Mother told us when we were little. With the goats and the bridge."

"This is quite different, Margaret," Lucy replied as she walked left and right, the goat tracking her in defense of his domain. "It was the goats who wanted to pass and a troll who wanted to eat them. And, frankly"—she glared at the animal—"I shouldn't mind if a troll ate you."

As if offended by the comparison, the goat aggressively edged toward Lucy.

Margaret, though amused, had the protective instinct of an older sister and the determination to follow through when required. Lucy was so confident a personality that such protection was seldom needed, but a farmyard-animal attack matched the criteria. Margaret strode forward with a smooth swiftness and firmly took hold of the creature's horns. Shocked and defensive, he immediately tried to twist away and kick, but his stubborn nature was matched by the grip of Margaret Elliot. She pushed down the goat, dropping to her knees on the grassy path, over-powering the animal with all the considerable strength she could muster.

To Lucy's amazement the stunned beast seemed to give up the fight entirely.

"I am going to release you now," Margaret stated in a gentle yet forceful tone. "And if you trouble us again, I shall throw you in the stream."

Whether or not she was able to make good on her threat was not to be tested, the animal trotting meekly back to the safety of Birkenshire Farm.

"That . . . that was utterly unmannerly, Margaret!" Lucy exclaimed.

Margaret huffed. Her dress was scuffed with dirt and grass stains, and her shoulders and part of her back had torn through as she exerted herself. She was unharmed but flushed, with her hair considerably more disordered than it had been. In addition, a faint but unmistakable scent of goat clung to her. She was, as their mother might have phrased it, in quite a state.

"Whatever should we have said if someone had come along?"

"There is nothing to be done about it now, Lucy. Perhaps it will be an excuse for dress shopping."

"Surely you do not intend to continue to town?"

"I most certainly do. I just wrestled a pugnacious goat for that exact purpose."

"You are utterly disheveled. It would be quite inappropriate. It was quite inappropriate to lay hands on the creature at all."

"Sometimes there are things that must be done, Lucy!" her sister snapped back. "Whatever rule or decorum you might cite, there are times when help will not come and you must take affairs in hand, sometimes literally. If it is poor manners to defend my sister from injury, then I should be the rudest woman in England."

Lucy paused as her next admonition evaporated into the warm spring air, and she felt the sudden urge to giggle. The quirk of her lips set Meg off too, and soon the quiet path was replete with laughter.

Gathering herself, Lucy slipped her shawl from her shoulders and passed it to her sister. It matched neither the color nor style of Meg's dress, but it did a passable job of concealing the rips in her seams.

The remainder of their walk was mercifully uneventful.

CHAPTER 18

ANY CONCERN THAT LUCY HELD ON THE APPEARANCE OF HER SISTER DI-
minished as they reached the outskirts of town. Groups were
talking with unusual enthusiasm, with serious expressions and
somber nods. Lucy concluded that there had been definitive *talk*.
Even if their incident on the way had somehow arrived before them,
Margaret's impromptu goat-wrangling would not have risen to the
level of *talk*. Such an incident might be commented on in casual
conversation, perhaps over breakfast or tea. To rise to the level of
talk it had to be something spread actively, not passively.

Lucy's deductive mind immediately went to work. It was not
likely to be a scandal. There was an openness in the conversation
she saw, not the furtive giggles and tut-tuts that might accompany
a sordid revelation. Nor was it likely to be major political news
from elsewhere. How curious that she could hypothesize on the
mood and interactions of a crowd but have such difficulty reading
a conversation in an intimate setting.

She kept her observations to herself, confident the story
would be revealed in time and aware that it would be poor manners to ask.

Their first stop was the dress shop and tailor run by Mrs. Calloway and Mr. McDonald. She was a spry Welshwoman, he a slow
and precise Scotsman, each attending to the garment needs of
their respective genders. They both lived in the apartments above
the store, and their exact relationship had been the cause of considerable speculation on their arrival in town, and more than one
sermon by the vicar. Despite gossip and speculation, no further

evidence could be pried from them. Over time the novelty wore off and they became an accepted part of the landscape. It was generally agreed upon that they bickered like a married couple and that was good enough.

"Oh, Miss Elliot, whatever have you done to yourself?" Mrs. Calloway exclaimed as Margaret removed her shawl.

Lucy's disheveled sister then explained the incident with the goat in a casual manner Lucy felt she would have been quite incapable of herself.

"Glad to see someone teach those Birkenshire animals a lesson," said Mrs. Calloway. "They're a menace they are. Mr. McDonald dropped off a pair of trousers there once, and he was mobbed by chickens."

"I suspect we might have had better luck with chickens," Margaret mused.

"Don't be so sure. He said they were terrors. Now the good news is that the seams can all be patched up. I can do that now if you want. But those grass stains won't be coming out. You'll need a whole new panel to replace them."

"I think that shall have to wait for another day. But if you can do some repairs now, then I'm prepared to wait. Lucy, if you wish to go elsewhere, I shall not take offense."

Lucy politely took her leave as Mrs. Calloway continued her tale. "Pecked him, they did. Great stab in the side of his coat . . ."

Outside the store, Lucy looked up and down the street, considering where she might best attain the knowledge she knew was out there, when a tall figure emerged from the post office and she recognized the stern features of Oliver St. Martin.

"Miss Elliot," he greeted her.

"Mr. St. Martin. How are you this day?"

"I am quite well. Just sending some business correspondence to London. It is an odd thing to be witness to misfortune so close to home."

"Misfortune?"

"Robbery, Miss Elliot."

"Robbery? At St. Martins Hall?"

"No. Our home was untouched. But a delivery destined for my father never arrived."

"What manner of delivery?"

"Brandy. A whole case of the stuff. Some fancy brand, difficult to get these days with the war in Europe. Father was hoping to use it in his preserves, and recreationally of course. But the coach never arrived. No, that is an error—the *coach* arrived."

"I'm not sure I understand."

"The coach and horse were found by a farmer this morning by the roadside. No driver and no cargo. It could have wandered there from anywhere. George thinks the driver went and got drunk somewhere and lost the cart."

"You disagree?"

"A trusted driver taking a whole case of expensive brandy? Nonsense. At worst he'd steal a shot for himself. Someone got to him in the early hours of the morning."

"He was traveling at night?"

"Quicker road out of London, apparently. He was scheduled to arrive just before dawn, but he never did."

"And now it's the talk of the town."

"My father is not known for his subtlety. He came to town as soon as he discovered the cart had gone missing, and he's been talking to the magistrate for some time. I decided to go about other business."

"You are not overly concerned?"

"It was a frivolous expense for a hobby I do not share. While it is a concern there may be highwaymen in the district, there is little you or I can do about it—unless you are aware of any unsavory characters that frequent the roads at night."

Lucy smiled and hoped desperately that her expression did not give away her discomfort. "What other errands do you have?" she asked. "I'm free to roam if you wish for company."

"Thank you, Miss Elliot. My next port of call is"—he checked a list—"to collect a pair of trousers from the tailor's."

"Might I suggest postponing that briefly?"

"For what reason?"

"My sister is currently there having her dress repaired. While she should not admit to embarrassment, I daresay she should feel it."

"Then I shall delay that visit until later. Good day, Miss Elliot."

He tipped his hat and headed off in one direction while Lucy turned to walk the other along the river. The market stalls offered some distraction, but the path of her thoughts led repeatedly back to the possibility of foul play on the very roads she'd sped along the night before.

CHAPTER 19

THERE WAS NO END OF GOSSIP AND SPECULATION AS TO THE NATURE OF the disappearance of the coach's rider and cargo. Seldom had a missing case of brandy been such a subject of interest. Theories ranged from the mundane (such as George's belief in an absconding driver) through to the wild (that the coachman had chanced upon a secret Napoleonic invasion force) and the supernatural.

Charlotte Wyndham was a young woman whose excellent amiability was matched by her tendency to leap to the most outlandish of explanations.

"They say that the Night Mare only rides on the blue moon, a ghostly figure whose hooves are cursed to never quite touch the ground and ridden by a pale rider with no head. It's been abducting people in the district for centuries." This she opined some days after the incident, when she and several ladies were engaged in collecting cherry blossoms for decoration.

Lucy was not given to flights of fantasy, least of all ones that were demonstrably and logically false. While governed by politeness, she had been worn down by some of the other absurd theories offered. The casual certainty with which Charlotte told her tale finally pressed her past the bounds of civil silence.

"Are you quite sure about that, Charlotte?"

"Oh, yes. My mother told me stories of the Night Mare when I was a child. Once, I even heard it on the night of the full moon."

"You heard it?"

"Yes. From my window."

"What did it sound like?"

"Well, like clopping hooves of course."

"But you didn't actually see it?"

"Of course not. If you ever see the Night Mare, then you will be swept away by it and never seen again. That's what I think happened."

"So what does it look like?" asked Sarah Mayhew, so enthralled by the tale that she had managed to get several blossoms tangled in her hair.

"A headless white rider atop a huge white stallion, with eyes as dark as coals."

"A stallion?" Lucy asked.

"Yes."

"Then why is it called a Night Mare?"

"Well . . ." Charlotte paused, blushing. "That's . . . just the name I heard."

"And if its hooves don't touch the ground, why would it make the sound of clopping?"

"I—I hadn't really thought of that," Charlotte stammered.

"Perhaps it's a ghost sound?" Sarah offered helpfully.

"And if it whisks away anyone who sees it, how could anyone tell what it looked like?" Lucy continued.

There was an uneasy pause as Wyndham fancy came to an embarrassing collision with Elliot reasoning.

"In my experience," Margaret chipped in for the first time, "horses behave very differently around different people. I should imagine the same applies for ghost horses. It would be utterly tiresome to carry away every single person who chanced to see you. More likely it would only take those out at night for wicked purposes. Don't you think so, Charlotte?"

Sensing a lifeline, Charlotte grabbed it hastily. "Yes. I think that would make much more sense. Perhaps the driver was up to something illicit."

Lucy almost replied, but a stern gaze from her sister suggested she should leave the topic for now and the conversation was diverted by Anne Mayhew pitching her pet theory that the "brandy" was really gold being transported to finance the war in Europe. While Lucy found it improbable, it did not rise to the level that she felt a need to correct it, so the remainder of the outing did not see another uneasy contradiction.

Only once they were returned home did Margaret take her aside.

"Was it quite so necessary to treat Charlotte so ill, Lucy?"

"Her story made no sense."

"It was the story of a ghost horse. Of course it made no sense. It was no more than a harmless tale she spun to amuse herself and her friends."

"It wasn't even internally consistent."

Margaret sighed. "There are times, Lucy, when I wonder how a young woman of such intellect and insight can be so detached from the feelings of her fellow man."

The statement stung Lucy, who considered propriety and detail the most effective way to achieve contentment in herself and others. "I do not mean to be so."

"Could you not tell from the first time you poked a hole in the story that she was afraid of being humiliated?"

"No!" Lucy replied in frustration. "I could not. I had no intention to humiliate her."

"But humiliate her you did. Out of a desire to correct details that no one else in attendance cared for in the slightest." Seeing her younger sister shaken, she took her hand softly. "Lucy, you are not unkind. Nor are you thoughtless. But your need to always be right and say right has consequences in a world where imperfection abounds."

The polite correction stuck with Lucy for the rest of the day. She had intended to prove Charlotte wrong, that she could not deny, but as to her motive she was less certain. The story had irritated her, clashed against her sensibility and her reason. Was it not possible that she had spoken with frustration or spite and that logic was merely her justification? Had there been a better way to speak? Different words to say? Cues she had missed?

Alone in her room, pondering this riddle deeper and deeper, she kept herself busy by taking her model coach apart and reconstructing it. The pieces were familiar and easy. They went in the right place every time, in a way words and faces never seemed to be. By the time dinner arrived, she had dismantled and reassembled the coach on her floor almost as many times as she had dismantled and reassembled the conversation in her head.

CHAPTER 20

OVER THE FOLLOWING DAYS, PERHAPS TO DISTRACT HERSELF FROM her indiscretion, Lucy continued to ponder what might have happened to the missing driver. It was one thing to ridicule the story of a ghost horse, but thus far no other outcome had proved itself either. George's theory seemed less and less likely as the days went by, with neither driver nor brandy resurfacing. George himself admitted this and now wondered if the man had gotten drunk and stumbled into Longburn Mire. There was talk of a search, but the roads were long, the mire itself impassable, and while there was concern for the fate of the driver, the case of brandy—expensive as it was—seemed a poor use of manpower.

Lucy, however, had a different perspective. If the driver had absconded, he would likely have taken the cart with him. He could have changed vehicles, but there was little to be gained by leaving the horse and the cart to be discovered the next day. Traveling on foot was out of the question, as the case would have taken at least two men to carry, and even then it would have been slow and heavy work.

Foul play was the most likely option. While coincidence was certainly possible, Lucy could not dismiss the fact that the robbery occurred on a night where several expert coachmen were assembled in the district. Lord Rathbone seemed the least likely culprit. He seemed too honorable to engage in villainy, too wealthy to bother with such petty spoils, and too stern for it to be some kind of prank at Sir Walter St. Martin's expense.

The other suspects all seemed much more probable.

The coastal party, having had their coach ruined, might have taken out their frustrations on a driver later that night. If they were longshoremen or transporters themselves they would likely have recognized the value of rare brandy. It might therefore have been a crime of opportunity.

Though she had a respect for Torres and his team, she also knew little of them outside the Night Races. That they might make a living through questionable means was entirely possible. If she were to ever put together a group for the purpose of coach robbery, then it would include the daring precision of Dante Torres, the owl eyes of Ulcha, and the craftsmanship of Hekili and Elsa Reinhardt. If they set themselves to it they could pluck the cargo from a coach without the driver even knowing it.

And then there was Captain Dashwood. He was a talented driver, reckless at heart, but with more than a little cold steel in his manner and skeletons in his closet to match. She had raced with him and danced with him, but there was much she did not know and much he clearly did not wish to be known. She recalled her observations of the ball at Elsworth—Dashwood eyeing the room and endearing himself to his neighbors. Was he gathering information on potential targets? But why would he indulge in such a theft? For the pure thrill of it? Or perhaps his gambling debts were not as settled as some believed. If he was responsible, would it be a solo act?

This was the very train of thought she was following, sitting alone in the garden, when she was interrupted by her father.

"My dear Lucy, there is a matter on which I desire your perspective."

"And is my perspective to be one of objective thought or subjective opinion?"

"Both, as it happens. We have been invited to dinner at Elsworth Manor."

"By Captain Dashwood?" she asked, surprised. The invitation itself was not out of the ordinary, but she had been assessing the possibility of him being a highwayman only moments earlier, and the change in direction was jarring.

"Indeed. I encountered him while doing some business about town. There has been discussion of the local regiment patrolling the night roads after a recent delivery went awry. An overreaction if you ask me, but the idea has been floated, and Captain Dashwood has been asked for his input on it."

"Has he indeed?" she asked.

"Did you know he has a history with coaches?"

"It . . . had come to my attention."

"Well, he was happy to give some thoughts, but he didn't want to be dragged into local affairs."

"How curious." Lucy noted. "One would think as a man in uniform he would feel a responsibility to his home district, however temporary."

"I cannot disagree. However, I suppose he is not here in any official capacity and his consultation was a favor rather than an obligation."

"Yet how does this relate to a dinner invitation or my perspective?"

"After he explained all this, he asked if we should like to attend a dinner. At first it seemed it referred only to myself, but he clarified that it was also for your mother, Margaret, and you."

"It is not uncommon for our family to visit friends and neighbors."

"No. But to visit the home of a bachelor, without the company of neighbors, might be seen as having certain connotations."

"And you are wondering about the propriety of this invitation?"

"I am. Though I cannot pin down a solid reason, I must confess something about it seemed . . . askew."

She nodded, her thoughts passing over possible ulterior

motives. But if Captain Dashwood could have such motives, then she could too.

"Well," she began, "you cannot think it odd that we might invite him to dine here?"

"Not at all. He would be most welcome."

"Then those who sit at the table shall be the same either way."

He laughed. "That is a fine way of putting it. But there is another aspect I feel must be addressed, one of a more personal nature."

"Which is?"

"We are being asked to the home of a bachelor, and I have two unmarried daughters. It is not unreasonable that the thought of a potential union should cross my mind. It has certainly crossed your mother's."

"It is . . . not unreasonable to give thought to the prospect," she replied.

"He did dance with you at the ball."

"He danced with a lady from every household. He showed no greater favor to me than any other that night."

That night, she repeated in her head to assure herself she was not engaged in deception.

"And you can think of no other exchange that might have hinted at this?"

"I can assure you, Father"—she considered her words precisely—"that I have never given the man words or actions that would lend themselves to my being considered for his wife."

Unless he wanted a wife with an encyclopedic knowledge of coach mechanics, she supposed.

"And Margaret?"

"I cannot speak for her. Though to the best of my knowledge she has not exchanged one word with Captain Dashwood."

"Well, then. It is possible that it is his intent to explore this possibility even if it has not yet been broached. I do not wish to throw you or Meg into an unwanted match, and my accepting this invitation stands on your deference."

"You are too good to us, Father. Many a parent would engage in relentless matchmaking had they daughters of our age."

"Of your ages, perhaps, but not of your dispositions. You are both of you quite singular in your own ways."

"I am undecided as to Captain Dashwood. There seems to be both good and ill in him, and I cannot weigh one greater than the other in my estimation. Yet I should in no way be opposed to a family visit."

"I am glad to hear it. If Margaret has no reservations, I shall send word at once that we shall attend at his convenience." With that he left his daughter to her contemplation.

It appeared at first that fate had placed an opportunity in Lucy's hands to better acquire the very information that was at the heart of her considerations. Yet, she cautioned herself, there was an equal opportunity for reconnaissance on the part of Captain Dashwood—continuing, in a more intimate fashion, the observatory behavior he had exhibited at the ball.

It remained to be seen to whose greater advantage the visit would be.

CHAPTER 21

ETURNING TO ELSWORTH MANOR OUTSIDE THE CONTEXT OF A BALL was a curious experience for Lucy. The event had formed a singular impression on her and it felt strange to be seeing it in a different light. The decor and architecture was as fine as it had ever been, though notably less illuminated. With only the Elliots and Captain Dashwood in attendance, the place seemed much emptier.

It appeared that their host had retained his small staff numbers, which she found both perplexing and reasonable. Perplexing because, as befitted the status of the manor, a greater number of staff should be employed now it was an official residence; reasonable because, as a single gentleman of simple tastes, there was only so much attendance required.

"Do you plan to stay long in the district, Captain?" Alice Elliot asked as they sat at the dinner table awaiting the arrival of the main course.

"It is not entirely of my choosing. To be sure it is a charming spot, but my father is the owner of several properties, some of which have received little use in recent years due to his poor health. While I am here for the season, I cannot say whether my services shall be required in other places."

Or, Lucy thought, *whether a season will be sufficient time for whatever trouble you are hiding from to settle down.*

"Has that played a role in your decision not to employ a staff?" Margaret asked.

"To some degree, yes. Plus I am accustomed more to an army life on the move, where attendance is far less than it is in society.

The Marbrooks do well enough to cook and clean, and it is not so demanding a property that a groundsman cannot manage it, with occasional help from local farmers. I have my footman, Jim, who served me well abroad. That is a sufficient number to meet my needs at this time."

"But you do plan to put down roots someday, I hope?" Mrs. Elliot asked.

"I am certain the inclination will one day come upon me. Not too late I hope. My father married late, and I have seen one too many retired colonels reliving the stories of their glory days but too old to make any new ones. I should admit that if I were to retire my commission, this would be a fine place. A comfortable abode, amiable society, and smooth roads."

"Though not always safe ones," Mr. Elliot noted.

"Do you refer to the missing driver and brandy?"

"Of course. What else could I mean?"

Captain Dashwood smiled. "What indeed?"

Lucy shivered as his eyes met hers and the secret knowledge silently passed between them.

"I should not be too concerned," the captain continued. "Sir Walter St. Martin is making a large amount of noise over a minor incident. Though I am given to understand he is particularly sensitive on the matter of preserves."

"He is." Mrs. Elliot chuckled. "I myself am especially fond of the pastime but not so much as to match his vigor."

"Surely it is not so much the object, but the novelty of the disappearance that marks the incident," Lucy chimed in.

"There are elements of curiosity." Dashwood nodded. "What conclusion have you come to, Miss Elliot?"

"No conclusion as yet. But I lean toward theft by an unknown party."

"Such speculation would bode ill for the driver."

"I do not wish for the outcome. I merely conjecture it."

"And what other conjecture accompanies it?"

"A cart traveling at pace would not offer a great chance to be set upon by opportunists. Therefore the robbers were familiar with the route, and waiting," she offered.

"A reasonable estimation," said Dashwood. "And yet the manner of such an ambush would be difficult. The road was examined for signs of incident, but no obvious roadblock or similar was found."

"Which would suggest the cart was taken in motion? Quite improbable."

"But not impossible if one was sufficiently skilled and determined."

"It seems a lot of effort," Margaret interjected, "for a case of brandy."

"They may not have known it was brandy," Mr. Elliot suggested.

"But by your daughter's logic, they did know the route," said Captain Dashwood. "It would be curious to know the details of such a delivery but not the cargo itself."

"Curious," Lucy agreed, "but not impossible."

Dashwood chuckled. "Quite right."

Further exploration of the topic was delayed by the arrival of the main course. The meal consisted of roast pheasant, simply but well prepared in such a manner that Mrs. Elliot insisted on prizing the recipe from Mrs. Marbrook, which also provided a fine chance for them to catch up on the past years.

Once the party had retired to the sitting room, Margaret was persuaded to play upon the pianoforte. Despite her determination to achieve a level of competence at the instrument, Lucy had never found great success. She certainly had the focus and precision for such a task, and she had an ear for enjoying music; her limitation lay in her insistence on perfecting her skill at one song before attempting another. After a decade of practice, it was possible that few amateur musicians in the isles could match her skill with Ignaz Pleyel's Sonatina in E-flat Major. However, most in the district would be quite content if they never heard Lucy play the song again.

Margaret lacked her sister's proficiency but had a considerably greater repertoire. Like Lucy, she worked hard at the skill, less out of a desire for mastery and more from awareness that any ability to offset her limitations as a prospective marriage partner should be explored. As she tested the keys of the instrument, she found it had a pleasant tone and was now eagerly engaged in one of her favorite Dibdin pieces.

"As you would expect, it was quite out of tune due to disuse," Dashwood explained. "But I felt it prudent to have it restored for the benefit of entertaining."

"It is indeed of excellent craftsmanship, far exceeding the simple instrument we have at Atherton." Alice Elliot smiled. "Do you play, Captain?"

"It has been a good many years since I touched the keys. I am more capable on the violin."

"And would you be amenable to a demonstration, perhaps?"

"Alas, I must decline at this time. I am out of practice and should not make for a comparable companion. Yet I promise to commit to some study that we may share at a later date."

"It is, I suppose," Lucy mused, "a decidedly more portable instrument than a pianoforte."

"Indeed. And I find it slightly more adaptable to the varying tastes that may be found among differing classes."

"Different classes?" Mr. Elliot asked curiously.

"A violin may serve to entertain an audience at an assembly, or it may bolster the spirits of troops after a long march. One must be flexible to the circumstances in which one finds oneself."

"A fair assessment," Mr. Elliot agreed, though Lucy wondered if there was a hint of suspicion in her father's voice.

"I hope you will not hold such an admission against me, Mr. Elliot. The practicalities of active service place one in circumstances that defy explanation in polite society. I make it a habit to neither dwell on nor conceal this truth. Some soldiers I have known delight in the sharing of macabre battle stories and I am most certainly not of that fold. But nor shall I deny my history for the pretense of elevating my station."

"You are not a man given to concealment, Captain?" Lucy asked blithely.

"No more than yourself, Miss Elliot." He met her challenge with one of his own, and she was inclined to hint at their secret acquaintance no further.

"I think there is an admirable nature in earnestness," Margaret noted as she came to the end of her piece. "To be true to oneself is a standard one should always aspire to."

"And yet," Dashwood continued, "to be true to oneself, one must know oneself—a task perhaps more formidable than honesty."

"I believe I am in fair estimation of my character," Mrs. Elliot proposed.

"I do not doubt it, madam. But one can only measure against what one has experienced. I have seen bold officers crumple at the first cannon fire and timid soldiers risk life and limb to rescue their comrades. There are a great many tests we may face in life, and we cannot say how we will fare until they occur."

"If that is true," Lucy pointed out, "then you render your claim dubious."

"How so?"

"If self-knowledge only comes through trials and the nature of those trials is indefinite, then to truly know oneself becomes an impossibility."

"Perhaps it is more an ideal than an attainable goal, Miss Elliot. Unless you believe otherwise?"

"I do. While there can be no certainty, there can be relative confidence. I need not know the nature of every type of wood to know it will burn in a fire in almost all given circumstances. Nor do I need to know the particulars of every moral challenge to have insight into how I might react to it."

"And if time does not allow such insight?"

"Then one should endeavor to think faster."

At that Dashwood laughed, which for a moment Lucy feared dismissive, but from the reaction of her sister, she realized it was in admiration.

"I must credit you, Mr. and Mrs. Elliot, for raising two daughters with not merely sharp wits but the willingness to use them."

"We are indeed blessed." Alice Elliot nodded politely, with just the faintest hint of a sigh.

"I should also commend your playing, Miss Margaret. There is a fine elegance to your music."

"Thank you, sir. And now I must rest my fingers. It is a shame that we are one too many in number to play at cards."

"Unless Mrs. Elliot could be persuaded to play the piano while the rest of us play cards?" Dashwood mused.

Lucy caught sight of her mother's eyes as they lit up. Her mother's talent exceeded them both, but with two eligible daughters there was seldom an opportunity to share it. Lucy had noticed more than once in the past half hour that her mother's eyes had strayed over the fine instrument. Clearly these glances had also not been missed by the watchful gaze of Captain Dashwood. Even in small company he had the eyes of a hawk.

CHAPTER 22

WHATEVER SUSPICION LUCY HAD ABOUT THE MOTIVES OF CAPTAIN Dashwood, she could not deny that he made an excellent partner at cards. This, of course, did raise further concerns in her mind and she wondered if his aptitude for the game was behind his current exile. They were so effective a pairing as to bring the first game to a premature close. Dashwood proposed a second, pairing Lucy and her father against himself and Margaret. This game was a much closer affair, and the tight victory came down to a well-played queen from Margaret on the second-to-last hand. Andrew Elliot declared the round to be the most enjoyable game he had played in quite some time, aided by the soft and steady tone of his wife's pianoforte music.

With the hour moving on, Mrs. Elliot wondered if it might be time to return to their coach and to Atherton.

"I apologize if it was poor manners not to send a coach of my own," Dashwood offered.

"Not at all," Mr. Elliot dismissed. "We are more than happy for our horses to get some exercise, especially in such fine spring weather."

"I am fortunate you were able. My coach is currently somewhat ill-disposed for use of any kind."

"I do hope you had no issue with our roads?"

"Not at all. I have seldom seen finer. I am in the process of rebuilding my coach."

"Our Lucy had a fondness for that in her younger years," Alice quipped.

"Really? You built coaches?"

"Models," Lucy replied.

"Were you inclined, I should be quite happy to show you my progress."

"You are too kind, Captain, but the hour is drawing late," Lucy demurred.

"Well, I should like to see it," Margaret said confidently.

Lucy glanced at her in surprise.

"Go along, then." Mr. Elliot sighed. The evening had been going so well, and now the odd nature of both his daughters had been revealed in swift succession.

"Are you coming, Lucy?" Margaret asked casually.

"I believe I shall."

"Perhaps a duet while we wait?" Mrs. Elliot suggested to her husband.

"That would be most welcome, my dear," he replied.

As the sisters followed Dashwood, Lucy smiled at the fading sound of pleasant notes from a well-matched pair.

Lucy was not entirely sure what to expect as they entered the stable rooms and Dashwood lit the lamps. His coach had been lost to Torres, and it seemed a curious thing to build a coach himself when a completely new one should likely be superior. Captain Dashwood was at least wealthy enough to have wagered horses and coach on a race. Then again, perhaps it was an indicator more of recklessness than capital.

"Why, pray tell, did you ask to see a deconstructed coach?" Lucy asked her sister quietly. "You have never indicated the slightest interest in such a thing."

"No. But you have."

Before Lucy could reply, their host returned, ushering them in.

Laid out on the flagstone floor was something that might barely be recognizable as a coach. It was broken up into pieces and parts, just the way Lucy might do with her models on her bedroom floor.

Instinctively she began putting together the components in her mind—wheels and spokes, axles and cross braces, all coming together bit by bit. It was woefully incomplete, whole sections missing, including the front, a wheel, and . . .

She paused as she recognized what she was presented with. Her initial failure to recall was easily forgivable. The last time she had seen the coach intact it was flipping head over tail, about to come to pieces. It appeared that Captain Dashwood had followed through on the stakes of the race and had all salvageable parts delivered to him.

"A Pemberley Cross," Lucy noted, "partly complete."

"I do hope you have not been swindled, Captain Dashwood," Margaret commented.

"Fortunately not. It was involved in a crash. I hope to rebuild it better than before. I believe the Pemberley Cross is a versatile model."

Margaret gasped. "You plan to do the work yourself?"

"My footman, Jim, has experience in building. I have talked with your local blacksmith, as well as a firm in London that will ship me the parts. I have been considering a double cross brace under the carriage."

"You cannot have a double cross brace on a Pemberley!" Lucy countered indignantly. She took a moment to compose herself before explaining. "The cross brace is already reinforced. Putting in a second will remove all flexibility from your base and transfer imbalance to the axle points."

There was quiet as the authoritative engineering settled on the flagstones.

"That is a shame." Dashwood shrugged. "I have heard good things about Harding suspension and was hoping to try it."

"There should be no need to install a double brace for that, so long as the anchor points have reinforced lateral bars."

Again, there was a pause.

"Miss Elliot, would I be presumptuous in asking for your assistance on this work? You appear to have a most adept mind for it."

"I must decline, Captain. To come here alone would be overstepping the bounds of propriety."

"I am sure Mrs. Marbrook would be happy to chaperone," Margaret suggested. "She was a nurse to us for many years and has a fond connection to our family. If she and you are amenable to such, I see no reason why Lucy could not offer her insight."

Dashwood remained silent, turning to Lucy in expectation of her reply.

She weighed the choices in her head. Chaperone aside, the connection was still decidedly unladylike and would certainly be cause for gossip in the district. Though in truth, what would such gossip say about Lucy Elliot that was not already known?

And she could not deny the appeal. The chance to work on a real coach was assuredly unique. Should she decline it now she might never have another such opportunity. And there was also the mystery of the gentleman, which, over the course of the evening, had in no way diminished. If anything, her desire to solve it had grown to rival any other such conundrum she had previously tangled with. How else could she explain the nervous flutter she felt in her stomach?

"I should be delighted to assist you, Captain Dashwood," she replied evenly.

"I am glad to hear it. We shall correspond to arrange an appropriate time, with the permission of your parents, of course."

"Of course."

And with that it was settled, the trio returning to the warmth of the sitting room and the sounds of a contented duet.

The coach ride home was a quiet one. Margaret fell asleep, as she often did on such return journeys, leaving Lucy to ponder and appreciate the efforts of her sister, willing to overstep propriety to forward the interests of her sibling. Had Margaret not expressed her interest in seeing the coach, then Lucy would never have accessed this opportunity.

A double cross brace. She shook her head in disbelief as she recalled the exchange. That a man so familiar with coaches should suggest such a thing was absurd. Completely absurd—

Lucy groaned, though not so loud that her parents noticed. Of course he would not make such a mistake. And of course she could not help but correct it.

Halfway home and far too committed to back out now, Lucy Elliot realized she had taken the bait—hook, line, and sinker.

CHAPTER 23

After two days of contemplating ways to get out of her obligation, and of considering whether it was even her preference, Lucy finally reconciled with herself that she would follow through as planned. So it was that some five days later, she found herself on her way to Elsworth once more. Were the visit to be a social one involving company, her parents would have insisted on her taking the coach, but as it was a spring day and she was not attending a tea party she was able to convince them that she might ride. The day was sufficiently fine, and the pace sufficiently easy, that Daisy, a horse with whom Lucy had a strained relationship, was mostly behaving herself. Even the Elsworth grounds seemed fresh and ready for opportunity, having reclaimed some of their natural growth following the manicuring they had received prior to the ball.

As she drew up the horse to the front door, she saw a familiar face, though one that had been altered by the years.

"Miss Lucy." Thomas Marbrook tipped his hat. As a groundsman at Atherton he had on occasion overlooked Margaret's more adventurous exploits or Lucy's rapacious curiosity as they explored their surroundings. When the children no longer needed nurse or minder in the form of his wife, the couple were fortunate enough to find this position, caring for Elsworth.

"It is good to see you again, Thomas. The state of the grounds does you credit."

"I can only claim so much. It is a fine estate that does well in caring for itself."

"I hope the new master of the place is treating you well."

"Aye. He is a straightforward man. Having met his father but once I cannot say how he compares, but he assuredly has an affection for the place. My Theadora tells me she shall be chaperoning you today."

"She is. Is she well?"

"Her hearing is not what it used to be, but I daresay her cooking improves year by year."

"We were fortunate enough to sample it last week."

"If you wish, I shall lead your horse to the stable. Mrs. Marbrook awaits you."

Lucy nodded, handing him the reins and stepping up to knock upon the front door. With surprising swiftness she was met with the warm and welcoming face of her old nurse.

"Miss Lucy."

Though it did not come naturally, Lucy felt it right that she should hug her former companion. While she had a fondness for the woman and mostly good memories, she was aware that the Elliot girls had not always been the most gracious of charges. They were not so much ill-behaved as they were beholden to their characters—Margaret cooperative but impulsive, Lucy shy but stubborn. Mrs. Marbrook had tended them with patience, though it could be sorely tested. As they had grown, so too did their respect for the woman. A sad aspect of reality was that by the time they were old enough to truly appreciate their nurse, they were also old enough that her services were no longer required.

"I take it you are well here?" Lucy asked when they broke apart.

Mrs. Marbrook nodded thoughtfully. "I could ask for little more to satisfy me than the life I have."

"Thomas mentioned your hearing has been troubling you?"

"Pardon?" The older woman paused for a second, then grinned. "Oh, I'm not so bad. I've heard most of his stories anyway."

"I hope it is not too great an imposition to request your time today."

"Not at all. Our Sally and Thomas Junior are off at the town school, and I had no plans but to knit them up new woolens. They're growing so fast they shan't fit them by next winter."

"Is Captain Dashwood in?"

"He is expected back from town within the hour. I hope it is not impertinent of me to ask how things are at Atherton."

"It would only be proper of me to inform you of such things."

"My dear Lucy, it seems your sense of duty drives you as fiercely as ever."

"I should like to think that the perspective of an adult means that I am able to discern when propriety is appropriate to the situation."

"Whether it is proper to be proper?" Mrs. Marbrook asked with amusement.

"Yes. I suppose that is an apt summary."

Half an hour passed in pleasant reminiscing before they were interrupted by the sound of hooves and cartwheels. They exited the manor to the sight of Captain Dashwood on horseback and a cart covered with a cloth, drawn by a younger man.

He rides very well. Lucy recalled her sister's words. It was a claim she could not fault, for he sat upon his horse with a comfortable appearance she had never seen him in before. It was as if at any moment he could just as easily casually dismount or burst into action.

Or sweep a maiden off her feet.

That, she realized, would be quite impractical. Without stirrups she would have to hold on tightly, arms wrapped around his waist, pressed to his back and—

"Miss Elliot. I hope you have not been building without me."

"Whyever should you make such an assumption?"

"Your complexion is somewhat flushed. Then again it is a hot day." He dismounted gracefully, wiping his brow with a necker-chief.

"Yes," she said abruptly. "Yes, it is."

"I apologize for my delay. My expedition took longer than planned."

"Not at all, Captain. It has been a pleasure catching up with Mrs. Marbrook. Your expedition?"

"Parts ordered from London. Jim, would you take the cart around to the stables? Miss Elliot, I must excuse myself to change garments for the workshop."

She nodded politely, taking a breath, and only briefly visual-izing what that act of him changing might look like. She followed the cart to the stables at the rear of the house, where the young man uncoupled the horses.

"Ma'am." He bowed in a polite but slightly awkward manner.

"Did I hear your name was Jim?"

"Yes, ma'am."

"You served with Captain Dashwood?"

"Yes, ma'am."

Lucy swiftly assessed that the boy was not to be a wealth of in-formation about the captain. Then again, perhaps he was simply shy about new company, something she herself could certainly attest to. Even so, it struck her as curious that Dashwood should bring an army attendant with him on a family affair.

Jim drew back the covers on the cart to reveal an assortment of parts and pieces all jumbled in a manner that instantly offended her sensibilities but equally challenged her instinct to identify them. There were, she concluded, more than enough parts to fully construct a coach and have some left over, depending on which customization they chose.

"Were you with the messenger cavalry, Jim?"

"No, ma'am. Engineers."

"Engineers?"

"Yes, ma'am. I come from a long line of shipwrights."

"Then shouldn't—"

"Shouldn't I be in the navy?" he finished with the familiarity of someone who had answered the question many times before. He caught himself and resumed a more humble tone. "Apologies, ma'am. I meant no offense."

"Nor is it taken," she replied. "But I expect there is a tale to it."

"Not much of one. No sea legs. I can swim all day, but I get ill in a rowboat. So no navy life for me."

"Well, you're better than me. I can't swim at all."

"I don't suppose you'd need to. Luckily there are plenty of things to build on land."

"So how is it you are here with Captain Dashwood?"

"Not my place to say, ma'am. I go where I'm told."

"Of course."

She said no more but watched as he moved the parts, assembling them in her mind, deconstructing and rebuilding over and over again. One model for speed. One for maneuverability. One for stability.

But how to achieve them all? Was it even possible?

As in life, coach racing seemed to be a world of compromises.

She was halfway through mentally remodeling the front rigging when Captain Dashwood reappeared, accompanied by Mrs. Marbrook. Her host had changed into looser trousers, and a jacket that had seen better days and would have had him quietly expelled from some of the more expensive parlors of the district. And yet he seemed perfectly at ease in the clothes. *How many worlds can this man comfortably inhabit*, Lucy thought, *when I find it hard enough to abide one?*

"Thank you for waiting, Miss Elliot. Forgive my impertinence earlier. It was in jest. I didn't really think you had started building without me."

"On the contrary, sir, I have been building for several minutes."

"You have?" He looked about in confusion.

"Perhaps 'designing' would be a more appropriate word. You have the makings of a passable coach here."

"If that is what we have, then I have no doubt that between us we can make a great one."

Lucy couldn't help the tiny smile that curved her mouth at his words. She turned studiously back to the parts, before he could see it.

CHAPTER 24

AND SO THEIR WORK BEGAN: EXPLANATION AND DISCUSSION FIRST, backed up by sketches when Lucy was unable to fully translate her thoughts into words. Occasionally Dashwood would be forced to bring her fancies down to earth, Lucy reluctantly conceding that theoretical design sometimes must give way to practical experience. At other times he would be amazed at the potential of her innovations, able to see how they might impact racing.

There was an ease of flow in the work, the chance for her to lose herself in the task at hand, as she had during racing. She had found peace in such tasks before, but never with such ease in company. There were moments she forgot there was a world beyond the two of them.

Of course, there certainly was, with the calm eye of Mrs. Marbrook, knitting steadily, occasionally glancing their way, but otherwise seemingly content that her charges were behaving themselves. Not that such supervision was strictly necessary. They had maintained a respectable distance and had never even made contact. Except, that is, for one instance of him leaning over her to pick up an iron brace pin just as she moved in his direction. Lucy had stiffened abruptly as her shoulder brushed his chest. Though her outer body was still, she experienced a disorienting feeling of her insides briefly floating upward. She was quite sure he had felt something too, momentarily pausing as he did, but perhaps it was merely a reaction to *her* strange response.

As for the manual labor, Captain Dashwood was able to assemble the basic parts, the pins and braces, with an ease that impressed her. He'd done this before, she was certain, for he was familiar with construction at a practical level. As an army driver, she supposed a knowledge of emergency repairs would be a vital skill. In the Battle of Roliça perhaps? She recalled it as something Torres had mentioned. The captain was a man of untold stories and Lucy realized she wished to know them not only for information but also for personal gratification. It was not a feeling to which she was accustomed.

Nor was she accustomed to the deference and praise with which he treated her opinion. She recalled their discussion at the Night Races and how remarkably easy it had been, and now it struck her once more. She did not need to check herself for over-speaking or being too technical. Her family tolerated her eccentricities, but it seemed that Captain Dashwood not only accepted but also admired them. That alone, in her eyes, made him a remarkable man.

Lucy was surprised Mrs. Marbrook announced it was time for lunch, for she had not estimated much of the day to have passed. In truth she had quite lost track of the hour and, once reminded, became aware of her hunger.

Having washed her hands thoroughly of various smudges, she joined her host at the lunch table. He had changed back into a more formal shirt for the occasion, his hands equally clean, though rosy from meticulous scrubbing. As their eyes met, Lucy couldn't quite hold back a smirk at his look of slight awkwardness as he sat across the table from her. Perhaps he wasn't entirely impervious.

His brow furrowed. "What amuses you?" he inquired.

"Forgive me, but you looked somewhat uncomfortable."

"And that is of amusement to you?" He raised an eyebrow.

"Only in its rarity. You are always at ease with your company. Be it a ball or a family dinner or on a coach. I can scarce imagine a setting where you are not a fine fit."

"I can assure you, there are customs of society that do not

come naturally to me. I learned manners as a young man and un-learned many of them in the army. But, to use a military device, one wears the uniform that befits the battlefield. I may wear a fine dress coat to a ball but I find it . . ."

She filled the pause. "Inflexible."

"That is a fine way of phrasing it. I will admit they do chafe at times. The customs, not the coats. You, however, seem well at home with them."

Lucy took in his words in earnest. She took a bite of her sand-wich, giving herself time to contemplate her reply.

"It is . . ." She struggled to articulate. "It is not wholly that I am a woman beholden to the rules of society, Captain Dashwood. I am born to a world where social cues and notions are of the most vital importance. And yet those notions that come to others with so little effort, are so often unfelt by me. Should a companion not shriek or yawn, I could scarcely tell if they were afraid or bored. The jest of a smile. the jibe of an inflection—they sail past me. I navigate the seas of society by set rules as a captain navigates by his charts. Without them I am adrift."

There was a long pause as the words settled upon them both. It was perhaps the most wondrously insightful description of her character that had ever been spoken; more wondrous still that it had been spoken by Lucy herself. It took her a moment before she was able to turn her attention to her companion to gauge his re-sponse. There was in his features a stern contemplation she had not yet seen, and she feared she had crossed some unobserved barrier of decorum.

"You impress me with your earnestness, Miss Elliot. It is a trait to which I wish I were more naturally inclined."

"You are not an earnest man?" she asked, aware of her suspi-cions in the matter, but surprised at the admission.

"To dissemble is, I like to think, not in my natural character. I cannot deny that I have an aptitude for it, though not a prefer-ence. You speak as if you have perceived such in me yourself."

"I have. Your actions have led me to wonder at the level of calculation to them. It seemed to me that your behavior at your ball had the intention of insinuating yourself into the good graces of the district."

"That I cannot deny, though it is also in my nature to make connections where I find them. I should just as likely have done it were it not my specific design."

"But it *was* your specific design." She was again shocked by the confession, her mind following the threads of logic. "A gentleman new to the district might do so for reputation or to advance himself. Yet you had a deeper purpose. You became familiar with the shopkeepers and tradesmen, with the staff of your manor, even with . . . other circles. You cast your net wide and you would not do so without the most specific of goals."

That was the heart of the mystery. The one that had puzzled her from the moment she had first heard of the gentleman.

When in doubt, acquire more information, she reasoned. She sipped her drink while gathering her wits.

"Swiftly becoming familiar with the local community would be important for a man who was a target. There are rumors of a gambling debt that forced you to return home. What exactly is the story behind it?"

"I fear you will not like the story."

"All the better I should hear it."

"True. I was, as you know, stationed in Sierra Leone. Their capital, Freetown, is home to some less-than-savory establishments where the best cards are played. I was doing quite well until a rather devastating loss. I was convinced they were cheating, but could not prove as such. Then the rather dangerous group made an offer. There was to be a horse race a few days later, which I was to enter and to lose. I had something of a reputation as a skilled rider, so I was a favorite to win. Especially among my men."

He paused, but Lucy remained silent and attentive.

"So I ran the race, feigning a modest ride. Until at the last stretch I put on speed. I assure you it was not pride, rather I could not bear for my men to lose their hard-earned wages. I crossed the finish line first, then kept going all the way to the port. My father had pulled some strings to arrange a berth for me. I returned to home soil with nothing but the clothes on my back and was packed off here to be safe and to avoid embarrassment."

The tale hung in the air of the dining room.

"What do you think?" he asked after some hesitation.

"I think it needs work," she replied bluntly.

"I beg your pardon."

"Your father arranged a berth?"

"Yes. Though elderly, he is not without sway."

"But you said the race was a few days later. How did word get to him and back again so swiftly?"

"Well—"

"You came home with nothing but what you were wearing, yet you showed up to the races with a coach you used in Africa. Hard to believe it was shipped back here at the request of a disgraced army officer." She tried in earnest to read his expression but could not decide between consternation and admiration.

"Indeed." He gave a wry smile. "I did say you wouldn't like the story."

"So," she asked calmly, "why are you here, Captain Dashwood?"

He took a breath, and his expression became one of unmistakable seriousness. "I confess this to you with the utmost confidence, Miss Elliot. What I tell you now is known to no one in the district. Not to Jim. Not even to Mrs. Marbrook, who watches us intently but whose hearing is such that she cannot make out our speech from this distance."

Lucy glanced over her shoulder to the older woman in the far corner, who smiled but gave no indication she had heard mention of her name.

"If you do not wish to know, I shall not tell you. But if you do, then I am placing my life in your hands. Are you certain you wish to know?"

For a reason Lucy could not discern she was reminded of a moment in the moonlight years ago: her entrance to the world of the Night Races and a choice that had changed the roads she traveled.

"Yes," she replied. "Yes, I am."

"I am not here to assess my father's lands, though Elsworth Manor is indeed his, and he is suffering from old age and poor health. Nor am I an exile forced to flee a gambling scandal. That is a fiction contrived to divert the attention of those inclined to dig deeper."

She nodded in assent.

"I am here by express military command. The robbery of Sir Walter St. Martin's brandy was not the first in this district. Two army couriers have vanished in the last six months, both times carrying payroll and some documentation. I have been sent here to uncover the culprits and bring them to justice."

Whatever suppositions she had formed around Captain Dashwood, this revelation was well outside them. There had been a hint of truth in her suspicion about his connection to the robbery, but it had been wholly inverted. Rather than being a culprit, it seemed he was searching for the very same answers she was. She felt a sense of guilt at having thought him a gambler, yet as that was the impression he deliberately crafted, she could scarcely be too hard on herself. She shook off such thoughts, instead focusing on the case at hand.

"Surely a couple of thefts could be handled by local magistrates," she said.

"In normal times perhaps. Since the Treaty of Schönbrunn, Napoleon has solidified power in Europe. Our blockade is holding, but the military is afraid of any weakness. Hence my being tasked with the responsibility."

"Have you any theories on who may be behind such acts?" she asked.

"As yet, I do not know. It could be someone high up engaged in treason, or someone from common stock merely seeking money. That is the reason I have endeavored to make as many connections as possible."

"But why do you confess this to me now? That I dissembled your fiction seems poor motivation."

"On the contrary, it is a vital element. Firstly, you possess a unique insightfulness, a capacity to see the world in a different manner. You are one of the smartest people I have ever met, and I would be foolish not to utilize such intellect."

Her heart jumped at the words, and she was dumbstruck, which prevented her from humbly contradicting him.

"As my efforts," he continued, "have been of limited success, it seems reasonable to add such a perspective to mine. Secondly, through my interaction with you and your family, I have come to trust you. I am quite certain you are in no way involved in these crimes."

"Could not my behaviors be a deception?"

"If that is the case, then your skills are of such a talent that my operation will be doomed either way. No. I trust in your innocence. Thirdly, you have a knowledge of the district that, for all my connections, I cannot emulate. And . . ." He paused momentarily. "That is why I have chosen to admit the truth to you."

And fourth, she thought. She was quite sure he was about to say a fourth thing before he stopped himself, though what it might have been she could not guess. She put the thought aside and returned to the topic at hand.

"You wish *me* to aid you in investigating a string of mysterious highway robberies?" she said, realizing how outlandish it sounded spoken.

"That is the sum of it."

"Is the construction of this coach a pretense to enlist me?" Lucy asked, unable to hide the hurt in her voice. She could not deny that the promise of building a coach had been as appealing as the promise of riding in one, not to mention the company of Dashwood himself to be an attractive component.

"The coach is a means to an end. My request for your help is because I cannot conceive of a better heart and mind for the task in all of England. I neither deny nor regret that my actions in the district have ulterior motives. But I should not ask these things of you if I did not believe you wholly capable of and enthusiastic for them."

"Over the past months," Lucy began, "there have been two mysteries that have plagued my attention. The most recent, that of the missing driver, and before that the strange behavior of yourself. Since it appears that one has been solved, it stands to reason that I might devote my attentions to the other."

He nodded politely. "Well, then, Miss Elliot. Welcome to the defense of the British Empire."

CHAPTER 25

"IT WAS INITIALLY SUSPECTED," DASHWOOD EXPLAINED AS HE SORTED through a selection of bolt pins, "that the robberies were the result of foreign agents, hence my being assigned to the task. As you are no doubt aware, we stand in a tense state of affairs with Napoleon in control of most of Europe. We have superior naval forces, which give the isles a strong defensive position. But secrets and information are a vital point of military strategy, and while the robberies themselves did not involve the loss of especially critical intelligence, there remained concerns."

Lucy nodded, still comprehending what it meant to be part of a second secret world in addition to the Night Races.

Their conversation continued as they worked, breaking only when Jim and Mr. Marbrook were required to lever up the frame of the coach so that the wheels might be attached. The finessing and customizing were left to Dashwood and Lucy.

"But the latest robbery surely does not fit the pattern," Lucy mused.

"Perhaps not the pattern but certainly the style. Each coach has been found with the persons and cargo missing, but little to no indication of damage."

"Given that the previous robberies were not common knowledge," she said, "it would be an unlikely coincidence that the missing brandy is the result of a different party."

"I concur. But it may also suggest that the robberies are not the action of foreign agents after all."

"But rather the work of thieves, or at least those with money as their prime motivation."

"Precisely. Military information can be valuable for anyone with the right continental contacts. And yet . . ." Dashwood paused, twisting a bolt in place with impressive strength. "It seems curious that one would start with harder robberies and work down to easier ones. The previous coach had five men on it, four of them armed."

"Perhaps they simply found the brandy too easy a mark to ignore."

"That is my supposition also. I believe the robbers are likely very experienced in this activity."

"Which is why you attended the Night Races."

"And why I intend to race again once we are able."

"You suspect Torres?" Lucy asked.

"I do. He is a skilled night rider with continental knowledge and a mysterious background. From what you know of him, might he be capable?"

"Torres and his team were one of the two most likely parties responsible for the crime in my theories."

"The other being?"

"Yourself."

He chuckled at her blunt admission. "A logical conclusion."

"Torres and his team are formidable, both in knowledge and skill. I know nothing of them beyond the races, for it is seldom done to ask about such things. In theory they seem the most likely suspects. But it does seem at odds with what I know of their character."

"I too have such reservations. A man like Torres has no love for Napoleon. Yet a man without a country may just as easily sell his services to another." Dashwood paused again, walking over to a workbench.

With the lull in conversation, Lucy returned her focus to the practical work at hand. At the moment she was fascinated by the expansion in scale she had known intellectually to exist but

had never considered. In her models, it was easy enough to remove a pin or a screw. Here it was a matter of positioning, filing
down, bending, and hammering, some of which took significant
lengths of time for what seemed like a simple part. Dashwood was
both experienced and fit for such a task, but the spring heat and
heavier work meant that he often mopped his brow of sweat. Lucy
was quite aware that it would be inappropriate for her to lend her
hand to the crafting, and imagined she should be of little assistance if she did. But for the first time she could recall since her
childhood, she felt a compulsion to get her hands dirty. Was it the
same feeling Margaret had had when grappling with the goat, she
wondered—the desire to get the job done under one's own power?
It took a combination of her will, her desire for propriety, and the
watchful gaze of their chaperone on the far side of the workroom
to resist the urge to pick up a wrench herself.

"Do you know anything of the rest of the group?" Dashwood
asked, returning her to the conversation.

"I know the most about Hekili. Most people call him Hercules. We have talked affably several times. He has a love of carving and cares well for the horses. He came here as a whaler from
the Pacific. I cannot imagine him a criminal, but I suppose if the
need arose . . . I have never truly known want, but I am told that
given deprivation there is little one cannot be driven to."

"Alas, that is true. And yet for some the call to crime need be
little more than a whisper. Desperation may lead a man, but greed
is far more often the bait."

"Elsa is his engineer. I have conversed with her only on technical matters. I believe she is Swiss in origin."

"And the messenger?"

"Ulcha. Irish. And that is the sum of all I know of her save
what I have seen her capable of at racing."

"So, a mysterious crew assembled from across the Continent
and across the seas, with no known home. Would they be capable
of seizing a coach in motion?"

"Without question, were it their object."

"If they are guilty, they shall not give themselves away readily," Dashwood posed.

"But you have a plan to fish them out?"

"I do. It is already underway. You have been a key compatriot in it. Next full moon I intend to outrace Dante Torres."

"That will be difficult."

"I do not doubt it. He is a man who lives for the chase."

"Like yourself?"

"I cannot deny there is a thrill in racing. The wind on your face and the reins in your hands. You've felt it too. I saw it on the road."

She nodded. It seemed her observations during the races had been reciprocated.

"But for Torres I think it is more than that," said Dashwood. "His livelihood at least. If I can beat him at the Night Races I hope I might see what manner of man he is beneath his mask."

"He will not be expecting you to race him again so soon," said Lucy. "But he is a canny racer, as you know. We can build a fast coach, but we must work in concert to defeat him. Horses, coach, messenger, and driver."

"That is my hope. I have had the axle reinforced and the pin double-locked so we shall not have a repeat of the accident that put this coach in my hands. But I am uncertain as to what modifications to apply."

"Dual-spring suspension."

"It would lose speed on the corners."

"This can be adjusted for by the driver, but not completely," she said. "We would need a way to gain it again on the straight."

Dashwood began to hook one of the coiled springs onto a pin, and, without thinking, Lucy swiftly stepped forward to stop him, putting her hand over his.

Again they both froze. She had applied no pressure, but her merest touch halted his movement. Without a word he seemed to divine her meaning, gently lifting his hand away with hers still on it before she came to her senses and pulled back.

"That spring is for the crossbar," she managed after a moment. "It runs sideways, not lengthways. Had you continued to apply pressure it would have slipped and you could easily have been hurt with the backlash."

"I see," he replied. He was not looking at the crossbar but holding her gaze.

Something in her felt like a spring itself, coiled and tense. She took a breath, knowing her nerves well enough to calm them.

There was the scent of iron, mahogany, lavender, and lemongrass. Had she missed lemongrass in his cologne during the race?

No, Lucy, she reminded herself. *The lemongrass is yours.*

She felt the tension slowly unwind.

"Thank you, Miss Elliot." His voice broke the silence, a shade rougher than usual. "I am less familiar with this element of design. Perhaps you could direct me to—Miss Elliot?"

She raised a finger but did not reply. Her thoughts were already several steps ahead. Would the mathematics work? The materials? The construction?

"Lucy? Are you all right?" he asked.

"I am . . ." She considered. "I am in need of a pencil and paper."

As Dashwood went to retrieve it without question, she continued to sketch in her mind. Perhaps victory over Torres was possible after all.

CHAPTER 26

BEFORE ANY THEORY OR DESIGN COULD BE TESTED, LUCY WAS RE-quired to return to her other world, which now held only distrac-tions from her two fixations of the moment—the potential of her coach and the mystery of the robberies. Captain Dashwood was absolutely not a third fixation.

The events of her day took precedence in Lucy's mind even as Margaret did her best to engage her.

"I suppose it is a match that could be most sensible," the elder Elliot sister opined as they sat in the parlor.

Spring at Atherton could be a difficult season—too warm for the fire but cool enough to require a shawl if seated for too long. Margaret was working on her sketches, another craft in which she had improved more through effort than natural talent and in which she had overtaken her sister in their teenage years. Lucy had a precise hand and an eye for detail, but beyond the technical she found it difficult to improve. She struggled when sketching nature or animals and was worst of all with people. It confounded Lucy to the point of frustration that she might draw a precise like-ness yet somehow capture nothing of the character of the subject. Her images always appeared as if a sketch of a waxwork, somehow a step removed from the real thing. It was a hurdle she saw no path to overcome, so she had abandoned her practice.

"Though it seems curious that one may call the match sen-sible when neither party is particularly of that nature them-selves." Margaret glanced up at her sister, sitting silently at her needlepoint. "Do you not think so, Lucy?"

"It is frustrating," she replied, "that steel cannot be produced in effective quantity to be used in coaches." She paused for a moment then turned to Margaret. "You said something about sensibility?"

"You have not heard a word I've said, have you? I cannot imagine your thread work is so enthralling."

"In truth, I do it only to keep my hands busy while I think. I apologize. My thoughts have been on coaches all day."

"And shall be for a good few days more, knowing you. But might you pay attention long enough to absorb what I am saying? If you express surprise at it later, it will reflect badly upon both of us."

Lucy nodded and tried to focus her attention.

"George St. Martin and Charlotte Wyndham are engaged."

"To each other?" Lucy expressed her surprise.

"That was my reaction too." Margaret laughed. "Though I did a better job of stifling it in company. Upon reflection, it is not so odd a match as it might seem. They are both of a flighty nature, given to cheerfulness and storytelling. I daresay they might make a happy couple so long as their personalities balance and not amplify."

"The difference of standing is of note," Lucy mused, momentarily distracted from her other thoughts. "Sir Walter St. Martin might have some reservations. It would make sense if they were ill of fortune, but they are well furnished."

"The Wyndhams have acquitted themselves well enough since moving to the district," Margaret countered. "Though their wealth may have been amassed through the colonies, they have no scandal or disrepute to their name. However, the moods of their daughter might lean toward fancy."

"How could a headless horseman even see where to go?"

"That is not the point, Lucy."

"I suppose not. I have noted in the past that the character of George is ill-suited to you or me, so Charlotte might fit him well."

"I never thought the man would be an ill match for me. Only I for him."

"You should not hold yourself in such low esteem."

"There is a simple and idle nature in him, Lucy. I should not trust him to put effort into seeing past my imperfections."

"Then that is his failing and not yours," Lucy asserted. "Had you the wealth of Charlotte Wyndham, you should make a fine match for Oliver St. Martin."

"Perhaps. But we do not have the wealth of the Wyndhams."

There was a stillness, and Lucy felt a sense that she had offended her sister in some way. Out of a fear of worsening this offense, she allowed the silence to stretch on until her sister broke it.

"In any case, I should think that if the district were to wager on which Elliot sister were to marry first that you should have the greater odds."

"Now you do yourself a greater wrong," Lucy exclaimed. "My nature is known by all to be a peculiar one and that surely puts me below you in marriageability."

"Perhaps in the past. But recent connections cannot be overlooked."

"Connections?"

"Lucy, you cannot be so obtuse as to think that technical acumen was the sole object of Captain Dashwood's interests. It is unthinkable that he does not have at least an awareness of other motives."

"You mean . . . marriage?" she asked uncertainly.

"Of course. What else would I mean?"

Gambling, racing, and espionage? thought Lucy. Marriage was a topic she had done her best to avoid thinking of, not least of all because it arose more anxiety in her than the other three put together. As she focused on steadying her heart rate her sister filled the silence.

"He is an eligible gentleman, Lucy. He invited the family to dinner and you spent the day together engaged in an activity he knew interested you. Coach-building cannot be his sole focus. Can you honestly say you were blind to this?"

"It is, upon objective reflection, a reasonable conclusion to be reached by anyone."

"Well, that is not exactly a heartfelt endorsement of the possibility."

"I am . . . uncertain as to my feelings. I thought it prudent to . . . reserve judgment, as I did not consider it primary among his intentions."

"What other intentions do you know of?"

"My impression is that Captain Dashwood is a man dedicated to his profession. I cannot tell if marriage is in his intentions at all. He has lived a life of travel and may do so again."

"That is a fine evasion, and an unconvincing one, as he seems quite content to spend a season in the district at the behest of his father."

Sworn to secrecy as she was, Lucy could defend neither her claim, nor the loyalty of Captain Dashwood.

"If it were his intent to marry, what should be your reply?" Margaret asked.

"It is quite irrelevant!" Lucy sputtered, wishing she were able to answer to herself as well as her sister. "There are, to date, a great many unknowns, both of myself and him, and to think of a proposal is not a sensible use of my time."

"There will always be unknowns, Lucy. Life is not an equation that can be neatly balanced." Margaret put her sketchbook aside and stood. "I am going to bed. We have both been invited to see Charlotte tomorrow morning and extend our good wishes for her impending marriage. As to your possibilities, I should never wish for an option that was not your ardent intention. I merely address it to make sure you give thought to those opportunities, as frightening as you may find them."

"I shall. Good night, Margaret."

"Good night, Lucy."

Left alone in the parlor, Lucy replayed their conversation. She was aware of her opportunities. Before the arrival of Captain Dashwood she could never have imagined herself to have so many. Were it not for the Night Races or the mystery of the coaches, she might have no hesitation in accepting a proposal from such a man. But without those two elements would they even be drawn together at all? If their connection was only one of utility then she could hardly expect a proposal, let alone a future. Their conversations had been captivating and he seemed to enjoy her company, but she knew her instinct for assessing such things could be sorely lacking.

He trusted her, that much she was sure of. Twice now he had instantly replied to her urgent warning without hesitation. He had entrusted her with a dangerous professional secret and should not have done so frivolously. That thought brought her mind back to a sticking point. Were it simply a matter of marriage and society, she might have puzzled it out from the rule book she knew. But faced with secrecy and the security of the state, she found herself hurtling into the night with no idea of what path lay ahead.

The memory of orange and lavender crossed her mind. The room really was uncomfortably warm. Sleep, she knew, would not come easily yet. She placed her needlepoint aside and took up Margaret's sketch pad. Furniture, she found, made for an unexciting, but cooperative subject.

CHAPTER 27

T HE FOLLOWING DAYS FELT LIKE SOME OF THE MOST TEDIOUS AND drawn-out that Lucy had ever experienced. It was not for the lack of activities, for the pending nuptials of Charlotte Wyndham gave rise to several events that Lucy was obliged to attend. Normally she would have managed the dress shopping and picnic celebrations despite her usual discomfort for social events, but what dragged out the time was the anticipation and focus of her thoughts on the approaching full moon and the racing it entailed.

The appeal of this was threefold. First and foremost was the chance to see her construction and design come to practical form in a racing coach. Ever since she was young, fascinated with her model, she had dreamed of one day having that chance on a grand scale, and better yet to see it race.

Racing itself was the second attraction. Her skill as a messenger in the prior race and the compliments from Dashwood had proved to her she was more than capable of the role. She was well aware of the physical risks and of the unseemliness that would reflect on her if her part were to become known in society. Yet in the world of the Night Races, it did not seem inappropriate at all. Perhaps what concerned her most from her one and a half races was that they had given her a taste of something she could not deny she wanted more of. But the rush of wind, the speed of the wheels, the pounding of her heart—those were more visceral desires, ones that could not so easily be rationalized.

Nor could the third attraction: the company of Captain Dashwood. She silently chastised her sister for bringing that to her attention. Yet Margaret had only given words to something that clearly already existed.

She had found in the gentleman a level of ease she had seldom known. He took no offense at her eccentricities, and in doing so made it that much harder for her to critique herself in his presence. In fact, he seemed to approve of some of the habits she had long learned to keep hidden. For all his admirable talents his greatest might be that of allowing Lucy to feel at ease with herself while around him.

Whether constructing, conversing, or careening through the night, it was clear she wished to spend more time with him. This was something entirely new to her and she was not, for the most part, inclined to new things. Ever since her sister had mentioned it, Lucy had begun to overthink it. Were it a normal connection, in good society, she could have made use of society's clear rules. But it was definitely not a normal connection. Those were formed at balls and picnics by gentlemen seeking a companion of good character and good family, not a fellow racer, coach builder, and defender of the realm. Such a courtship fitted nowhere into the framework Lucy was familiar with. It was a game she did not know the rules for. More frighteningly, it might be a game for which there were no rules at all.

And so, as frustrating as Lucy found them, there was at least order and distraction in the social events she was taking part in. Had she been at home alone she had no doubt her mind would be whirling, so the brakes of society at least had a practical purpose.

She had never been close to Charlotte Wyndham, but there could be little doubt that the woman was happy and excited about the upcoming events. A supper party at the Wyndham manor was among the least appealing of the activities for Lucy, but one she knew she must attend. The young women in attendance were not great in number, just under twenty, but the noise they were able to generate seemed to exceed that of a full assembly. Lucy found herself trapped in a conversation about fashion with Sarah Mayhew, Katherine Dyer, and Felicity King. They persisted in asking her opinion, which she answered with increasing difficulty, not due to the questions themselves but rather the rising cacophony around her. If either the questions or the noise stopped, she might be able to focus, but as they both persisted, she found herself in an increasingly agitated state. When she found herself contemplating whether Felicity would fit in the fireplace if pushed hard enough, Lucy decided to throw nicety to the wind and break away from the conversation without excuse. The spring evening air was no cooler than that inside, but she immediately felt relief as she stepped onto the empty patio, steadying herself on a railing.

"Underwood, Thornbrook, Rawleigh, Pemberley Cross, Norfolk," she listed quietly.

As she drew even breaths and felt her tension melting away, she heard a noise that attracted her attention. Charlotte Wyndham had stepped outside, and for a moment Lucy was afraid she was there to ask her back in. But there was an uncertainty about the woman's step, and her high spirits were far more muted than Lucy had seen them in many days. The out-of-character appearance made Lucy ease away from her inner turmoil and ponder what might have brought about such a change.

"Miss Lucy," the bride-to-be began, "I find myself in an oddly perilous position in talking to you. In a time where I am surrounded by merriment there is a matter I fear requires a more sober perspective. Thus, seeing the opportunity that we may speak alone, I thought it wise to take it."

"And what is the cause of this perilousness?"

"Perhaps I overstate myself. My fear is of you. Forgive me if I am uncivil, but you have been curt with me before in a manner that I have been embarrassed by, and yet now it is that very candor I seek. I must trust that you will keep this conversation between us . . . that you do not laugh at me."

"I swear I shall neither share nor laugh." Lucy nodded. "Though if it is a matter regarding marriage, I fear I am ill-equipped to offer any advice."

"Were it an issue of my engagement to Mr. St. Martin I should have no end of open ears and helpful mouths. This is a much more curious matter. I know I am given to colorful tales, but I assure you that I do not indulge in that now."

Lucy could not imagine where Charlotte was going, so she simply let her speak at her own pace.

"Last night, I dined at St. Martins Hall. My father had planned to be there, but business dealings in London prevented him, so I was the sole representative of my family. It was a pleasant dinner. George was his delightful self; his father was eager to know all about my family, and even the other Mr. St. Martin seemed in good spirits, when he is so often somber. I played at the pianoforte for a short time after dinner and then left in the St. Martins' coach to return home. It was all a perfectly ordinary and enjoyable evening . . . until we come to the part that I swear you to secrecy on."

Here she hesitated and Lucy was forced to coax her.

"I assure you, Charlotte, I have known greater secrets than what you are about to tell me, and I would not laugh when you are so clearly in earnest."

The other woman nodded, then continued. "As we left the estate, I heard a noise behind us, of hooves. My first thought was that I had left something behind and George had ridden after us that he might return it. But when I opened the shutters—I can scarcely believe it even as I tell it—there was a horseman following us, Miss Lucy. Not at pace to catch up but riding steadily."

"That does not seem so odd. There are many on the roads at this time of year, especially as the moon waxes."

"I have not yet told the extraordinary part. It was a horse and rider both all in white. I could see them in the moonlight. Yet . . . the rider had no head."

Whatever Lucy had expected, it wasn't this. She glanced

about, half suspecting this was some manner of prank. But Charlotte seemed genuine and shaken in her tale.

"A headless horseman?" Lucy said.

"I know how ridiculous it sounds." Charlotte sighed. "You understand my quandary? I am fond of telling ghost stories or local legends. They are entertaining. In moments of fancy I might believe them to have grounding. But it is quite another thing to see such with one's own eyes. So who now am I to tell? My friends are so fixed upon my marriage that I could hardly raise it, and if I did, then they would pass it off as another of my stories." She met Lucy's gaze earnestly. "So I turn to you, Miss Elliot, not in spite of your past bluntness but because of it. You have a rational mind that will not entertain foolishness. So it is to you that I hope I may unfold my story and be believed."

As strange as the entreaty was, Lucy did believe her, at least inasmuch as she was recounting the experience as best she could.

"How did you react when you saw the rider?"

"I was quite paralyzed. I wished to call the coachman but found myself unable to speak. It was quite a sense of dread that overtook me. I wondered at the absurd notion that the rider might have come for me in penance for all the malicious tales I had told about him. Foolish, I know, but in moments of anxiety one may think the strangest things."

"You say the rider did not gain on you?"

"No. If anything, we drew farther apart. This gave me some relief it might just as likely be an omen as a vengeful spirit."

"And how long did it follow you?"

"Some way. The last I saw it was upon Rushmore Hill, just after the branch to our grounds. Just as I was fearing it would follow me all the way home it stopped. I saw it briefly on the hilltop, then it turned and headed back the way we came. You cannot imagine the relief I felt, and yet I have tried ever since to make sense of it. What advice do you have for me, Miss Lucy?"

Lucy pondered what she might say that was both honest and

did not offend the poor girl, who was now trembling though the evening air was still warm.

"If the rider meant you harm, I should think it was quite capable of it, so that threat may be disregarded," Lucy explained. "If it is an omen, then it is an ill-defined one. If it wishes you to amend your behaviors, then it must work harder to clarify its intentions."

To this Charlotte chuckled slightly, which Lucy approved of.

"In all honesty, Miss Charlotte, I think you were perhaps the subject of a strange prank. The rider neither appeared nor disappeared as a spirit might. It rode upon the path as you or I would. Were it not for the absence of a head, I am sure you would not have thought it anything supernatural."

"Perhaps not. But the absence of a head is not easily dismissed."

"A misdirection, I should think. There are many ways such an effect might be achieved. You were in a moving coach, some way off, in the night. And the horse, I take it, was of no ethereal nature whatsoever?"

"It was white," Charlotte countered. "Though I see now that is hardly cause to assume it a spirit."

"It is a curious incident, Charlotte. That I do not deny. But we cannot derive meaning of it yet, be it of this world or another. You should not trouble your mind on events uncertain and beyond your control."

"Thank you, Lucy." Charlotte nodded gratefully. "You swear you will tell no one?"

"No one. But it is most peculiar. You must speak to me if it occurs again."

"I most certainly shall," said Charlotte. "Shall we go back in? I am sure they will be noticing my absence by now."

Lucy agreed and they walked back toward the house. She dismissed the idea of ghosts, but a mysterious rider on roads plagued by highwaymen? That was most certainly something to keep note of.

CHAPTER 28

THE WALK TO THE NIGHT RACE WAS NEVER A SILENT AFFAIR, HUSHED but steady whispers rippling among the fields. But Molly had seldom been so energetic in conversation as she was as they headed toward this gathering. Having learned of the previous month's events and of the rides of Lucy Elliot, she now showered her with more questions than Lucy could at any moment respond to. The maid sorely regretted missing the event and, now she had recovered from her illness, was eager to know whether she was to witness a repeat.

Wishing to raise the hopes of neither Molly nor herself, Lucy did not reply either way. It was certainly her hope to race, and that she might do so on a coach she herself designed, but until it arrived there remained a sense of uncertainty, one that lingered until the moment she finally entered the clearing. Of the assembled coaches, two were unknown drivers from other districts. As the seasons grew warmer it was more common for racers to travel farther afield to test themselves, and their district seemed to be a popular meeting point for the east and west coast rivalries. Torres and his team were present, but tonight it was not their coach that drew her eye. It was the remodeled Pemberley Cross, a fine new coat of paint on the timber, polished and ready to race. The last time she had seen it, all the parts were in place but it was in need of cleaning, tightening, and tuning. Here it finally stood, finer than she had even imagined it.

Captain Dashwood smiled as he walked over to her. "I hope it meets your expectations, Miss Elliot."

"We shall see. An inspection is in order."

Lucy slowly paced around the coach, checking various parts and features closely, examining the links, the reins, every spot and joint with diligent focus. The only element she had not anticipated were the horses, a pair of fine chestnut-brown animals. They were remarkably nondescript, though clearly well cared for, both aspects she suspected were the deliberate design of Captain Dashwood; the air of normalcy tended to lower the expectation of others, a trick she now saw from the other side. Even the coach itself, fine though it was, gave little sign of being customized for racing.

"It is remarkable," she commented as she finished her examination of the coach.

"If it is, then it is to your credit. I might have added a part here and there, but your insight has been invaluable."

"And our addition?"

"In place. But untested. I am torn between trepidation and temptation as to its use. My hope is that it shall not be needed."

"If we are to race Torres, then I suspect it shall be."

No sooner had she spoken the name of their rival than she caught the unmistakable flick of the braid of Elsa Reinhardt approaching. The woman's eyes swept over the coach with a careful study.

"An interesting choice," she commented, "to rebuild a ruined coach."

"A necessary one," Dashwood said. "My previous coach was lost to me."

"Indeed." Elsa smiled, peering over her glasses. "I see you have imitated my suspension model."

"If one is to copy, one should copy the best," Lucy replied.

"A philosophy I cannot fault. However, the reinforced axles create excess weight."

"I balanced it through a lighter rear cross brace."

"Better for acceleration, difficult for slowing down."

"Well, we don't intend to slow down." Dashwood laughed.

As they spoke, Torres himself appeared, his eyes equally curious and a smile forming on his face.

"Looking for a rematch, I see?"

Dashwood nodded. "If you will oblige me."

"If you want to lose another coach, be my guest."

"I am not so foolhardy to make the same mistake twice. But it seems only fair that we have some stakes."

"What do you propose?

"Dinner," replied Dashwood after a moment of thought.

"Dinner?"

"The loser shall host the winner, and his team, for dinner."

A look of novelty and disbelief crossed the face of the usually unflappable Torres. "You're telling me that you'll host the four of us at a dinner at your manor?"

"Of course not," Dashwood replied with an aloofness that surprised Lucy. But before anyone could comment, the expression shifted to a sly grin. "Because I'm going to win."

Torres laughed. "The loser hosts the winner for dinner," he said with a nod.

They shook hands, and the driver and his engineers headed back toward their coach.

"A strange wager to make," Lucy commented.

"Do you know where Torres lives?"

"No."

"Neither do I. And I have been unable to learn its location by any connections. So what better way than having him invite us to his home?"

"So this was another maneuver in your investigation?"

"It is. An extra incentive to win."

"And if you lose?"

"Then they shall dine with me at Elsworth."

"And how will you explain this to society?" Lucy exclaimed. It seemed unthinkable to her to so confound the barrier between the social and racing worlds.

"I do not plan to tell them."

"Oh. That does seem an obvious solution."

"And, in any case, by having them to dinner there is still much more I can learn about them."

"It is somewhat distressing to think they might be guilty of such crimes."

"We know it is within their capabilities. Thus we must learn more of their character." He turned to check on the horses, then, perhaps sensing her anticipation, turned back. It took him a moment to recognize the expression of a young woman waiting to be asked to dance.

He stepped forward and extended his hand. "Miss Elliot. Will you do me the honor of riding with me this evening?"

She reached out to accept his offer.

"Yes, Captain Dashwood. I would be delighted."

The first race of the evening was watched with interest, the locals eager to see how the visiting teams would fare against each other. The west coast team had a heavier coach, adapted for the harsher Atlantic winds, but with the coach came an attitude of plowing forward with little regard for life or limb. The east coasters were driving a lighter coach, more influenced by continental designs—bright and ornamented, faster, but in need of a sharp driver.

"The west coasters to win, I think," Lucy mused as they waited for the race to begin. It was local tradition for visiting racers to go first if facing each other.

"They're slower," said Captain Dashwood.

"On a straight road. The east coasters will lead, but I wager they'll lose it through overconfidence and overcorrection."

"You wager? Upon what stakes?"

"I was led to believe your gambling proclivities were a pretense, Captain."

"One must keep up appearances." He gave a roguish grin.

"And what might you care to wager?"

"The same as Señor Torres? Dinner? I cannot imagine your parents would object to your inviting me."

"Very well." She smiled, and they proceeded to observe silently the beginning of the race.

To some surprise, the west coasters took the lead from the opening, charging into the night fearlessly. But then the lighter coach began to gain ground, overtaking on a corner where the heavier vehicle had to slow. From there they held the lead, gradually inching ahead of their rivals. True to form, the west coasters pursued relentlessly, never letting up even as the gap between them grew larger.

"Foolish," Dashwood remarked, peering through his spyglass. "The east coasters have a comfortable lead that cannot be taken. Why risk speeding up?"

"Boastfulness." Lucy nodded. "Did you spy the flair on the coach? Designed to make it look fancy but actually slowing it down."

Following this very prediction, the east coasters extended their lead farther and farther until the very last turn. Finding it sharper than it appeared, they overbalanced and were forced to slow and correct course. In their moment of panic, their steady rival came from behind and took a narrow lead. Back on the straight, the east coast coach began to catch up, but there was only so much the tiring horses could do. The west coast driver kept his pace steady, leaving no error or opening until finally crossing the line with a clear lead.

"Well picked, Miss Elliot. You have an eye for human character."

A laugh burst out of her, bright and loud, and he gave her a questioning look.

"My apologies." she replied. "Human character is certainly not an area in which I have natural talent."

"One need not have a natural talent to cultivate a skill. Perhaps you lack an innate social ease that some of our peers value, but you have insight nonetheless. How is it that you were suspicious of me at the ball at Elsworth?"

"That was a matter of noting small things in your actions that struck me as out of the ordinary."

"And what is that but perception of human character? I should commend it as a rarer skill than your fellows. Among all those assembled that evening, I daresay you alone noted me as unusual. Sometimes it is more important to see the snake than the grass."

She nodded and accepted the compliment, not adding that she had not been wholly alone in her observation—that Oliver St. Martin had shared some of her perceptions.

The first race complete, there were various barbs and insults exchanged between the winners and the losers, though their tone suggested that, tonight at least, the rivalry would go no further than words.

With that, it was time to turn their focus to other matters.

"Ready to race, Miss Elliot?" said Captain Dashwood.

Under the light of the moon, his eyes found hers and her heart rate rose. For once, she welcomed it.

"Most certainly."

Chapter 29

At the start of her third race, Lucy still felt apprehension, perhaps owing to the new level of uncertainty involved. The past events had relied only on her insight and sharp wits. Here her design—her very worth as a creator—was to be tested.

Dashwood was silent, knowing her well enough now to leave her in the moment. He turned his attention to the coach beside him, the messenger with her eyes closed, the driver confidently holding the reins.

"Just so you know," the Spaniard offered, "I have a preference for spicy food."

"Excellent. I shall know what to expect when I come for dinner."

Torres laughed, clearly enjoying the novelty.

Both riders and messengers had closely watched what they could of the race prior, putting into their minds the various twists and turns. But there was always a keen difference between perception and practice. As the starter signal went, the two elements merged into the instant and both coaches accelerated into the future.

Lucy found herself balancing three areas of focus at once—the road ahead, the performance of their coach, and the tactics of their rivals. Now that they were in motion she could hear the roll of the wheels, feel the shift of weight beneath her, her mind translating the forces that the coach was bearing on each joint and axle. She committed to memory the sound of smooth running, listening for any change. When she was satisfied she had a sense of it she adjusted her primary focus to the road.

It was a simple circuit with only a few twists and turns, and she was certain her driver had already held them in his mind. With the road ahead clear, the remaining obstacle to their victory was the team in the other coach. Torres was riding at a swift but steady pace. Unsure of the rival coach's capabilities, he was cautiously testing them. Dashwood kept them in line, eyes fixed on the road and reins as the horses galloped steadily. The first turn would be the key point.

"First corner. Medium turn," said Lucy.

Dashwood nodded as the turn approached. Torres took the outside, steering the curve tightly. Dashwood fared well, but with a tighter angle he was forced to slow a little and their rivals inched slightly ahead.

It was just as Lucy had suspected. Both coaches bore Elsa Reinhardt's suspension springs, but Torres was more experienced with taking the turns, knowing just how much he could manage. Dashwood, on the other hand, was cautious, learning how his new coach handled.

"Rough ground ahead. Hold speed."

Where the other carts earlier in the evening had both slowed, now both racers kept their pace. Hooves clattered over the path, unimpeded by the slight imperfections in the stones. But the wagon wheels had no such flexibility. It wasn't an issue for daytime travelers—who simply dropped speed for a time—but for racers, speed was the difference between victory and failure. Here the suspension system came into its own, and Lucy was pleased that what she had installed was a match for her Swiss rival. Engineering had its limits, though, and she still held the rail tightly as the coach shook beneath them, Dashwood hooking his feet into iron loops, legs tensed to hold him steady while he gripped the reins. Lucy briefly caught a glance from Ulcha, seemingly taking note of their matched pace.

On the second turn, Torres again took the outside, but this time Dashwood was ready, pulling an even tighter angle, losing a little speed but gaining ground. They gained no distance on their rivals, but nor did they lose it. Again they were back to matched pace on the straights, the Pemberley Cross holding its own against the custom coach, Dashwood matching reins with Torres.

If there were to be a change, it would come from the messenger catching a surprise early. Without looking, Lucy knew Ulcha would be thinking the same, equally alert with her night vision piercing the darkness ahead.

But despite Lucy's heightened alertness, no challenge appeared, only the next turn approaching. Lucy turned her attention to Torres, trying to gauge his next move.

"If he moves off the line, slow and bank long," she said quietly.

Dashwood cast her a curious glance but returned his focus to the road with a nod. He might not know precisely what Lucy meant, but she knew he trusted her judgment.

As soon as Torres began to move as Lucy had suggested he might, Dashwood reacted.

The Spaniard turned in, veering sharply and cutting across them to take the inside turn. In doing so he denied Dashwood the sharper turn he needed to keep level. A cutoff turn was a brazen move, dangerous but effective, forcing opponents to suddenly change tack.

But Dashwood was forewarned, guiding the horses into a slower turn without need for correction, so that when they came back into the straight, Torres had strengthened his lead but nowhere near as much as he had expected. The Pemberley Cross built up speed again, closing slightly on the lead coach, but Torres held his nerve, riding at a steady speed, knowing he held the advantage.

"Last turn. Tight," Lucy offered.

"Can he try a cutoff again?

"Only at risk. And he has the lead."

"Take the inside and hope it works?"

"Yes."

Now in front for the final turn, the Spaniard had no need of taking risks, once more taking the longer curve that allowed him to retain his speed. Dashwood turned sharply again, faster than ever. There was no doubt he was a swift learner.

With no turns left, they entered the final straight. The excited spectators watched from the distance. It seemed as though it might be a repeat of the previous race, a coach giving chase but unable to catch up. Dashwood coaxed the horses, but there was little speed to be gained. Torres held firm, steady and cautious, not trying to push harder than needed, knowing that a win was a win.

As the finish line came into view, it was clear that Torres could not be overtaken. Dashwood and Lucy simply did not have the power in their horses.

Despite Dashwood's earlier confidence, Lucy had always suspected the race would come to this. The skill of Torres and his team meant they had been able to anticipate everything the new team and their rebuilt coach could bring. Nothing short of the unthinkable could gain her and the captain victory.

So it was time to do the unthinkable.

"Pull it?" she asked, the calmness of her voice disguising her pounding heart.

He nodded, gripping the reins and urging the horses. "Pull it."

Lucy reached to her side, drew back a cover, and pulled the cord.

In the workings below them, a pin was pulled, a bolt springing out to remove a larger pin. With that, the foot-wide coil of wound spring unfurled with fearsome force, teeth locking into the cog by the axle. The full force of the coil now spun into the wheels, driving them faster.

As the wheels spun, the horses, briefly relieved from the load of the coach, sped forward, urged on by Dashwood. He and Lucy were pressed back into their seats by the sharp acceleration. It took only three seconds for the full energy of the spring to exhaust itself, but that was all they needed to boost them into the lead.

Lucy caught sight of Torres, looking on in disbelief at the sudden burst of speed out of nowhere. It was as shaken as she had ever seen the stoic Spaniard. Seconds later they crossed the finish line with a slim but clear lead, to the roar of a crowd that could not comprehend what they had just seen, but recognized a phenomenal last-minute triumph.

Though they came to a gradual halt, Lucy still felt as if she was racing. Her heart certainly was.

"It worked. It really worked!" she exclaimed, staying seated as she didn't yet trust her legs.

"Was there ever a doubt?" Dashwood smiled, stepping down from the coach, circling and checking the horses.

"Well, yes. There was at least a five percent chance it would rip the axle off."

His grin faded. "You might have mentioned that before."

"I thought it might throw off your focus."

"It probably would have."

"But it worked." She stood excitedly. "Of course we'll need to check whether anything was damaged when it engaged and—" She peered toward the undercarriage, misplaced her foot, and tumbled into space only to find herself standing on solid earth facing the captain, her face inches away from the lapel of his coat.

Unlike hers, Dashwood's reflexes were unhindered by the race, and he had caught her about the waist, spinning her smoothly so she reached the ground safely in his arms.

She was standing safely now. Why, then, did she feel weightless?

She stepped back, the arms that had caught her effortlessly making no attempt to contain her. It was as if it was her first race again, time slowing, but rather than the road ahead she saw only his face.

"Thank you" was all she could muster.

"You're . . . welcome," he replied, his tone as awkward as hers.

In her every encounter with the man, Captain Dashwood had seemed unflappable. Why now did he seem to have trepidation in his gaze?

"Now that was a nice trick." Torres laughed as he approached, his eyes carrying a mix of equal amusement, curiosity, and caution.

"Perhaps I'll share it over dinner." Dashwood had snapped back to his sociable self.

"A deal is a deal." Torres nodded, drawing away to meet his team.

Hekili was laughing heartily and Elsa was already peering at Lucy's coach, trying to understand what had happened. Lucy watched them happily for a moment before a darker thought struck her.

"You realize that if they are behind the robberies, you're going to be walking right into their territory without backup?"

"I'll have backup."

"Who?"

"You."

Lucy's gaze whipped to his.

Dashwood shrugged, a sly smile lighting up his face at her expression. "I do owe you dinner."

CHAPTER 30

WHILE MOLLY'S FAWNING ATTENTION ON THE WAY BACK TO ATHERton was somewhat discomforting, it also provided a welcome distraction from the situation Lucy found herself in. Captain Dashwood might be at liberty to travel to Torres's mysterious lair (why she fixed upon the word "lair" she wasn't sure), but she surely had no such option. It was one thing to spend the day at Elsworth under the watchful eye of a chaperone, quite another to abscond for an evening to an unknown spot, especially when a certain gentleman was absent at the same time. The idea that she might dine with a group so outside the borders of society as Torres, Ulcha, Elsa, and Hekili should be utterly unthinkable.

She would simply have to refuse the offer of Captain Dashwood and hope she could do so in a manner that would prevent further questions. Further questions were something she'd had quite enough of recently.

"Did you know beforehand that the race would be so close?" Molly asked intently.

"It was a suspicion, knowing the skill of the parties involved."

"It was a truly remarkable race. I have never seen the like. However did you manage to find speed from the horses in the final stretch?"

Lucy smiled. That their last-minute victory was the result of the horses was the talk of the Night Races. It was a reasonable assumption. After all, where else could speed come from? Lucy imagined that only Elsa Reinhardt knew any different and she would be most eager to learn their secret.

The question left unanswered, Molly rolled on to the next, and any need for Lucy to keep her secret from the maid was left in the past.

The return to Atherton after the Night Races was often a strange affair. As the party neared the buildings, the conversation ceased and an easy stealth guided them on. Due to good preparation, there was to be no repeat of the previous incident where they were locked out and they entered near the servants' quarters without issue. Once inside the threshold of the house, no words were spoken, the formal divide of class silently slipping back into place.

The group branched off in ones and twos until only Lucy remained. Having removed her boots, she walked in her stockings up the stairs. There was still a little moonlight, but she knew the house so well she could have easily navigated it in darkness.

Inside her room she found her nightclothes where she had left them, changing and slipping under the covers, the night chill soon leaving her. She fell asleep with the thought of her coach, of her mechanical success, and what might be the possibilities in the future. Possibilities drifted into impossibilities and dreams of curious coaches formed of geometrical paradoxes and impossible lengths. The only constant in them was that, whatever shape they took, Dashwood was riding them alongside her.

"I have been giving thought to the discussion we had the other evening," Lucy announced to her sister after some period of silence on their morning walk.

"Regarding?" Margaret asked.

"The intentions of Captain Dashwood."

"Have you had correspondence or spoken with him since?"

"There has been no social occasion for us to communicate," Lucy replied diplomatically. "And I cannot speak to his intentions or indeed, with certainty, to mine. However, there is by extension a matter that arises if such a union were to pass."

"And what matter might that be?

"I am unaware as to the whole nature of what income Captain Dashwood might be in possession of, but as Elsworth is only one of his father's properties, even if the others are of a lesser standing, he has wealth enough for a comfortable living."

"That may be assumed."

"If I were to marry into such a comfortable living, it is most likely that any share of our inheritance might be freed up for yourself."

"Lucy, it would be up to Father as to how that might unfold."

"But not without the input of both his daughters, I should suggest. He is a kind and reasonable man, and I think he should see sense in the face of a united front."

"It is a kindness for you to offer, Lucy, but to what end? I should be comfortable enough at Atherton knowing of your happiness and my security."

"Security perhaps, as you should one day be lady of the house. But happiness? That is a matter of equal concern to me, Meg."

"Speak plainly, Lucy. I still do not comprehend your meaning."

"If money was not an issue, who would you wish to be your husband?"

Margaret demurred, but it was clear the question elicited an answer in her.

"I felt when we spoke of the matter that the affection you and Oliver St. Martin once felt was not altogether extinguished," Lucy said carefully.

"He is a fine gentleman." Margaret blushed. "I would say that we shared a passion for knowledge and a modest disdain for the shallower of our peers. It is important, I think, for a couple to share dislikes as well as likes. It is curious, really. I daresay many discussions in the district paired us off because of stature alone. But truth be told, I think I should be as fond of the man were he as short as Napoleon."

"In actuality, Napoleon is not short, Margaret. It is . . . I am taking myself off the topic, aren't I?"

"Almost." Her sister smiled.

"Oliver is heir to no fortune beyond his saved allowance. And yet, if it was you who had income, it might not be so great an issue."

"There would be, for many men, an issue of pride."

"For many men, no doubt. But I think Mr. St. Martin might be trusted to put such aside for a chance at happiness."

"It is most kind. But I implore you, Lucy, that you not put my happiness ahead of yours. I should not have you marry out of deference to your sister."

"Nor would I wish to place such a weight upon you. I promise you, Margaret, if I am to marry it shall be for my own happiness and ends. But that need not preclude an outcome that is favorable to us both."

"That is true."

"As I have noted, I am unsure how things may develop. I merely wished for your thoughts and feelings on the matter. I should suggest, for the time, that such possibilities remain between the two of us. It is unfair to bolster our parents' expectations too early."

"Agreed."

The topic concluded, they entered the town with a new appreciation of the day.

"Will you come to the dress shop, Lucy? I have alterations to be done for my dress for Charlotte's wedding."

"I understood that the bridal party dresses had been made to size."

"It seems the London store made an unfortunate assumption. Alteration is perhaps an understatement of the truth."

"You should not want your shoulders undoing a dress at a wedding."

"The shoulders are the least of it. It is a dress tailored to my dimensions quite neatly, but for the lack of a foot."

"A foot?"

"It is a dress for a rather large woman of five foot, one inch."

Lucy only partly managed to suppress a laugh.

"My attempting to wear it should pass from the indecent to the impossible. So Mrs. Calloway is to do her best at patchworking what she can in the hope that Charlotte and her mother never learn the truth."

Lucy chuckled. "I think I will leave you to this work alone."

Parting from her sister, Lucy briefly browsed the bookshelves of the town store for new publications. There were a couple of novels and a gazette on the Lake District, but nothing of such interest that it held her attention for more than a glance. Strolling idly outside, she caught sight of the blacksmith, alone and working on sharpening an ax in his storefront.

Taking the opportunity, she crossed over toward him, standing by a railing, facing away from him, but clearly within earshot.

"Spring is becoming warmer, Mr. Kelly."

"Aye, Miss Elliot. To my dread. Summer is too hot a time for my line of work."

"I should like to commend you on your work. The coil functioned just as anticipated."

"I heard about your race the other night. Put two and two together and figured the difference might have been your secret gadget."

"I trust it will remain so?"

"I'll not speak a word. But as my father used to say, the only thing harder than steel is keeping a secret."

"Diamonds are harder than steel," Lucy replied. "Thank you, Mr. Kelly."

She was already several feet away before she realized her excessive literalism, and by then it was far too late to do anything other than sigh.

Secrets. Lucy felt she had never held so many.

CHAPTER 31

MARGARET WAS CONTENT THAT MRS. CALLOWAY'S ALTERATIONS HAD been successful.

"I can only hope that the change is not so noticeable as to stand out from the others or to cause offense to Charlotte," she mused as they walked.

"I daresay that if your dress is the center of attention at the wedding, then a great many other things must already have gone wrong," said Lucy.

"Have you ever given thought to what your wedding might be like?"

"As I have said, I am unsure of the intention—"

"I meant only in the hypothetical sense," Margaret said with a laugh. "Many a young girl plans out how her wedding will look long before she meets her groom."

"I must admit, it is not something I have ever set my mind to."

"That is most unlike you. I should have thought you would know precisely how every aspect should be."

"I do not mean to say that there is not a proper way for such an event to be held. Merely that without the particulars, one cannot formulate it. The variables are simply too great."

"The variables?"

"Yes. The primary being the groom," said Lucy. "Where should you get married, Margaret?"

"I should say the parish church."

"But whose parish? What if your groom is from far afield? Might it be more likely that the ceremony be held closer to his home?"

"I see your point."

"Even one's own choices must affect the situation. Surely my dress must complement or please my husband. Without knowing when the proposal might be, one cannot predict the season, which influences so many elements. Which guests should I invite? Supposing some have moved a great distance? Supposing I have gained new acquaintances? No, you see it is all quite futile. It is a subject not worthy of focus until the facts are before me."

Margaret chuckled into the afternoon countryside. Lucy remained silent and, despite her rational declaration, found herself wondering what manner of dress might catch Captain Dashwood's eye and, indeed, what cut of coat might please hers.

Upon their return to Atherton, the sisters found their parents in a heightened state of curiosity and anticipation. An official-seeming letter had arrived, addressed to Lucy, and they were anxious to know the contents. For a moment she wondered if it might be from Captain Dashwood, and if that were the case, she would certainly wish to read it in private.

But the formal-looking envelope appeared more business than personal, and she decided to open and read it in the sitting room. She read through it in silence and, upon completion, passed it to her eager family with the hope that by the time they had finished, she would be able to explain the contents. This was to be a challenge, for she was still in the midst of processing the words herself.

FROM THE OFFICES OF REINHARDT AND CO., TRANSPORTATION ENGINEERS

Dear Miss Elliot,

It has come to our attention that you have recently been involved in the reconstruction of a Femberley Cross

*model coach. Through our connection with its owner,
Captain James Dashwood, we are most eager to review and
discuss some of the alterations and additions you have
made. Advancing the engineering of coaches is at the very
heart of our business, and we are always interested in new
innovations, which your designs certainly reflect.*

*We would like to invite you to our headquarters that
you might meet with our design team, discuss your work,
and give assessment of some of our prototypes.*

*If you are amenable to this, we will arrange
transportation, chaperone, and accommodation on a date
preferable to yourself.*

Yours in appreciation,
E. Reinhardt

Genius, Lucy thought. The story was all so utterly plausible. In
fact, even more insidious, every word was technically true.

She could not deny any part of it without exposing her connection to the Night Races. She could possibly refuse without
explanation and her family might pass it off as one of her eccentricities. Yet it simply didn't feel right to decline what was an un-
deniably well-crafted invitation but also one that preserved her
secrets.

There was, she suspected, a stroke of Dashwood's input in
this, for it not only met his ends but also had all the hallmarks
of the snares he seemed so adept at laying in people's paths. For
a moment she was aggravated at the thought, deciding she should
refuse out of principle. Why should she put herself in danger just
because he wanted company?

Was there danger in answering the invitation? And if so,
could she truly live with herself if she let Dashwood face that danger alone?

"It is quite extraordinary," her father exclaimed after they
had all finished reading the letter. "I shall admit my surprise,

Lucy. As clever a mechanical mind as you possess, I should not have imagined it would invoke so keen an interest."

"I must offer a degree of caution in this," said her mother more somberly. "While I have never been one to deny your interests, we must be prepared for such a connection to be the cause of talk in the district. It would be seen as most unladylike for you to follow through on such a course, however much it might bring you joy."

"It is not necessarily a course, Mother, merely a couple of days. Should it be so different to the gossip that would follow were I to go off in study of art and music?"

"I fear it should. Art and music are womanly pursuits. Mechanical engineering most certainly is not."

"Perhaps we should say I am sculpting, then. That has a partial truth to it."

"Perhaps we should tell them nothing at all," Margaret cut in for the first time.

Her parents and sister turned to her, drawn by the sternness of her tone.

"What business is it of anyone in the district? Tell them she is visiting friends. That she is engaged in studies. Charlotte Wyndham is to be married in two weeks. She will be all people are talking of. If someone pries so deeply that it cannot be denied, by all means tell the truth, but I doubt that shall ever come to pass. The person who thinks less of Lucy for following her talent is a person who neither knows her nor cares to." Her outburst completed, Margaret stood silent.

Any argument against Lucy's going seemed to have been silenced forever, even that of Lucy herself. There seemed no way out of such a spirited defense.

Lucy was uncertain of what to expect, and being uncertain of what to expect was one of her least enjoyable states to be in. However, since she was committed, and a great many elements were quite out of her control, she instead focused on the aspects she could manage.

An easy element of consideration was what she might take on this excursion. She decided on a casual spring dress, and a heavier winter dress that was long due for retirement due to wear and tear, and a wine stain that refused to be shifted. The only reason it had remained in her wardrobe so long was that it was eminently comfortable both materially and emotionally, having carried her through many seasons. She anticipated that, at some point, she would find herself examining the underside of a carriage and a free-fitting, sacrificial dress was just the sort of thing she needed. A cloak would keep her warm enough if they experienced a shift in the weather—not likely, but not impossible even in this late spring season. Such a garment would also serve as additional bedding if the accommodation was cold.

The accommodation. The word, so official-seeming yet so ill-placed, reminded her that she really had no idea of what she was getting herself into. Arrangements had been made for lodgings in Hackney, but she very much doubted this would be the case. She was entering a different world. If the Night Races were a moonlight dance in a fairy circle, then she was preparing a visit to enter the fay kingdom outright.

The odd thought triggered a recollection of old stories that fairies disliked cold steel, prompting her to visit the kitchen and secure a small but sharp paring knife. Lucy did not believe in fairies any more than she believed in headless horsemen, but she did believe that, in a desperate moment, a knife might be as effective against a person as a mythical creature. She slipped it into a small leather pouch that had previously housed a comb and now fitted snugly within her boot. She placed a few other items into a small bag: a hairbrush, a handkerchief, a notebook, a pencil, and, as an afterthought, a small pack of bonbons she had purchased as a Christmas gift but not given away.

A fine guest you are to be, Miss Elliot, she thought, coming with sweets in her pocket and a knife in her boot.

When she felt there was no more that she could pack or prepare for, she passed her time writing letters. One was to Charlotte Wyndham, to be given along with their gift on her wedding day. And one was to her family. This second letter was the most difficult to word, and she started over several times before she was satisfied. Once complete, she placed it in an envelope, sealed it with a drop of wax, and wrote her name upon it. By her calculation, having one's own name upon a letter provided security against all but the most prying eyes accidentally reading it.

She then passed through the house with casual caution until she came to a room that was in the middle of being dusted.

"Molly," she said quietly.

The maid turned, surprised to be addressed by the young mistress of the house in this place and at this time of day.

"Yes, Miss Elliot?"

How strange it was that the girl who had been so talkative only nights ago was now so timid a creature. But then, by all appearances, Lucy Elliot was a different being by moonlight too.

"I would like you to hold on to this letter for me. I am to be away for several days, after which I shall reclaim it from you. If . . ." She paused to consider her wording. "If I am not returned in five days' time and I have sent no other word of my whereabouts, please give it to my sister to read."

"Yes, miss." She nodded, taking the letter and tucking it into her skirt pocket. "Are you . . . not likely to return?" she asked, her curiosity and care overstepping her station.

"I believe I shall return without incident. But, as we both know, accidents can happen."

There was a moment of unspoken understanding between them.

"Take care, Miss Elliot."

"Thank you," Lucy replied, leaving the girl to her work.

CHAPTER 32

WHEN THE DAY OF LUCY'S DEPARTURE NEARED, HER FAMILY SHARED her anticipation but little of her nerves. They saw their daughter as visiting an established craftsman and business. Correspondence had been made several times from the Hackney address, which involved either an established cover or an expert interception of Royal Mail. Lucy was uncertain whether the subterfuge was the product of Dashwood or Torres, both seeming equally capable of it. Her family did not know the invitation had come from an eccentric Swiss inventor living in parts unknown with a mixed band of rogues. The band of rogues in turn did not know they were being investigated in regard to a string of robberies. Lucy and Captain Dashwood did not know if their subjects were guilty, or dangerous, or some combination of both. There were so many unknowns that Lucy was envious of the simplicity her parents and sibling were managing.

But there was nothing for it now. If all went well, they would never know anything different.

On the morning of the arranged collection, Lucy waited nervously, sitting, then pacing, then sitting again when she felt her pacing threatening to turn into a sprint. One way or another, she knew that coaches awaited her so she focused on that.

Underwood, Thornbrook, Rawleigh, Pemberley Cross, Norfolk.

She pictured each coach in her mind, visualizing them in motion.

She was so focused on this thought that she initially wondered if the hoof steps were imagined, but as they drew nearer she realized there could be no mistaking the sound of a real-world coach.

"My goodness," Alice Elliot exclaimed. "Have you ever seen such a fine vehicle?"

Lucy did not reply. As it happened, she had seen that very coach before, up close and in motion.

It was the racing coach of Dante Torres, carved lovingly, tuned to perfection, and now out in the daylight for the first time that she knew of.

The lone driver came into view and Lucy repressed the brief urge to give a familiar wave to Hekili, seeming quite at ease in the driver's seat and less so in the jacket and trousers. It was an old but smart suit, one she imagined not out of place for a man of his style in London. He drew the cart to a halt and tipped his hat.

The door to the coach opened, and a smartly dressed woman exited.

It was the first time Lucy had ever seen Elsa Reinhardt without a long coat. She wore a light green dress, her hair was, for once, in a respectable bun that suited her very well, though she retained her glasses.

"Mr. and Mrs. Elliot. I am Elsa Reinhardt." She curtsied politely.

"Reinhardt?" Mrs. Elliot commented. "You are related to the business?"

"I am from a fine line of engineers and inventors," she replied. "And you are Lucy?"

"I am," she played along.

"It is a pleasure to be formally introduced. Your bags?"

Hekili dismounted and helped steer the valet to the rear of the coach to load Lucy's bag. She was certain the luggage carrier was an addition, as she had never noticed it during racing before. Other aspects of the coach looked faintly different too, but she dismissed it as possibly being simply the daylight view.

"I am grateful for your permission for Lucy to come work with us. We are quite excited about what can be learned together," Elsa said to Lucy's parents.

"You are an inventor yourself?" her father exclaimed.

"In a family business it is difficult not to be. But I can assure you that the well-being of your daughter is my focus until she is returned safely to your doorstep."

It was a fine performance. Her parents certainly believed it. Had she not known the truth, Lucy might have been wholly convinced too.

Joined by her father and sister, the Elliots exchanged brief farewells. Concerned she might give away her greater trepidation, Lucy finished these and stepped up into the coach and Elsa followed. Lucy leaned to the window, ignoring her travel mate for now, waving to her family one last time as the coach began to move away.

It was not until they were finally off the grounds of Atherton, and her family was well out of sight, that Lucy sat back in the coach.

It was the Swiss woman who broke the silence.

"You're wondering what you've got yourself into."

"Yes," Lucy admitted.

"Well . . . that is another thing we have in common."

She was silent again, observing Lucy as if waiting for something.

Unsure of what that might be, and content to wait it out, Lucy reclined in her seat. It was surprisingly comfortable, especially when—

"You cannot possibly race with such seating!" Lucy exclaimed. "The mass of the fabric alone would create needless deadweight."

Reinhardt laughed at the outburst, and Lucy realized it had been precisely what she had been awaiting.

"The interior is crafted to be flexible. The seating can be removed in its entirety."

"But that in itself is an inefficient element for racing."

"You assume it is meant solely for racing. Not everyone has the luxury of a separate coach for separate needs."

"No. I suppose not. The luggage compartment?"

"Today it is a coach for transporting a gentlewoman. It can be many things when the need arises. But I think we should dispense with the small talk and get to the heart of the issue." Elsa leaned forward with a knowing smile.

Lucy returned the smile, thinking briefly of the knife in her boot. "And what issue is that?"

"Your speed booster, of course! I know full well it wasn't the horses. I've been trying to figure it out ever since."

"Your best guess?"

"Galvanic magnetism. But I cannot conceive of a storage mechanism for such that would not be of impractical size."

Lucy smiled further and wondered just how far she should wind up her companion before she came to the answer like clockwork.

If there was any intention of keeping the path to their destination a secret, Lucy could not see it. The coach followed the main route south and she wondered at first if it might be misdirection, but as they continued it became clear it was their route.

After an hour they exhausted their initial topic of the mystery mechanism, with Elsa impressed at its simplicity and frustrated she herself had never thought of it. Their talk came to a natural end, and the Swiss woman turned her attention to a small book. Lucy, who found reading in coaches made her unwell, instead considered the scenery and her own state. She was nervous, but that was natural given the uncertainty she was entering. But there was no excessive anxiety like she might feel before a ball or similar occasion. That, she was aware, might come later, but for now she felt in control of herself.

After an early lunch in Witham they continued, but veered

sharply south well before Chelmsford. They were quickly surrounded by trees and Lucy abandoned any attempt at plotting
their location, though she did stay alert for forks in the road. The
woods grew denser as the path grew rougher, suggesting they were
heading away from commonly used roads. Briefly, they were off
the gravel path altogether on what sounded like earth, and then
the unexpected sound of wheels on cobblestones found her ear.
At the same time the shade diminished, opening out into what
seemed more like a clearing.

Peering out the window, Lucy was surprised to see an ex-
panse of stone ruins, reclaimed by vines and trees. She wondered briefly if it might be simply a landmark in passing, but
the coach was slowing and then came to a halt, indicating they
had arrived.

Elsa opened the door and exited the coach. Lucy, unsure what
to expect, followed. The ruins spread out before them, buildings
in various states of overgrowth. With forest all around, the property seemed out of sorts and yet clearly it had once held pride of
place. Her analytical mind examined the structure and recalled
what she knew of historical architecture. She could see where the
outer walls used to be, the courtyard, the keep. She estimated that
the ruins were of fourteenth- or fifteenth-century construction.
No one had lived here for several hundred years.

Yet that was not quite true. There were paths visible, some
trodden by human feet, some larger. There were vines and foliage
trimmed back, walls rebuilt. The castle had been abandoned long
ago, but someone most certainly lived there now. Existing and re-
constructed walls had been repurposed, with several buildings of
varying size spread between the stone, with thatched roofs, timber frames, and one or two chimneys. What was once a sprawling
castle was now a small settlement.

She noticed Hekili leading the coach and horses toward a
large stone building off to one side. Stables. They had their own
stables. They had their own everything. There was even a small

stream running past for fresh water. And here it all was, built in the middle of the woods where no one ever came.

"Quite a sight, isn't it?"

Lucy turned to see Captain Dashwood strolling over to her. He was dressed in his stable clothes, remarkably at ease. She had to admit there was something tranquil about the setting; dwellings in the midst of nature.

"It is indeed. Whose land is this?"

"Blakes Woods. Crown land. They're living off the grace of King George. They even have chickens."

"Is that legal?"

"Keeping chickens?"

"Living on Crown land?"

"Almost certainly not. But I shan't hold it against them."

Lucy instinctively flinched at the casual disregard of the law, but when she forced herself to look at it logically, she could see no harm. If people did not claim the castle, the forest certainly would.

"It's not every day one gets to visit a secret hideout," Dashwood mused.

"I never said it was a secret," came the voice of Torres as he appeared from one of the buildings. "I just didn't advertise the address."

"Oh, do allow me some kind of boyish wonder. A secret hideout is so much more adventurous."

"If that is what you are looking for. Most of the time we live a quiet life."

"A racer like yourself wants a quiet life?" Dashwood asked.

"I said most of the time."

With that, Torres began to lead them on a tour of the grounds, which Lucy had decided to call the space, rather than the ruins, which seemed uncharitable. She had never doubted that Dante Torres was a proud man, but as they walked, she saw for the first time a different kind of pride, an eagerness to show others what they had accomplished as a group. They each had their own quarters, with several other rooms to spare. There was a food store, a dinner room, even a rebuilt forge and smithy. Where possible the remaining stone of the castle had been used, but additional beams and walls had been added over time. In a courtyard was a large patch of various vegetables with chickens wandering among them, scratching the earth.

It gave Lucy a peculiar feeling as she took it all in. On one hand it was all makeshift, thrown together with what was available and without concern for aesthetics. And yet it was all so efficient, everything built for a purpose, without waste or frills. Gutters channeled rain back to the stream, walls faced to make the most of the sun. She could not help but respect the engineering of what had been built here.

"However did you chance upon such a place?" Dashwood marveled.

"As you say—chance. Some years ago, I found myself traveling apace and in need of concealment, for reasons I shall not bore you with. I passed through these woods using back ways and came across this place. I made myself a shelter, which expanded over time, as did my family. Someday, perhaps we will have to move on. But for now, we put down our roots."

"And what is that?" Lucy pointed to a fresh mound of rocks and earth. It was not something that would have held her attention but for the fact it seemed to be smoldering.

"That"—Torres smiled—"is your winnings."

To her amazement he had not spoken in jest. The meal had been prepared in a style Hekili had imported from far away: a firepit, burned down to embers and hot stones, upon which food was placed, covered in leaves or cloth, then piled with earth and left to cook in a natural oven.

Lucy was both horrified and intrigued as the large man explained the process to her, explaining how it was done with the volcanic rocks of his homeland, and how it was a delicacy he missed, enjoying the chance to share it on special occasions.

It was a wide world indeed.

When the time came to dig it up, Captain Dashwood insisted on helping Hekili and Torres. In the early evening of a warm day, over the hot earth, it was hard work, and when Lucy's traitorous gaze wandered back to the men—*one man in particular*—her eyes widened on the discovery they'd discarded their shirts. A stray gust must have blown her way, for she felt a sudden flush of heat that could have only come from the fire. She swiftly averted her eyes, though not before an entirely objective assessment of Dashwood's well-defined frame.

Even from a distance, she thought she'd seen a red scar crossing his right shoulder.

Definitely not a shaving cut, she mused, averting her eyes yet again.

Perhaps sensing her discomfort, or perhaps aware of her role as chaperone, Elsa ushered Lucy away to show her the workshop. Lucy swiftly agreed though could not resist one last peek at Captain Dashwood amid the steamy air.

CHAPTER 33

Inside the workshop Lucy found the air suddenly cooler. It was every bit as neat and ordered as she might have hoped. There seemed a perfect place for every tool, some of which she recognized, but a great many she did not, from larger levers all the way through to fine clockmaking instruments.

"My father makes watches," Reinhardt explained as Lucy looked over the workshop. "He taught my brothers the craft, and, while he would not teach me, he could not stop me observing. I had never thought of scaling coiled springs into other forms. Your contraption is quite ingenious. It is a shame it could not be used for other purposes than a quick burst. I cannot yet work out how it might be put to use on a longer journey."

"I am perfectly happy for any recommendation you might have to improve its efficiency," Lucy said.

There remained a rivalry between them, but during the coach ride much of the dislike Lucy had felt toward the woman seemed to lose its edge. There was more in common in their way of thinking than she once cared to admit and it seemed foolish to foster an irrational prejudice, however irritating Elsa's braid remained.

"A gear system would allow you to reduce the size and weight, I think. It would require considerable fine-tuning. If we are so inclined, we might be able to fashion a version over the next few days."

"How do you afford such things?" Lucy asked. "Some of these more specialized tools cannot be of small expense."

"Well, how do you afford things?" Elsa asked.

Lucy considered how she might diplomatically reply. "Atherton is a sizable estate with surrounding farmland. These are rented to farmers. In addition, I believe there is a modest investment managed for us in London."

"You are most fortunate, and more aware of your fortunes than many. A great number of your class never give thought to such matters. As to how we afford things? We work for them. Custom craftsmanship may be required from time to time, or custom carving. We have a wealth of wood and Hekili has time. Perhaps we tinker with something and sell it at a market. If not our crafts, then our skills. There are times when things need to get somewhere in a hurry. Or unseen." She left the words hanging in the air, awaiting Lucy's response.

Lucy turned her attention to a selection of seats and boxes stacked on shelves. The shape and size looked familiar, and she matched them to the interior of Torres's coach. In her mind she assembled them, impressed by the modular nature and how seamlessly they might fit into the conveyance. It could be a simple cargo coach or an elegant travel vehicle. Her eyes were drawn to a curious step and box, upholstered on top, elegantly carved with wooden detailing.

"Things that need to get places," she echoed the Swiss woman. "And sometimes people?"

"You are a dangerously perceptive woman." Elsa smiled, though it was clear she was a little disturbed to have her secrets revealed quite so readily. "Were more border guards like you, I fear we should seldom succeed. But you are quite right, particularly at present. There are people of note attempting to escape the Continent and the clutches of Napoleon. Sometimes this calls for a driver with nerve and a coach with seemingly impossible compartments. Dangerous work, but rewarding."

"I have always felt detached from the war," said Lucy, "as if it were taking place in a different world."

"In a way it is." Elsa nodded. "But worlds have a gravity. They draw on each other despite distance."

"Of course they do. Kepler's laws of planetary motion."

"I was speaking more metaphorically. Of the interactions of people."

"Oh." Lucy paused. "Well, then I'd quote Isaac Newton."

"Saying what?"

"I can calculate the motion of heavenly bodies, but not the madness of people."

Elsa smiled, eyeing Lucy in a curious way she could not interpret.

"Come, then." The Swiss woman changed topic. "There will be time for coach work tomorrow. Dinner will be almost ready. Hopefully the men will not be too distracting."

Lucy followed after her. For someone so completely out of her familiar element, especially one who disliked change, she was slightly concerned at how readily she was adapting to it all.

It was a train of thought that persisted, even as they gathered about the embers of the fire, seated on sturdy wooden benches. Dashwood seemed perfectly at ease beside her, eating with a fork from a tin bowl, chatting around a campfire. There was an exhilarating freedom to the evening, an escape from the social rules that Lucy clung to, but did not always agree with. Propriety was about doing what was most appropriate to the circumstances. But that only applied in relation to the expected norms of that circumstance. It was not so vital to know which piece of cutlery was the salad fork when all everyone had was a fork and a tin bowl.

A strong earthy flavor permeated the meal: potatoes, lamb, carrots, and greens. The meat was tender and flavorsome, and Lucy wondered where they had sourced it, and if that source had been entirely legal.

"Like it?" Hekili asked with a grin.

"It has an excellent texture," she replied. "Is this how you normally cook?"

"Mostly stews for us. Or roast. This we save for special occasions."

"It is a remarkable home you've built here."

"It is. Never imagined when I was a boy that one day I'd be living in a castle. The sea takes us strange places."

"That it does," Dashwood interjected. "I can see how being a whaling shipwright might lead you here and how coaches might attract an engineer, but what brings you to this place, Señor Torres?"

The Spaniard paused, clearly weighing up the question and the man who posed it. "My father was a courier," he said eventually. "I was learning to drive a coach before I could walk. I grew into the same profession. But when the wars came it got harder. If you didn't work for the army, work got slimmer and slimmer. My father and mother were getting older then; I was bringing in the money. Not enough money. So I started finding other jobs. Getting things places fast. Or unseen. With less to go around, well, that meant there was good money in the things people wanted most. I stopped asking questions. People paid the most for that."

Torres flicked a piece of gristle into the embers and it crackled briefly. "One day I transported a coachload of crates. I never found out what was in them, but the emperor of France wasn't happy with me. And that's not an eye anyone wants on them. So I left my parents every coin I had spare and ran as fast as I could. They must have chased me for damn near a year. Never caught me though, obviously I tried to stay in Europe. I figured if they were chasing me anyway, I might as well give them trouble while they did. The trouble with heat is that it can always get hotter."

As if to punctuate his point, a brief shower of sparks rose into the air as the stones and embers shifted. Torres watched them as they drifted away into invisibility.

"The Flight of Lisbon?" Dashwood asked. "The Portuguese royal family escaping under the French army's nose?"

Torres nodded. "Not all of them got out by ship. I think on

that day if Napoleon could have chosen the Crown of England or my head on a pike . . . he'd have chosen the Crown, but he'd have thought about it first. So the only safe place for me was on this side of the channel. Not so much work here for a man like me, but enough coin to survive, good racing, good company. What more could a man ask for?"

"Some would ask for more."

"Not me." Torres shook his head. "And what about you, Miss Elliot? What do you ask for?"

Lucy, aware of all the eyes on her, took a breath and wondered what Margaret might say in this situation.

"I believe," she began, "that in respect to self-knowledge, it is important to know the difference between what one needs and what one wants."

Torres laughed, and she wondered whether she had embarrassed herself, but when she looked up, he was nodding in agreement.

"That, I will drink to. Elsa, fetch the good drink, please."

The Swiss woman smiled, stood, and headed to one of the buildings.

"We should have company more often," Torres said. "But then privacy has its advantages too, especially when one is living off the land as we are."

"Privacy is a strange thing, really," Dashwood observed. "I am an only child, so I was often left to my own devices. Then, upon joining the army, I found myself surrounded by people and noise. Now, once again, I find myself mostly alone in an estate far too large for me."

"The solution to that is to find a family," Torres replied.

"Perhaps. It is certainly expected of one of my station that I marry a woman of good standing."

Lucy, so recently involved in wedding preparation, was struck by the improbable image of Dashwood and Charlotte Wyndham at the altar. The invasive thought so unsettled her that she felt a twinge in her stomach. She kept her gaze on the fire, unsure quite what this tense new feeling that kept plaguing her was.

"I said a family, señor," Torres replied. "This can mean many things. Ah." He waved to Elsa as she returned, carrying two bottles and a handful of cups. Torres took a bottle and passed it to Dashwood for approval.

"Have you tried Spanish wine before, Captain?"

"Certainly not of this vintage. A rare commodity these days."

"A fringe benefit of some of the work we do." He opened a bottle, pouring the wine into mugs, and sharing them about.

Lucy was faintly amused at the thought of drinks being served in such a fashion at a dinner party.

"A toast," Torres proposed.

"To racing," Dashwood suggested, turning to Lucy with a grin, "whether it gives us what we need, or what we want."

There was a clinking of mugs and sipping of wine.

It was a fine wine indeed, Lucy noted. A mellow texture, with strong aromatic fruit flavor and subtle hints of tin mug.

CHAPTER 34

THE EVENING PASSED WITH MERRY STORYTELLING, RECOUNTING OF past races, and liberal amounts of Spanish wine. Lucy marveled at how rare and exhilarating it was, not only to talk freely about her topics of inclination but also to have her knowledge treated with respect. The tension she had felt at Dashwood's proximity seemed to fade as she became more settled in her own skin. She doubted she could have achieved such comfort without his presence by her side and as the night moved on she found herself, eyes closed, not retreating into her mind but absorbing the world around her; the warmth of the fire, the chatter of voices, and the weight of his shoulder as she leaned in toward him.

"Lucy?"

She opened her eyes, straightening up and looking into his face, eyes reflecting firelight. As ever, she could not interpret his subtle expression. But how remarkable it was that she felt no need to do so.

"I think," he said softly, "it might be time for you to retire for the night, Miss Elliot. Tomorrow will be a busy day."

The sun had long faded, and the woodland shadows were beginning to overcome the glow of the fire. Dashwood proffered his arm to accompany Lucy as Elsa led her to a small stone hut, walls overgrown with vines but topped with a well-tended thatched roof. Perhaps it had once been a guard post or a storeroom. Inside was a small space with a wooden bed, a straw mattress, and a table.

Elsa hung a lantern on a hook and stepped away, leaning

against a wall, arms folded. As many a pretense as the racers had layered to bring their guests here it was clear the Swiss woman held her duty as chaperone with utmost severity.

"I trust you will be comfortable enough for the night?" Dashwood asked politely.

"Yes, of course," Lucy said. "This will be perfectly sufficient." It was, without doubt, the most modest sleeping arrangement Lucy had ever experienced. And yet she found herself suddenly so tired all she wanted was to curl up and sleep.

"Good night, James," she said drowsily, quite tired or content enough to forget the propriety of names.

In the silence that followed, she looked up to see him watching her with the strangest expression on his face.

Then he seemed to catch himself, cleared his throat, and replied, "Good night, Lucy." And then he turned and walked back across the camp.

While she herself was weary, she marveled that he seemed to walk with a sudden and lively spring in his step.

She closed the door and turned to the bed. After such a long and unusual day, and more wine than she was accustomed to, sleep easily overcame Lucy Elliot.

She woke somewhat later than usual, barring the morning after the Night Races. She arose and changed into her simpler dress, suspecting that the day would be ill-suited to her fine traveling garments. She hoped no one at Atherton would give too close a thought to her clothes smelling of a campfire.

When she walked outside into the morning light, the sun was already high enough to be brightening sections of the broad clearing. Here and there she caught sight of the daily routine of the settlement. Hekili was gardening, diligently plucking out weeds from among the vegetables. Elsa was working a contraption by the stream that involved turning a box with a crank. Dashwood and Torres were by the firepit, which had been turned over, rekindled, and was now being used to roast a bird on a spit. Of the group only Ulcha seemed to be absent, possibly elsewhere or still in her room.

"Good morning, Señorita Elliot. You are just in time for roast pheasant. A fine morning's hunting."

"Well," Dashwood noted casually, "this is Crown land. Technically it was poaching."

"Fair enough. If the king comes looking for his bird, I'll replace it."

Lucy was slightly shocked by so jovial a comment and yet Dashwood seemed quite at home with it. Perhaps it was an army thing. Besides, she could hardly maintain her sensibilities when her stomach rumbled at the fresh, fire-roasted breakfast.

Torres, sitting on a bench quietly, watched her as she approached.

"Captain Dashwood, I understand," he said. "But how is it that a lady like yourself has such an eye for coaches?"

"I am . . . of a curious disposition. Since my youngest days I have been inclined to order and precision. There is an elegance in putting things right that I have always reveled in, in many ways to the detriment of other perceptions."

"Other perceptions?"

She recounted to him what she had previously expounded to Captain Dashwood: her challenge with the reading of others, preferring instead the calculable and quantifiable.

"So, you see, I am quite unique in my ways of thought."

"Perhaps not as greatly as you would believe," came the accented voice of Elsa Reinhardt as she joined them. "I wondered yesterday if it might be the case. You remind me of my older brother. He has an exceptional mind. I saw him put a watch together the first time he saw my father take it apart. He can look inside a clock and know in a moment what is wrong and what must be done to fix it. It is more than study. He sees the working in his mind. Yet whenever anyone outside the family ever visited, he would hide in his room."

"Did he ever say why?"

"No." Elsa smiled sadly. "He has never said a word in his life. I wonder about him. Had he not been the son of a clockmaker, would it have been music? Needlepoint? Perhaps he could have been the son of a farmer, mute and doing no more than cutting wood all day. A genius never given form. There are stranger minds than yours. And there are worse things than coaches to be drawn to."

"Perhaps. But it is hardly an acceptable pastime for a lady of my position."

"And yet here you are." Elsa laughed. "With the approval of your family, no less. Perhaps not to the precise circumstances, but certainly to the visit to Reinhardt and Co., Engineers. It may not be right for Miss Elliot of Atherton, but I daresay it suits Lucy rather well."

Lucy found herself in resigned agreement. Twice during the conversation she glanced over at the coaches with a lingering curiosity. And once at Captain Dashwood.

But let's not think too much about that, she scolded herself.

By early afternoon, as Lucy had anticipated, her dress was quite beyond saving. Though blankets were laid, the constant kneeling, crouching, and sliding beneath the coaches had taken a hefty toll on the already aged fabric. But Lucy was quite oblivious to it, absorbed as she was in the mechanical world. There were four coaches in the camp: Captain Dashwood's; Torres's modular coach, which had brought her here; the weathered army coach Torres had won in their first race; and a smaller phaeton, stripped back to bare basics.

The latter was a project of Elsa's, stemming from a desire to build something small and incredibly fast.

"Imagine," she explained, "a coach that could travel as fast as a galloping horse. One with so little weight and drag that it was hardly there at all."

"With such a conveyance," Dashwood inquired, "would it not be more efficient simply to ride a horse?"

"Efficient perhaps," she said. "But you overlook the thrill of the challenge."

"Are those sails?" Lucy asked, wondering at the collapsed piles of dark fabric.

"My attempts at a land yacht. Like a small sailboat. It's been effective on a beach, but as you can imagine, it's not overly practical on the roads."

Such an idea had never occurred to Lucy, and it was to be the first of many discoveries for her. As they examined the coaches, every board, every point and connection, Lucy found herself learning from someone for the first time in many years. Most of what she knew she had drawn from books. Out here she was learning things that no book taught. A mathematical table might calculate a stress load, but the Swiss woman taught Lucy how to hear it. How to see a gear slipping. To feel an axle turning and know how many revolutions.

And as they talked, Lucy realized that Elsa possessed something she had long envied in others and lamented lacking in herself.

Instinct.

But there and then, talking to an expert, she began to perceive her instincts better than ever before. She could see the end of the process being described even before it was completed. She could see potential.

Sometimes Elsa sighed at Lucy's suggestions and explained why they would never work in practice. Other times, she was intrigued, hastily making notes in a foreign longhand on the pages of a small notebook. Instinct could jump you to the right or the wrong conclusions, but tempered by knowledge, it could lead to inspired invention. This was the world Lucy now found herself swimming in. She dived in and she dived deep.

"No, Lucy." Elsa sighed wearily. "You cannot remove the rein brace to adjust for less weight."

"Whyever not? It seems most—"

"Because it is two in the afternoon and I am hungry."

Lucy was skeptical of this announcement, until a pocket watch was produced to demonstrate its accuracy. She realized that in the future she should not argue the time with the daughter of a Swiss clockmaker.

It appeared she had been so caught up in her interests that the time had passed without her mind or her stomach noticing. Resisting the urge to tinker with one last part, she joined Elsa, who was now slicing bread and cheese. As she waited for her share, she noticed Ulcha for the first time, emerging from a hut.

"She sleeps most of the day," Elsa explained. "A night creature."

"She is . . . most unusual," Lucy noted, in full acknowledgment of her present company.

Elsa nodded, passing her guest a slice of bread and cheese, and a mug of water. "She's not like my brother, you know. Or like you. She wasn't born that way."

"If it is not proper for me to know her story—"

"It is not a secret. She just won't tell you. We've barely spoken more than a few words in years. She speaks to Dante a little more. What I know I learned from him, and even that is only pieces. You know she's Irish?"

Lucy nodded, watching as the dark-haired woman disappeared silently into the woods.

"What do you know of the rebellion of 1798?"

"Nothing, I'm afraid."

"Well, there was an uprising against the British," Elsa began. "It went down about as well as you might expect. The rebels got squeezed back. One point was a little village on the coast. They knew the Crown was coming. Leaving by sea meant the ships would catch them, so they decided to stay and fight. But one man, a fisherman, sent out his daughter on a small fishing float, on a line off the beach. He told her to keep her head down and stay silent no matter what happened. She would have heard the attack, and what came after. They burned that village to the ground, and she kept silent and kept down, even when they cut the fishing line and she started drifting out to sea. It must have taken days to drift across the channel. By day she hid. By night she paddled. Eventually she was picked up by a Welsh patrol. Of course they didn't know who she was. She didn't speak, so there was no accent to go by. She became a thief. On the darkest night she could walk as well as if it were day. One night she tried to steal from Dante's coach. Maybe he saw someone with talent. Maybe someone to save. Maybe just an outsider in search of a family to replace the one she had lost."

Finishing her tale, Elsa bit into her cheese and bread.

Lucy wiped her face, considering the story. With such a history, the Irish girl would have no love for the Crown. But would losing family in such a way be sufficient to steer someone to hijack army coaches?

"There are servants at Atherton," she thought aloud. "I have never once entertained the idea of being without them. Or the grounds. Or my family. There are so many who have so little and yet they must suffer losing even that."

Elsa nodded. "Some think our minds are elevated from the world around us, but I am not so sure." She lifted a small stone and dropped it into the stream. "If the stone had not wished to fall, it would have made no difference. The position we start in, the forces upon us, are as inevitable as the laws of motion."

"But we make our own choices surely?"

"Perhaps. My point is that you cannot change the place where you begin or what comes from it. But we may do what we can to make a better world for those around us."

"If our choices are predetermined, what use is there in trying such?"

"If they are predetermined, then I can hardly do otherwise." The Swiss woman smiled.

"I daresay you and my sister should have an excellent philosophical discussion," said Lucy.

"Our worlds are not the same. You are welcome in my home. I fear I should not be welcome in yours."

Lucy reluctantly agreed, eating her small meal in silence. When she had finished, another question occurred to her.

"I know why I am here, working on the coaches. But why is Captain Dashwood here? They took a coach out this morning and have yet to return, so I may assume they have a task at hand."

"That, I think, is a question to be asked of your captain himself. While his attitude to class is decidedly more flexible than most of his station, it does not seem likely that he is here without purpose. That is what Dante believes."

"Then why host him at all? Surely the debt of dinner might be repaid more easily."

"A coach may travel both ways." Elsa shrugged. "He wants to learn about us; we want to learn about him. People in our position do well by finding opportunities."

Lucy was unsure what to make of the words, but could detect no menace in them. Then again, identifying intention was not her strong suit.

The day had been so engaging that she had largely forgotten that she was far from home, outnumbered, and surrounded by a group of smart and skilled people who might be thieves and murderers. The bread and cheese suddenly sat uneasily in her stomach.

Dashwood seemed confident in his ability to maintain subterfuge. The best she could do was to attempt the same.

"Upon first meeting him, I had a similar curiosity," Lucy confessed.

"You did?"

"As you noted, he is a curious gentleman. I wondered at his intentions."

"And do you know them now?

"The entirety of his intentions remain frustratingly veiled to me."

"I should not be surprised at that." Elsa chuckled, washing her hands in the stream and drying them on her coat. "Now, then. Rein braces."

CHAPTER 35

W̲HEN ELSA RETIRED TO FOCUS ON SOME MORE COMPLEX WORK, LUCY'S care was passed over to Hekili. At present he was working on an intricate carving on the back of a wooden chair. As her eyes traced over it she saw a story unfolding and she began to recognize the familiar images compacted into the wood.

"Is that the Bayeux Tapestry?" she asked in admiration.

"I think that's what they called it. I only saw a print in a book. But that's what the client wanted. He has Norman ancestry."

"It depicts 1066. The last time someone successfully invaded Britain."

"Let's hope it stays that way."

"You don't mind selling your creations like this?"

"Not me. My work is for sale but not my stories. See these?" He pointed to his arms, dark skin covered in tattoos. "These are my story. My family. My journey. Myself. Those aren't for sale. But my work? Sure. But isn't that the same for all of us?"

"Not all of us. But I see your point." She gazed around the clearing, the late-afternoon sun drifting through the leaves. "Do you miss your home?"

"Sometimes. Mostly the water. It's too cold in this country. I think one day I'll go home again. When I've made enough coin. When I feel it's time. Until then, this is home for me."

"Your family?"

"Ohana. That's a word my people use. Family but . . . not just blood or marriage. Far as I can tell, there's no word for it in English."

"And Torres, Elsa, Ulcha. They're . . . ohana?"

"Must seem like a pretty strange family from the outside."

"I think that's most families," Lucy mused.

"Speaking of . . ." He looked up as a familiar coach came into the clearing, Torres in the driver's seat and Dashwood as messenger.

They pulled up next to the workshop, clearly in a good mood, which Lucy found infectious.

"Where have you been all day?" Lucy asked, curiosity overcoming her tact.

"Shopping." Torres laughed. "We make an excellent team. I know where to get the best bargains, and he has the money."

"An allowance from my father in caring for Atherton. Thankfully the place looks after itself well enough that I have a little left over."

"So why not take advantage of the Chelmsford Markets?"

Torres hauled a sack from the back of the coach; flour, she guessed. As they offloaded she realized that, while there were some treats, most of the cargo was essential supplies. Once again, Dashwood excelled at ingratiating himself.

"Have you heard the local tale of the headless horseman, Captain?" Torres asked as they sat around the fire once more. It was midevening and they were partaking of a simpler meal of sausages, stew, and bread.

"I've heard mention of it. Soldiers are often fond of collecting ghost stories."

"Oh, it is simple enough. A ghostly white rider without a head. The story goes that he was a crusader who believed that as long as he rode his white horse, he would be invincible. He was captured during a battle and his enemies knew of him and his boast. So they cut off his head, tied him in the saddle, and sent his horse back toward the crusader lines. But the horse and rider kept going, all the way home, and never stopped."

The story hung in the air over the campfire, as all good ghost stories should.

"I daresay there are more earthly mysteries to be solved in these parts." Dashwood laughed.

"Such as?" Torres inquired curiously.

"Three coaches. All found riderless this year. No sign of crew or cargo."

"Ghost ships on land?" Hekili asked.

"I should say more likely the work of excellent thieves," Dashwood replied earnestly.

Lucy tried her best not to look awkward. taking a large mouthful of stew lest she was asked a question.

"And killers," Torres noted coolly.

"What makes you so sure?"

"One coach goes missing, perhaps it is an inside job. Three coaches? Not likely. Even if they were paid off, one of them would have slipped by now. So I'd wager those men are dead and buried."

"Buried where?"

"It's a big country." Torres shrugged. "We're living in a castle in the forest that no one even knows is here. Much easier to hide a body than hide a castle. Several bodies though? You'd want a regular spot." The Spaniard paused, thinking over the problem. "No signs of a struggle?" he inquired.

"Not so far as I've heard, though the tales might be exaggerated."

"A clean robbery like that . . . It's difficult work." Torres spoke with an air of experience.

"I'm sure it is." Dashwood agreed. "How are the sausages by the way?"

"Good," came an unknown voice from the other side of the fire.

Lucy flinched but saw the others had remained calm. It took her a moment to realize it was Ulcha who had spoken.

"If robberies are happening, perhaps some additional defenses might be added to the coaches," Elsa suggested. "As a precaution."

"Hard to do without knowing the nature of the robberies," Dashwood countered.

"Perhaps. But maybe some kind of a spring-loaded trap system." The woman put down her plate and began sketching in her notebook.

"I think, Captain"—Torres smiled—"that any robber would be foolish to attempt such a trick against a driver of your experience."

Dashwood nodded. "Likewise, Señor Torres. Likewise."

The next morning, when breakfast was done, it was time for farewells. Captain Dashwood suggested he return Lucy to Atherton under the pretense of having met upon the return journey, which was close enough to the truth that Lucy felt it would be accepted.

With an amicable mood and a promise to race at the next full moon, they loaded the coach and drove off into the morning. It amazed her how quickly the castle vanished behind them and, had she not made an effort to recall the path, she wondered if she might ever find it again.

"So. What do you think?" Lucy asked once they were well clear and on the road.

"I don't think they're our highwaymen," Dashwood replied, his voice a mix of relief and disappointment. "No signs of the spoils. No signs of excess or of deprivation. They don't need to rob anyone, which leaves only the thrill of the challenge as a motive. And perhaps that is enough. But it doesn't feel right, does it?"

"No. It doesn't. They seem like good people. Not always lawful, but they were open about that too. There is no doubt they have the skills for it. And that they each love a challenge in their own way. But such robberies ill fit them."

"Political motive also seems unlikely. Torres has every reason to oppose France. Ulcha has reason enough to dislike the Crown, but I doubt she would drive a scheme, and the others expressed little interest in politics at all."

"Again it seems improbable as motivation."

"Which leaves us at a dead end on this trail."

"There are other trails?"

"I hope so. Otherwise my superiors are going to start asking difficult questions and I shall be short of answers. Well, at the very least we had good company, interesting meals, and you hopefully learned a great deal about coaches."

"Most certainly." Lucy nodded.

"In that case, you had best tell me what you learned."

And for the rest of the journey, Lucy did.

CHAPTER 36

T HE ELLIOTS WERE SURPRISED WHEN LUCY RETURNED IN THE COM-
pany of Captain Dashwood, now with Jim seated between them for
propriety. The parents were neither displeased nor disappointed
at the chance meeting. Lucy imagined that, like her sister, they
were increasingly optimistic about a match between the couple
and such a meeting furthered that end.

With Margaret yet to return from town there was a spare
seat for lunch, which Mr. Elliot cheerfully offered to the captain.
Dashwood politely declined, citing other business to attend to,
but happily accepting such a request for another time. They waved
him farewell, and Lucy wondered if his route home might involve
any of the "other trails" he had mentioned. For the moment her
practical part in the investigation was, once again, on hold.

Her luggage unpacked and returned to her room, Lucy spent
several luxurious minutes lying on her bed, the familiar curves
and textures soft and comforting. Were it not morning, and was
her company not anticipated, she should have stayed longer. Instead she changed into a lighter dress, for the day was warm, and
went to join her parents for lunch in the dining room.

Lucy expressed her approval of the trip, and where questions
required she might have to dissemble, she instead sidetracked
into practical details of her experience that were entirely true.

After the meal, and once she had reclaimed her letter from
Molly, Lucy found herself back in her room, strangely unsettled
by her recent experiences—so different to the world she'd always
known. To focus herself, she decided to write down some notes, for

while she had taken a notebook with her, she'd been remiss in her scribing. Now, she found the memories and ideas flowing so that it was some hours before her focus was broken by a knock at the door.

She gave invitation and Margaret entered.

"I have heard your visit was most positive."

"Remarkable. And I have lost track of time since."

Margaret's mood was more somber than Lucy had expected, and one generally reserved for the bearing of bad tidings.

"Margaret? What is the matter?"

Lucy dearly hoped she was not the target of this disappointment. If the truth of the past few days had somehow got out, she was unsure quite how she should cope with it.

"I have bad news, Lucy. I have just spent the morning consoling Charlotte Wyndham. The marriage to George St. Martin has been called off."

"Called off? Whatever for?"

"There has been a rather disgraceful scandal, quite out of her control. Her father has made a string of imprudent investments, throwing good money after bad in the hope of recovery. They shall not be ruined utterly, but it is a great fall for them. The estate shall surely be lost. And, of course, it reflects so ill on poor Charlotte that she cannot marry into the St. Martin family now. George withdrew from the engagement."

"That at least is a consolation, though I am sure it offers her little solace."

"Lucy. How can you say such a thing?"

"Charlotte bears no shame for her father's deeds. George St. Martin does not want for money. If he truly loved her then he would offer to take her in. In the eyes of some, that would make him a greater man, not a lesser. The fact that he does not, shows he cared more for her status and wealth than he did for her. So there is the consolation: George St. Martin is a flighty man, and she is better suited to another. Though . . . that is from a detached eye. The girl herself, I imagine, is heartbroken."

"She is. I have seldom seen her more forlorn. Such a warm and animated creature as she normally is, it seems cruel that this has been taken from her. Had the news broken in only a few more weeks, then it would have been settled and she would have the comfort of the St. Martins. But perhaps it is, as you say, a blessing that time will reveal."

"How long has this been going on? Robert Wyndham is a respected businessman. Surely his losses must have been known."

"It is because of his success that he was able to hide it. Had he let up earlier it might have been a blow, but not such a tarnishing as this. It is an awful business, Lucy."

"I shall send her a letter. I cannot say my company would be of great consolation to her at this time. I should offer practical solutions when they are neither requested nor suited. But she has my sympathies."

"Perhaps when you are done we can discuss your trip. I daresay it would make a welcome distraction to my thoughts."

Lucy agreed, turning her notes aside to begin her letter. By the time it was done, and after a bath, it was the dinner hour, and so it was not until later that Margaret and Lucy were able to discuss the events of the past few days in private. Again Lucy was evasive rather than deceptive, but painfully aware that her sister was more likely to see through gaps in her narrative.

"I was told that you were returned home by our friend Captain Dashwood?"

"Yes. It was rather a stroke of luck to encounter him on the return."

"It is perhaps poor form to hope for such when ill luck is elsewhere, but it seems undeniable that there is an attraction between you. Did you learn any more about him?"

Lucy's mind flashed to an image of the shirtless captain shoveling earth.

"He is," she replied tactfully, "an admirable man, and the time spent with him has indeed improved my opinion of him.

But I still cannot be sure of his intentions of courtship. In light of recent events I would lean toward caution rather than assumption."

"Perhaps wise on a day like this. To think that when you left, everything seemed so bright for George and Charlotte. There wasn't even the slightest sign of ill fortune on the horizon."

Margaret's words reminded Lucy of something she had not thought of amid the excitement of her expedition and the sad news of the canceled wedding. Perhaps there *had* been a sign. A ghostly pursuer, who had been a harbinger of doom.

Lucy dismissed such foolishness.

But that night, as she drifted off to sleep, she had a nagging instinct that there was something to it after all; something she could not pin down. She dreamed of riding in a coach, trying to make repairs even as it sped through the night. So bumpy was the ride that every time she reached for her tools she found them to have moved elsewhere. She turned to Dashwood to ask him to slow down, only to see that he was ghostly white and missing his head.

Lucy awoke then with a start.

Despite being back in the comfort of her own bed, she slept more fitfully that night than she had for some time.

CHAPTER 37

Any of Lucy's fears that the truth of her trip might be discovered were assuaged over the following week. There was little talk of anything but the dissolution of the engagement and the fall of the Wyndham family fortunes. Lucy did not meet with Charlotte, who found herself both heartsick and forced into the uncomfortable business of cataloging and packing her belongings. In correspondence, Charlotte explained that for the time being, they were to move in with her mother's sister in Kent. She was a wealthy widow who, while openly derisive of her brother-in-law, was looking forward to company in her home. It would be a smaller and more modest life than the one Charlotte knew, but it was acknowledged that they had been fortunate to have a relative able to take them in. Lucy hoped that, once the shock of events had passed, Charlotte would be able to find a level of contentment. The recent visit to the castle ruins had shown Lucy that the stateliness of one's dwelling was not a barrier to happiness, so long as it was warm and dry. She also had no doubt that Charlotte's effortless cheer and charm should quickly ingratiate her with the society of her new home on the southeast coast.

Charlotte had thanked Lucy for her letter, for her past advice, and told her that, if there were no level heads to be found in Folkestone, she should write to Lucy again for her perspective. She made no mention of the phantom, either forgotten outright or perhaps set aside by the harshness of real-life affairs. Lucy thought it for the best, as she feared Charlotte might attach all manner of prophetic meaning to the curious event.

The Wyndhams departed with little fanfare and Lucy wondered if she might never hear from them again. They were moving to a different part of the country and into a different level of society. Now that the initial gossip had passed, she noticed that the family was seldom spoken of, as if people feared to mention their name lest a similar fate befall them. Or perhaps the discomfort came from the unpleasant truth that one's status in the world was not so set and secure as it might seem. If the Wyndham family could come to ruin then could not any family end up the same?

And so events and discussion in the district moved on, more often now focused on the weather and the growing heat of summer. Lucy also turned her attention back to more familiar elements: the sketching of engineering designs and the mystery of the coach robberies. In more practical terms there were other elements of her trip that needed addressing. The dress she had worn while examining coaches was, as she had suspected, beyond salvage. That was the opinion of Mrs. Calloway when presented with it. A full laundering had failed to remove all the dirt and oil marks, and several tears were now visible. The seamstress tutted and shook her head as she looked over the garment.

"Are you quite sure this is yours, Miss Elliot? It wasn't borrowed from a chimney sweep or a ditch digger?"

Lucy shook her head, and the woman glanced about the store to check the place was free of prying eyes and ears.

"Miss Elliot. It is not my place to question your activities. But I do hope this is not a sign of inappropriate behavior on your part."

"Whatever do you mean?"

"Not to put too fine a point on it, but this dress seems to have spent extended periods of time on its back outdoors. A young lady might want to avoid certain assumptions being made."

"Oh!" Lucy gasped, blushing immediately. "I can assure you it was nothing so salacious. I am quite ignorant of such things . . . well . . . not ignorant. There are books on anatomy. But I am wholly inexperienced . . . Not that I . . . I do believe I should sit down."

There was very quickly a chair behind her, and she drew deep breaths until the embarrassment had faded a little.

"I have," she explained, "recently been involved in the engineering of coaches, some manner of which required the examination of undercarriages."

Mrs. Calloway paused, briefly chewing the end of her pencil. "Are you perhaps involved in the Night Races?" the seamstress asked.

Lucy was so surprised to hear these words come from the woman that she could not conceal her amazement. "It is certainly tangential to that. But . . . I have never seen you at any of the races."

"Oh, I don't attend these days. But that was where I first met Mr. McDonald. He used to race back in the day. He was quite awful at it, but it made him seem ever so brave. He had a bad crash, and that was the end of it. I don't think he misses it. A foolish young man's game. But I know how alluring it can all be." She put the dress aside. "A little padding and it might make fine farm clothes for a young lady. I think its time at Atherton is done."

She turned her attention from the dress back to Lucy, looking her over. "I could work on something for you. In case you ever found yourself examining coaches again. Something a little sturdier to save you ruining another dress."

"I'm unsure if I shall have the opportunity again, but having such a garment would be sensible."

"Well, then, you leave it with me. I'm sure I can pull something together. Do you have a laundry girl with a level of discretion?"

Lucy nodded, confident Molly could add anything into the laundry pile without raising attention.

"That settles it, then. Is there anything else I can do for you today?"

"As a matter of fact, there is. In regards to Charlotte Wyndham's . . . no longer wedding . . ."

"I'm afraid I can't do much with the dresses. They were all tailored very precisely by the London firm."

"That is not my concern. I'm sure Margaret will have fine opportunities to wear hers. I am referring to Charlotte's wedding dress. I understand that she commissioned you to create it. Was it completed?"

"Yes. Completed and now folded up in a box in the back room. Costly as it was, I could not be so heartless as to charge the girl for a dress she could no longer afford or wear."

"I should like to pay for it."

"I appreciate the offer, Miss Elliot, but I cannot accept charity."

"It is not charity. I wish to purchase it as a gift to be sent to Miss Wyndham."

"Whatever for?"

"I know some might see it as a callous act. I do not believe it so. She is not to marry George St. Martin. But I must believe that a woman as pleasant and sociable as Charlotte will marry before long. I should like to remind her of that fact and outfit her in advance of that day."

There was a pause before the dressmaker replied. "You are a curious creature, Miss Elliot."

"I suspect that you are neither the first nor the last to say so."

Leaving the store, Lucy was surprised to catch sight of Margaret across the street, engaged in conversation with Oliver St. Martin. For a moment Lucy pondered leaving them to talk but, positioned as she was, she could neither stay in place nor move away without the pair catching sight of her. She crossed the street slowly, giving them adequate forewarning of her arrival.

"Miss Elliot." The younger St. Martin bowed his head to her.

"Mr. St. Martin."

"Was your trip to the dressmaker a profitable one?" Margaret inquired.

"Alas, the dress was beyond saving for purpose. But Mrs. Calloway was quite confident it would be of use as farm clothes."

"They are a credit to our town," Oliver noted. "I cannot say how fine it is to have a tailor so adept at alteration."

"Indeed." Margaret nodded. "Mr. St. Martin was just inviting us to a ball."

"A ball?" Lucy exclaimed. "At St. Martins?"

"Correct," Oliver said. "Though I must express it is in a wholly unofficial capacity that I make such an invitation. I hope I do not steal the thunder of my brother, for the misconceived notion is entirely his idea."

Lucy wondered at the somber tone to his words. "Why do you say 'misconceived'?"

"The breaking of the engagement with Charlotte Wyndham is still fresh in the minds of the district. My brother is of the opinion that such a social gathering will distract that attention and reaffirm the goodwill of people toward him."

"You do not agree?"

"It is ill-timed. It is more likely that people will perceive it as callous, perhaps even seeing through to his insecure motivations."

"Is that what you believe?"

"I have never been able to discern the inner workings of my brother's mind. But, thankfully, so many of his thoughts seem on the surface level that it is hardly necessary. He is impulsive, and his intentions seldom extend beyond his own self-interest."

"Surely you do your brother wrong?" Lucy was surprised to hear such open disregard. Oliver was always a taciturn fellow, but not given to spitefulness. "I myself have been critical of his behavior in this affair, but while his actions may be callous, I am sure they are done with no malice."

"There is some truth in that. I am sure he believes that holding such a ball is in the best interests of the district."

"And your father," Margaret pointed out, "would certainly not agree to host such an event if he too did not see merit in it."

"They have been quite the pair of late. First in the intention of my brother's wedding and now in the ball. My father is quite in favor of it, though I think it is an extravagance in such times."

"What times are those?" Margaret asked, for he seemed to intimate more than merely the canceled wedding.

"Robert Wyndham's fall came from a series of poor decisions. But the origin of it was in what appeared to be a good investment that went bad. The state of Europe and the former colonies has been erratic. My father has always been astute in his finances, but I cannot help but think his attentions would be better focused on his accounts than on celebrations. For my part I spread my investments thin and wide. The gains are mild, but it is safer than wild speculation. Had I known of the Wyndhams' misfortune . . . well, that much is done, I suppose. I pray that young Charlotte will recover herself in time."

"Was your brother hurt by the revelation?" Lucy asked.

"Bitterly so. For days after, he was dour and snappish, not at all like his usual self. Perhaps this ball is not so ill an idea after all, as it has elevated him from his melancholy."

"When is the ball to take place?" Margaret asked, sensing the topic of his brother was giving Oliver some discomfort.

"A fortnight's time. On Saturday evening."

"The full moon?" Lucy asked.

"Is it? I suppose it might be thereabouts." He shrugged.

Lucy reminded herself that the lunar cycle was not so prominent in the minds of the general population as it was in the thoughts of the devotees of the Night Races. But a ball would quite derail any plans for a race event that evening. Not only would many of the attendees be present at the ball, both guests and servants, but the traffic on the roads would make racing quite impossible. It was a shame, as the early-summer nights were ideal for racing, before the air got too hot and the nights too short to really enjoy them. But the real world held precedence over the races, and there was no way of avoiding it.

"Are you returning to Atherton?" Oliver asked politely. "If you came on foot, I should offer you both a coach ride home. It is not so far out of my way that it would inconvenience me."

"We should be delighted, Mr. St. Martin." Margaret smiled. "Are you done with your chores, Lucy?"

Lucy instinctively drew a map in her head. The detour was not as slight as he suggested, which indicated it might be offered to extend their company.

"I have been hoping to thoroughly examine the new book arrivals at the store," Lucy replied politely. "But it is a fine day, and I see no reason why you should not avail yourself of a coach ride without me, Margaret. I should enjoy a walk by myself."

The sisters exchanged a glance they both very much hoped the young man was not aware of.

"Indeed." Margaret nodded. "Mr. St. Martin, I shall gladly take up your offer. Lucy, I shall see you at home."

"Very well," Oliver said. "Good day, Miss Elliot."

"Good day, Mr. St. Martin." Lucy nodded.

The pair departed and Lucy strolled happily toward the store to peruse the books she had thoroughly examined not half an hour earlier.

CHAPTER 38

THE WEATHER BEING INDEED AS FINE AS LUCY HAD SUGGESTED, SHE discovered that the walk home was unreasonably warm. She had worn a good hat but regretted not bringing a parasol to offer shade. With this in mind she decided it would be more pleasant to take a slight detour down a longer but more shaded path, rather than her usual return route to Atherton.

The noises of the fields were soon replaced by the equally active but more muted tones of the woods. The temperature was immediately cooler and Lucy congratulated herself on the wisdom of her decision. She walked on the roadway, confident that any coach or horseman would be heard at enough distance for her to move aside. Her initial attempts to identify a particular songbird continued to elude her despite the name being on the tip of her tongue. Instead she turned her focus downward to the stones upon which she walked. Watching as they passed underfoot, she wondered if there might be some manner of improving the grip of wheels as well as their durability and suspension. Iron wheel rims were a good way to reduce wear and tear and increase grip, but they added weight and still made for a rough ride.

Perhaps she was looking at it the wrong way. After all, it was the traction of the horses that generated the power, not the coach. Until she could develop a way to retain greater spring-coil energy that would always be an issue. Was it possible though? A coach without horses. That would be truly revolutionary. But the amount of stored energy required would be enormous and no mechanism occurred to her. Perhaps some manner of mining pump? But the devices were so massive that she might as well stick with springs.

It was this she was pondering when a noise attracted her attention. She walked more slowly, the noise coming closer and more directed, off in the woods to the side of the road. She noticed the small overgrown path. It originated from behind a curious sight, a midsize oak that had grown from the decaying trunk of an older tree. She hesitated only for a moment before stepping around the tree and off into the forest.

It was a seldom-used path but not wholly overgrown, though the trees and bushes encroached upon her as she walked. Lucy resolved not to ruin a second dress in so short a period, so she took her time navigating the tangles, keeping the fabric clear of any malicious twigs or thorns. Here the air felt even cooler than on the road, the sunlight high above, filtering diffused light through the canopy.

Her slow movement meant she was near silent and was able to freeze in place once she spotted movement ahead. She perceived a small clearing, so small in fact that it might not be noticed as such were it not for the figure standing in the center. It seemed to be that of a man, wearing a rough dark cloak, which, with the addition of him facing away, quite obscured his identity. Currently he was in the act of digging, and it seemed he had been doing so for some minutes for there was a small mound of earth to one side. What his intention might be she was unsure, but she was quite confident that it was of no legitimate nature.

Lucy observed in silence, considering what her course of action should be. She could not turn on the tight path nor reverse course without giving herself away. She doubted she could run faster than him, certainly not for long enough to reach aid. Her dress was of a bright spring style, about as far from camouflage as could be possible. Dismissing instantly the option of climbing a tree, she slowly raised her hand and drew a large pin from her hat.

Given the element of surprise, she might find use for it, though she doubted its effectiveness against a determined opponent.

While she pondered this, the man in the clearing paused, shaking his head, seeming to scout the forest before him. She tensed, readying herself to act if she were seen, but instead his gaze seemed to fix on a point opposite to her. Lifting his shovel he set off on a course into the forest without once peering behind him.

Lucy realized she had been holding her breath only when his footsteps faded into the distance. She let it out slowly, remaining still until she was quite sure she could hear no more than a few songbirds.

A chaffinch. The name came back to her at the most inappropriate time.

Objectively she knew that she should return to the road, but there was something too tempting to pass up about a half-dug hole in a clearing.

It was absurd to check, really. Whatever the man had been looking for, clearly it wasn't there, and what clues were to be gleaned from turned-over soil? And yet the compulsion to see was irresistible. She brushed aside the foliage and stepped cautiously forward into the clearing.

To her surprise, the hole was not empty at all. She could see the edge of a wooden box, half exposed.

Why had he abandoned the task, half done? There was no practical reason that she could think of. Unless he'd known he was being watched. Unless he had known that whoever was watching would check.

Instinct overcame both curiosity and reason, and she spun about, racing back along the path. She made it several strides into the woods before she was stopped by a voice.

"Lucy?"

She froze, her heart pounding as she tried to locate the source of the call so that she could head the opposite way.

"At that pace it is certain that the woods or path shall do you more harm than I ever should."

The voice was so calmly opposed to the flight reflex in her mind that it took her a moment to process it.

"Captain Dashwood?" she asked in confusion.

"I apologize for the deception," he continued, unseen. "I was unsure of who might be observing me and circled about to catch sight of them."

Out of the corner of her eye she saw a hand waving through a clump of scrub.

"Had I known it was you I should have dispensed with subterfuge at once. If you wish to leave, I should neither blame nor stop you, but I hope you shall give me the chance to explain myself."

"I am at a loss," she replied. "Any attempt to flee would, as you note, likely do me more harm than good. I can only hope your intentions are honorable."

And if not, she thought, *I still have a hat pin*.

"If you would meet me back at the dig?"

She turned and walked back the way she had come. All she knew of James Dashwood recommended him to be an honest man, but she was equally aware of his talent for deception, and this strange behavior would require a solid explanation indeed.

She arrived before him, watching as he stepped out of the overgrowth somewhat sheepishly. Beneath the heavy cloak he wore rougher trousers and shirt than even his workshop attire. He still had his shovel in hand, which he pointed back to the hole.

"I suppose it would appear that I am digging up a hidden cache of some manner."

"It would be difficult to deny otherwise."

"I shan't deny it. Though I shall deny burying it in the first place."

"Please elaborate."

"It came back to the case of brandy. It would have been a unique thing to steal. Something that would attract attention even if sold by the bottle. How then to deal with it? When I perceived it from the angle of highway pirates, the classic method occurred to me."

"Buried treasure?" Lucy asked skeptically.

"Perhaps a fanciful notion. But all my other lines of investigation have thus far been fruitless. I concluded that if it were the method, the case would not be far off the road from where the coach had traveled. Likely off a path but not a common one, though one well indicated by a landmark, such as the oak by the road."

"And you happened to chance upon the right spot?"

"Not chanced. I've been scouting the area the better part of three days, finding a lot of dead ends and false trails. I almost passed over this one, but I noticed the leaf fall in the clearing was off for this time of year. Sure enough, I found disturbed earth. So today I came back with a shovel."

"It appears you were correct."

"That remains to be seen. Clearly something is buried here. Shall we discover the contents together?"

She nodded, stepping back so that he might work. She did her best to focus on the mystery at hand and not the unhelpful thought that she much preferred the sight of him digging *without* his shirt on.

Unhelpful, perhaps, but definitely not inaccurate, she admitted to herself.

After a few more minutes he had cleared the edges around the box, so he kneeled down and levered it open with a small bar from his pocket. There was no mistaking the contents now, a full complement of brandy bottles, destined for St. Martins and now consigned to a subterranean fate.

Dashwood replaced the lid and sat back on the ground thoughtfully.

"I must assume from your reaction that this is not entirely good news?" Lucy wondered aloud.

"It is positive news. But not easy. What do you think should be our next course of action?"

"Why, to inform Sir Walter that we have recovered his property."

"How did I discover it? Was it by chance? Or was I looking, in which case I abandon a good deal of cover that I have in the district as to my purpose. Whoever buried it here would surely suspect me of hunting them."

"Well . . . what if I found it? I heard something in the woods, went to investigate it, and found it half uncovered."

"I admire your willingness to help, but the outcome might be even less preferable. It might well mark you to the eye of the guilty party and I should not wish to be the cause of any harm to you, Lucy."

He glanced back at the case in the hole. "Every bottle accounted for. Were it a crime of opportunity or more callous thieves I should suspect at least one missing, consumed as celebration. It suggests a far more disciplined and organized operation than one might expect. Perhaps they have a buyer in mind. No. Something seems amiss. I think perhaps it is better our discovery go unknown for the time being."

"But what of Sir Walter?"

"I imagine he has come to terms with the loss by now. And the value of the case will only increase over time. Not quite a wine cellar, but no harm will come to it."

"Unless they come to reclaim it."

"That is a possibility. You see my dilemma. I can hardly post watch when there is no suggestion of how long it might be before they return. Yet to return it endangers either my cover or your safety."

"There is another option," she offered. "We could rebury it elsewhere. We should retain our secrecy but secure the contents. If the culprits return, they will know that someone found their stash but will not know who."

Lucy could read his face well enough to know he approved.

The crate was heavy, and Lucy mused that she was the inferior

Elliot sister for such a task. Yet she lent her aid as much as she could, for it was too much to ask of even a fit and healthy man to carry alone.

Lucy Elliot, helping to relocate stolen goods, she thought. *How much your life has changed in but a season.*

With the weight and the forest working against them, they did not carry the cargo far, taking it westward from the clearing by direction of Captain Dashwood's compass. Lucy found herself not the least surprised that he carried such an instrument on his person.

Beneath a fallen tree was an old badger tunnel, now uninhabited, which made a good start for a new hiding place, aided by the diligent shovel work of Captain Dashwood. She offered to help, but he refused, which she was quite grateful for, as she was uncertain of her usefulness in such a task. Instead she kept watch on the surrounding forest—and did her best not to keep watch on him.

Once the crate was reburied, the earth replaced and concealed by plants, they stood back and assessed their work. Lucy made a few more suggestions as to shifting plants and branches they had disturbed until finally she was satisfied. If one was searching the spot in detail, it might be discovered, but it was a large forest and even the most determined thieves would be unlikely to ever find their stolen treasure.

Dashwood pulled a couple of loose leaves from his hair, brushing his face with a neckerchief to soften a dirt mark on his cheek. Lucy sighed, for though he retained a rugged handsomeness, he was shamefully disheveled for a man of his standing. She inquired for a comb, was delighted when he produced one, and spent a minute returning his hair to an appropriate state. She was just finishing wiping his cheek with her handkerchief when one intense focus on respectability collided with another. She was alone in the woods, in the company of a bachelor. She met his eyes and in the instant saw he too had just now realized it. Defense of the realm and visiting potential highwaymen was one thing, but this, this felt dangerous.

Her hand hovered just by his cheek and she saw his throat move as he swallowed. Was he as nervous as her? She could scarcely imagine it was possible. Slowly his opposite hand rose, reaching over, touching her fingertips and closing the handkerchief into her palm. The touch of his fingers was light on hers, his hands still warm from activity. She saw the look in his eyes, waiting. It was her choice to be made, and she was certain he would follow her as surely as he had as messenger to driver. She felt the tension within her, a tightly coiled spring that only needed the pin pulled to hurl them into the unknown.

Lucy Elliot, a voice of reason whispered in the back of her mind. *You do not ride blind.*

She pictured the path. Exhilaration. Recklessness. Scandal. Disaster for them both. There would be slower paths for them to take. But not this one. Not here and now.

She withdrew her hand, lowering it, returning the handkerchief to her pocket.

"What is the time, please?" Her voice sounded too high-pitched.

Dashwood exhaled and he nodded as he checked his pocket watch, his steady rider's hands visibly shaking. "It is a quarter past one, Miss Elliot."

"It is later than I expected."

"Digging is hard work."

She closed her eyes, distracting herself with the practical from the personal, eager to follow the new thread of thought that had just sprung upon her. Turning her mind to the time and mentally plotting her route home had provoked an unexpected thought, and she fell deep into introspection for several seconds before she finally spoke her spontaneous thought aloud and opened her eyes.

"Longburn Mire."

Dashwood raised an eyebrow at the sudden exclamation. "Longburn Mire?"

Whatever spell they had been under was broken, and she was sure she saw a moment of both regret and relief cross the captain's features.

"It took us quite some time to bury the box," she explained. "But the brandy was not the only thing missing."

"The driver." He frowned, settling in to her line of thought.

"To bury a small case would be arduous enough, even for two people. You could not swiftly do the same with a body, even with several men. And the previous robbery, you said four men went missing. To dig a grave for four in so short a time would be impossible."

"And yet no trace of them has ever been found."

"Suppose you wanted to be rid of them in a way that would make them difficult to find, but not take undue effort?" Lucy posed. "I think the answer might be to dump them in Longburn Mire."

"I have heard the name, but not visited it."

"I'm not surprised, it is horridly cold and wet by winter, dreadfully stifling and fly-ridden in summer, and combinations of both in between. Swamp and bog with allegedly a few safe paths, but little reason for one to ever take them. It stretches all the way from the northeast of the St. Martins' property to the stream near Lord Rathbone's. I believe they each own some of it by technicality, but neither bothers with it as the cost to develop anything would be prohibitive."

"And yet, for the purpose you propose?"

"It would be deep, murky, and isolated."

"And they might have left behind traces of a visit."

"I am afraid I have neither the boots nor the wardrobe for such an expedition," said Lucy.

"Nor would I expect it of you. Your insight and knowledge

have been invaluable to me, but I assure you I have no intention of putting you in harm's way, or indeed any unpleasantness."

"I appreciate your concern, Captain, but I should be equally upset if harm were to come to you."

"Thank you for that. My profession is not one given to personal concerns. It is gratifying to hear you speak of me in such terms."

"I think, Captain Dashwood, it would be dishonest to deny of ourselves personal concerns."

He nodded, their shared moment passed but not forgotten.

They walked back toward the road, deciding to part ways at the wood's end. His rough attire was unseemly for company, and too many chance encounters might hold a risk of reputation.

"I shall not assess the mire today," he said. "If I am to do so I shall make preparations and have Jim for company. Company and a sturdy rope can offset the danger if not the muck."

"I am glad to hear it."

"I . . . I trust you can remember the case's location if you need to."

"Indeed. Good day, sir." She nodded, a tremor undercutting her attempted detachment.

After a moment's pause, they headed in opposite directions down the road. Lucy had utmost certainty she could recall the location of their buried treasure. She suspected she would remember that spot as long as she lived.

CHAPTER 39

With the upcoming St. Martins Ball Lucy found herself at least partially distracted from the discovery in the woods. It was yet another secret to conceal, and one that offered up little more information. Captain Dashwood might be able to follow other lines of investigation, but she was only left to speculate, which was as frustrating as ever.

Initially her parents were looking forward to attending the ball, but as it neared, circumstances conspired against them. Andrew Elliot caught an early-summer chill and found his throat sore and his diet limited to soup and apple juice. Alice Elliot avoided the illness, only to be struck by a bout of seasonal hay fever and her sneezes echoed throughout Atherton in daylight hours. They were, they both concluded, poor company for a ball and limited in any enjoyment they might experience themselves.

"I am quite sure that the two of you will be more than adequate as representatives for the Elliot name," their father croaked.

"Besides," said their mother, "it is far more important that two eligible young ladies attend than an old married couple. You are both . . . Achoo!"

Whatever Margaret and Lucy might both be in their mother's eyes was lost in a fit of sniffing and sneezing, though they both felt assured it was a positive sentiment.

"Of course, the coach will be available to you, as I cannot imagine any business that might draw us urgently away."

"Thank you, Father." Margaret nodded. "But I have already arranged transportation for the two of us."

"Indeed? By whom?"

"By Captain Dashwood. I sent a letter asking whether he might be able to transport all four of us as he has such a fine coach, one that Lucy helped build, no less. I thought it might be a treat for the family and he kindly agreed."

"What an excellent idea," Andrew Elliot rasped. "It is a shame we cannot share the experience. I wonder if—"

"Achoo!"

"No. I'm afraid it will be quite impossible. But I'm sure he will understand we mean no disrespect. Margaret, you shall have to report on your opinion of your sister's handiwork to us."

"Indeed I shall." Margaret smiled.

St. Martins Hall was one of the finest estates in the district, second only to Rathbone Manor. The vast grounds were always well tended, with an avenue of beech trees lining the road leading to the main house. As the guests arrived, they assembled in the eastern ballroom; the room was bright, colorful, and filled with talk.

The Elliot sisters walked in, each on an arm of Captain Dashwood, who was looking especially fine in his bright formal regimental coat. Margaret had chosen to wear the dress intended for the now canceled wedding. Lucy was initially dubious about this, especially given that the ball was at St. Martins. But Margaret dismissed her concern. Mrs. Calloway had put good work into the alteration, and it would be a great shame not to wear the fine garment. Besides, she'd noted, it was unlikely that George or Sir Walter St. Martin had the faintest idea what the wedding dresses were to be. This reasoning was correct, for there were so many in attendance and so many different styles and colors on display that Margaret's attire would not stand out among them.

As soon as they entered, Lucy excused herself, heading off to a far corner.

"I hope the ride did not make your sister ill." Dashwood frowned.

"I am certain it did not," said Margaret. "It was as smooth as I have ever ridden. It is a busy room. She will take some time to compose herself, then she will join us. It is her habit to do so at such events."

"I am glad to hear she is herself."

"You are fond of my sister, are you not, Captain Dashwood?"

"I am. She is a most singular creature."

"Then I hope your intentions are honest."

"Have I given you any reason to suggest otherwise?"

"To a protective older sister, no reason is required." Margaret smiled politely. "While Lucy sees a great many things that others miss, she misses a great many things that others see. She sometimes reads intentions poorly. And she thinks upon them greatly. So I must request, Captain, that you be open and honest with your intentions toward her, if not to me, then absolutely to Lucy herself."

He nodded. "I shall be as honest with her as I may and shall act to shield her from every harm I can."

"Thank you, Captain. I am glad we see eye to eye." The statement was more than metaphorical, as she spoke the words face-to-face with him, his eyes angled very slightly upward.

He bowed, she curtsied, and they went their separate ways with a mutual understanding of the protection of Lucy Elliot.

In a corner, as sheltered as she could manage, Lucy found a seat and drew in steady, deliberate breaths, letting the noise wash past her. Every crowd had its own resonance, formed from the numbers, the space, the atmosphere. But it could be processed, turned into background noise, the sound of chattering songbirds. There would always be an itch at the back of her eyes, the twitch of her hand, but those she could manage.

After a time, she opened her eyes, the bright ballroom filling out before her, people and voices all merged together. It was the sound of a ball, a single mass that she could filter as one.

She took another breath then stood, her feet solid beneath her. Society awaited.

CHAPTER 40

LUCY ENGAGED BRIEFLY WITH EMILY DANFORTH, A GIRL SLIGHTLY younger than herself, who was enchanted by the ball and lamenting that her friend Charlotte was not there to see it. Given that the ball existed only due to the dissolution of the engagement, Lucy failed to see how this would work, but she decided that Emily would not be given to discussing Hume's definition of causality. To Lucy's relief the girl was instead soon distracted by the arrival of another friend.

Lucy glanced around the room with a more analytical mind. It was certainly a fine assembly, with every well-positioned family in attendance. Captain Dashwood was speaking with Sir Walter St. Martin, Margaret with George St. Martin, and Oliver with Lord Rathbone. Having traveled here with the former two, she decided to approach Oliver. The young man was dressed in a fine blue overcoat, another excellent testament to the work of Mr. McDonald. Lord Rathbone, on the other hand, wore a very sharp, charcoal-gray suit that might have seemed dull on another man but on him somehow managed to amplify his presence as a strong, sober gentleman.

"Miss Elliot." Oliver bowed. "Have you met Lord Rathbone?"

"Not formally," she replied.

The older gentleman made a faint smile, seeming to approve at once of her honesty and discretion. "You have a reputation as having a quick mind, Miss Elliot," Lord Rathbone commented.

"Then I shall do my best not to disappoint. Though I must confess, I shall be quite adrift if the discussion is one of finance."

"Only by tangent," the lord replied.

"Lord Rathbone is well respected and involved in the war effort," Oliver explained. "It is vital that we be prepared for future engagements."

"Mr. St. Martin was gauging my opinion on what areas of focus we are currently engaged in," Lord Rathbone explained.

"And is that of interest to a man such as yourself?" Lucy asked Oliver.

"It is. Especially regarding current investments. For example, we have, at the moment, naval superiority over the channel, thus it is wise to invest in shipbuilding and associated elements."

"Unfortunately," Lord Rathbone interjected, "it is an area in which I cannot offer advice for speculation. It is true that we are attempting to catch up with Napoleon at present in many areas of industry. But I cannot speak in any detail for fear of secrets or hints slipping to continental ears."

"Then I shall ask no more," Oliver said, "for I should sooner be poor in pounds than rich in francs."

"Outside of the war, I should recommend investment in coaches. Would you agree, Miss Elliot?"

"Perhaps," she replied.

"I suspect there are some impressive advances on the horizon."

"If coaches are your interest, then I believe you will find Miss Elliot more than apt for such conversation. She once spent an entire card game opining on the benefits of rear-axle release joints."

"Front axle, surely," Lord Rathbone corrected.

"Obviously front axle." Lucy nodded. "Why would you even bother with a release joint in a rear axle?"

"Why indeed?" Oliver demurred, gradually realizing he had likely just eliminated himself from his own conversation.

The eastern ballroom of St. Martins Hall was as perfect for dancing as could be desired. The musicians were of excellent caliber, and the dancers moved with fine procession, circling the hall in grand swoops before easing to a close, all parties going their separate ways. Lucy hoped that Captain Dashwood, who had danced with Emily Danforth, would come her way, but she was met by the familiar smile of George St. Martin.

"Miss Elliot. Might I have the pleasure of this next dance?"

"I would be honored, sir," she replied cordially. The man was not, at present, high in her praises, but there was decorum to maintain and it would not do to refuse the host a dance.

They entered the dance in silence and she could not conceive of a topic upon which they might settle comfortably.

She was not alone in this observation.

"You are unusually quiet, Miss Elliot. I hope I have done nothing to offend you."

"Forgive me, Mr. St. Martin. You are an excellent dancer and a fine host. I must confess, with some regret, a part of me does wonder at the propriety of holding such a grand ball, marvelous though it is, so soon after the disappointment of your engagement."

A faint frown crossed his features, whereupon he nodded then turned to a muted smile. "I cannot fault you on such an opinion. I hope it should not reflect too ill on me. I was very fond of Charlotte. One should be as a groom, of course. I had hoped at first that the match might still go ahead, but the scale of the scandal made it quite impossible. I felt it was for the best for all involved that it be called off swiftly and decisively. I have never been one to dwell on the past, but perhaps seek opportunities too recklessly."

"It is through no fault of yours that her father fell from grace. And I do not deny the great weight that impressions may force upon our decisions."

"If it is any consolation, I think it has taught me some caution in approaching matrimony. I promise you I shall not get engaged again for at least a month."

"That is a grossly perfunctory delay, sir."

"It was a joke, Lucy."

"Oh."

She shifted discussion to the architecture of the ballroom and was more than happy to expound upon it for the remainder of the dance.

During a break for refreshment, Lucy found herself looking out at the full moon as it rose above the forest. She wondered what the Night Racing crowd might be doing with the usual races suspended. Some were here, of course, and Molly and the staff at Atherton were likely going about their regular business. But what of Torres and crew? Were they home at their castle? Were they out on some country road testing new designs? Or perhaps they were off challenging racers in another district altogether. Lucy was quite sure the next time Torres raced, his coach would feature a clockwork coil boost, quite possibly one superior to her original. And there would be more after that. Competition spurred innovation and there was certainly as much competition between Lucy and Elsa as there was between Torres and Dashwood.

Refilling a cup from a large punch bowl, her mind was already turning down a path of invention. She stared at the upturned silver lid. A lantern in front of a convex reflective lens would focus the light to better illuminate the road. But it would need a wind shelter. Did ships use the same? Perhaps Dashwood's footman, Jim, might know. Or perhaps the captain himself.

Since their arrival at the ball she had yet to speak with the man. He had danced with several ladies across the evening and she felt certain he would ask her at some point. During the one other dance they had both sat out, she was waylaid by Sir Walter St. Martin. He had seemed in an agitated mood, not unexpected for the host of such a large number of people, and he was happy to talk with a familiar face. He inquired as to the health of her absent parents and recommended that peppers were a fine remedy for hay fever and insisted that he supply her with a jar of preserves before she left. She had accepted politely, and they parted amicably, but by this point she had lost sight of Captain Dashwood, as busy as the room was, and did not see him until the next dance on the card, when she was already on the floor with someone else.

All at once she felt uniquely frustrated with the man. Whyever did he entangle her in his affairs in such a way? Investigation and espionage convoluted every aspect of their interactions so that no one knew the true nature of their connection, least of all Lucy herself. She was already predisposed to overthinking things. The addition of so many variables made for an indecipherable courtship. She knew she had felt several moments of genuine attraction toward him. Their experience in the woods had seemed to suggest he felt the same, but she was all too aware of her shortcomings in such areas. What if she had entirely misread genuine romantic affection from him? What if she had simply projected her desires upon him, just as she had done long ago with Ben Krippingworth? The thought of this possibility caused a momentary imbalance that threw off her step of the current dance, mercifully near its end. She curtsied, thanked her partner, then crossed to the side of the room, catching sight of her agitated features in a mirror.

She closed her eyes and took a breath.

Underwood, Thornbrook, Rawleigh, Pemberley Cross, Norfolk.

She opened her eyes again, this time satisfied that the young woman in the mirror looked more composed.

CHAPTER 41

SUPPER WAS EXCELLENT, AND WITH HER MIND MORE AT EASE, LUCY resolved to approach Captain Dashwood directly, but this time found herself waylaid by her sister. She was about to assure her that she was well when she realized it was Margaret who seemed more anxious.

"Lucy, it is an unusual request to ask, but would you dance with Oliver St. Martin in the next dance?"

"I am quite sure I can. But I am curious as to why."

"He has danced twice tonight, both times with me. It is something expected in the district given our statures, but a third time shall tend itself toward gossip."

Gossip indeed, Lucy considered. To be so forward with a single gentleman within one evening would definitely lead to *talk*.

Margaret continued. "He is hesitant to ask most ladies as both his proportion and demeanor often cause concern. But, if you were to dance with him, I think it should be seen more as familial closeness and alleviate some of the immodest perception."

"Immodest perception it might be, but would it be wholly inaccurate, Meg?"

"His brother has too recently been embroiled in engagement and scandal. I have no desire to cause him to be reflected in the same light, no matter my feelings."

Lucy's thoughts returned once again to the possibility of the match of her sister and Oliver St. Martin. Perhaps here was a chance to move things along that path more swiftly. Three dances in one evening was practically an engagement, and if the pair were not willing to make such a statement, then she should support them as best she could.

"I shall have no fear in dancing with Mr. St. Martin." Lucy nodded. "If my sister will defend me by manhandling a goat, then I am quite sure I can defend her by dancing with a tall man."

They made their way across the ballroom, to where Oliver was waiting, and exchanged pleasantries. Shortly after, the music for the next dance began, and the two made their way onto the floor hand in hand.

"You are most gracious to do this for your sister." He bowed as they stepped into the music.

"You do yourself discredit, Mr. St. Martin. There is no ill task to be undertaken in dancing with you. The worst I might say is that you are somewhat unpracticed."

"That is true. The woman who taught us dancing was barely up to your shoulder. My brother took it well enough, but it was not a school in which I excelled."

"We each have our strengths and weaknesses. Some are more pronounced than others. For example, I cannot draw portraits," she admitted. "Margaret exceeds me at drawing."

"The two of you do not seem competitive."

"Combative, perhaps. We bicker. But we are different enough that we have seldom been rivals. I am sure you and your brother are much the same."

"Perhaps you mistake all family connections as being as strong as your own. George is moderately fond of me and seldom does me any more wrong than a slight jibe, but we are not close. He is his father's son and I am my mother's. I am heir neither to his fortunes nor his attentions." He paused as they turned, Lucy passing under his arm with little effort.

"Forgive me." He smiled. "It is not that I lament my station. I am merely pointing out to you my respect for the connection you and your sister possess. Find family where you may, Miss Elliot, and treasure it dearly."

She nodded and smiled. Though she did not say it aloud, she felt that to call Oliver St. Martin part of her family one day was something both possible and desirable.

Lucy entered the Boulanger eagerly, knowing that, by the nature of the dance, she should have at least a brief chance to speak with Captain Dashwood as they passed each other, cycling through partners.

And yet even this seemingly obvious plan was thwarted as they got underway. for she could catch sight of him neither in the orbiting dancers nor the assembled observers. Where she might otherwise have lost herself in the pleasant patterns and repetitions, she instead found herself frustrated by the persistent obstacles that the evening had placed against her. She wondered how she might remedy this. The most obvious solution was to take a diversion tomorrow to Elsworth if she happened to pass that way. This was quite at odds with the very perception she had been trying to avoid of there being a strong connection between them, but the truth was that her family now assumed as much and her vexation propelled her to risk such speculation. If she could confer with him directly then she might have a chance to pin down the truth and so better explain it to others.

This course of action decided upon, and no further opportunity for dancing presenting itself, she resolved instead to focus her attention entirely on enjoying the evening for her own sake. She savored an excellent dessert, made sweeter by observing the third and final dance between Margaret and Oliver.

The dancing completed and the gentlemen heading to the smoking room, she dismissed any other chance of discussion with Dashwood, focusing her attention on the rather ruthless defeat of three other ladies in a game of cards. So absorbed was she in calculating the odds of the necessary card appearing, that she only faintly detected a snippet of the conversation of her tablemates.

"Pardon me." She broke her silence so sharply that one of the other ladies almost dropped her hand. "But did you say a horse-man?"

"Yes." Elizabeth Overton nodded. She was a married woman with a predisposition for gossip and for overexaggeration of her children's virtues, but otherwise quite sensible in Lucy's percep-tion. "My husband and I were returning home from a visit to Lord Rathbone, and at some point we overheard hooves. When I looked from the side window, I saw a horseman following behind us at some distance."

"What manner of horseman?"

"It was too far off to make it out. My eyes are not what they once were. But it was ghostly white. It was a very dark night and yet I could still see the shape of it. My husband saw it too but dis-missed it as a night rider of some kind. A messenger perhaps."

"You were not convinced?"

"Well, I have heard the legends of the headless horseman. They say if you see him then you're doomed. So maybe these bad eyes saved me after all." She chuckled. "I glanced back when we turned into our gate, but no rider passed by on the road. It was a curious affair indeed."

"I do hope it was not a sign of misfortune," said Sarah Mayhew.

"Misfortune?" asked Mrs. Overton.

"Charlotte Wyndham once spoke of a ghostly horseman on the roads. And you can scarcely deny that an ill fortune came for her."

"As I said, I have heard the tales. But I am doubtful of such superstitions. What do you think, Miss Elliot?"

Lucy decided to keep what Charlotte had told her in confi-dence, but knew she had to reply with something in defense of reason.

"I find it most unlikely that a ghostly specter on the night roads should be a forewarning of improper stock speculation."

The women at the table all laughed cheerfully at the reply.

"Miss Elliot, you have a way of cutting through nonsense that I find refreshing," Mrs. Overton said. "I, for one, find it far more likely that such a figure is some manner of criminal marking out potential victims."

"Do you think so?" Sarah asked excitedly, the idea of highwaymen every bit as captivating as phantasms.

"Sir Walter St. Martin's wine was stolen from a coach."

"Brandy," Lucy corrected.

"Brandy." Mrs. Overton nodded. "And it hasn't been seen since. What better way to know of potential prey than to observe those regular users of the night roads?"

This made sense to Lucy, though she could not help but feel it was only a part of a more complicated issue. A night rider might observe coaches, but to what end? Neither Charlotte Wyndham nor the Overtons had carried anything of value on their trips. Perhaps that was why they had not been robbed. But then how was a robber to know what a coach did or did not hold from a distance?

Lucy pondered this in the back of her mind as she discarded, drew, then played a king of diamonds to muted sighs of despair from her fellow players.

As the evening wound down and the various guests and coaches departed, Lucy found herself wearied. She'd had her limit of socializing and now looked forward to the quiet comfort of her own home and bed once more. Before she was able to depart, however, there was one more obligation to uphold, that of the earlier offer from Sir Walter as to a remedy for her parents. While Margaret and Captain Dashwood waited for Jim to bring the coach around, Lucy followed her host down a quiet hallway in search of preserved peppers.

"You know, I have been most interested of late as to the curative properties of such spices. These are some of the strongest I have been able to cultivate, but I'm led to believe there are some wonderful exotic varieties in the Americas that might even be useful as ointments. You're not suffering from any maladies yourself, Miss Elliot?"

"My feet are somewhat weary from dancing, but I am otherwise well."

"I quite understand. I should not trouble you further with the basement steps. Ah, here should be a perfect spot for you to wait." He pointed to a small bench in an alcove, and she thanked him for his generosity as he descended into his pickling room.

For the first time in the whole evening there was a still silence, and she allowed the coolness of it to ease over her, every bit as pleasant as being able to rest her feet.

It was amid this silence that she caught the sound of voices moving down a nearby hall. She remained still as they approached, words and voices becoming clear. One of them was George St. Martin, and the other had the bearing of a servant.

"No trace of the stolen goods have been found?"

"No, sir."

"But you suspect that the Earl of Westchester is involved?"

"That is our best guess, sir."

"Well, hopefully the situation will be resolved before long. My father is becoming increasingly anxious about the whole affair."

The conversation continued, but it did so beyond earshot, as they had both walked on past her; seated on the bench in the alcove as she was, they had not sighted her as they'd conversed.

It was quite extraordinary information. Not only were the St. Martins still investigating the theft of the brandy on their own terms, but they believed it to be connected to the Earl of Westchester, a title she was unfamiliar with. She was quite sure it did not belong to anyone she had encountered in the district, and she had a quite comprehensive knowledge of local society. It was certainly intelligence that Captain Dashwood should find keenly interesting, if she should ever again have the opportunity to speak to the man in private.

Before she could mull this over further, she heard the sound of more footsteps, and Sir Walter returned. proudly holding a jar of preserves, swirling with crimson and amber. She took it with gratitude and held it with the reverence that reflected the way he had presented it.

CHAPTER 42

LUCY HELD THE JAR OF PRESERVES AS THE COACH SET OFF FROM THE ball. Sitting beside Margaret, she found herself facing Captain Dashwood at last but unable to address any of the subjects she wished to speak of. Margaret was nodding off to sleep, but Lucy would not risk being overheard. Small talk would have to suffice, something she neither desired nor excelled at.

"Did you find the evening enjoyable, Captain?"

"It was perhaps a little too crowded for my tastes. I enjoyed meeting a few new faces. And St. Martins Hall is well suited to such a congregation."

"I have encouraged George to host balls in the past for just such a reason, but he has been reluctant, more based on the wishes of his father than his own."

"Well, I am sure they found the event to be a success."

"Yes. All were well entertained, and the food and dances were excellent. I can scarcely imagine that anyone might find fault with the evening."

"And yet, if I may, your tone does seem to imply some disappointment."

She shuffled slightly, feeling caught out that she had given away her mood so obviously. Or was it merely the case that the man had become adept in reading her mannerisms?

"As you stated, it was a large affair. It can be trying for one disinclined to crowds. And in such a case there will always be missed opportunities. Those one could not speak to or dance with. Minor inconveniences."

"Indeed." He nodded, leaning forward, and speaking softer. "Is your sister well?"

"She often rests on the coach ride home."

Margaret was definitely asleep, but even in a smooth coach ride she could be jolted awake at any moment. Lucy avoided his gaze, fiddling with the waxy lid of the preserves, and when she glanced up again there was a soft smile on his face.

Surely he cannot be admiring the way I hold a jar of relish, she thought, though his expression suggested just that.

"Lucy," he said, and his voice sounded suddenly serious. "I—"

He paused as the coach came to a swift stop. Three quick taps came from the front of the coach, faint and from a boot heel. Seconds later there was the sound of their driver, Jim, descending.

Lucy saw Dashwood set his jaw.

"Remain calm. Wake your sister gently," he said with quiet authority.

Lucy faintly shook her sister, who opened her eyes to the sight of a finger pressed to the lips of Captain Dashwood.

"What is the matter?" Lucy whispered.

"We are being hijacked," he replied plainly. "Make no trouble unless your lives are in immediate danger."

"And if they are?"

He smiled grimly. "Then raise hell." He took a breath, and once again his countenance changed back to one of curious cheer. "Jim!" he yelled, thumping the carriage. "Why the blazes have we stopped?"

He opened the coach door and lurched out with such unbundled energy that, had she not seen him moments earlier, Lucy should have been quite shocked to think him drunk.

Outside the coach he seemed to sway for a moment, getting his head around the situation. Unable to see the rest of the scene, the Elliot sisters had to rely on their ears.

"Who are you?" Dashwood demanded with a slur in his words. "Are we being robbed? Jim? Are we being robbed?"

"It would seem so, sir," the young man replied quietly.

"Look. We really don't have much on us. I just—"

"Shut up!" called a sharp voice. There was no hesitation in his words. "Get over here!"

Dashwood nodded nervously, crossing to them, stumbling to his knees beyond view of the window.

"Please don't kill me!" he blubbered. "My father is a wealthy man!"

"I said shut up. Everyone else, out of the coach."

Lucy and Margaret exchanged a glance and nodded to each other. They exited the coach slowly, stepping away from it and standing as still as they might. Lucy was surprised that she did not feel the least bit panicked. If anything, she felt coolly detached. Then again, she also realized she was still holding the jar of preserves, so perhaps she wasn't acting quite as rationally as she imagined.

She took in the situation before her. Jim stood by the horses, hands held high. Dashwood on his knees nearby, hands on his head, whimpering. Lucy was certain it was merely an act, but it was a convincing one.

There were three assailants standing beside a fallen branch across the road. It was light enough to move, but heavy enough to force a coach to stop—a well-tested highwayman tactic. Dark coats and rough dress hinted at a sinister purpose. Their expressions of mixed scowls and cruel grins backed this up. The presence of the pistols they each held confirmed it.

"Over there. On your knees," the tallest of the men ordered, waving his pistol.

The Elliot sisters complied, stepping back from the coach, kneeling somewhat awkwardly, giving little heed to the state of their dresses on the roadside earth—this was no time for frivolous concerns.

"You too." The man pointed to Jim, who kneeled by Dashwood's side.

At a tilt of the tall man's head, one of the three moved toward the sisters. From a combination of moon- and coach-light Lucy could see he had a patch over his left eye.

"Jewelry," Eye Patch growled, singling out Lucy first.

Neither her necklace nor brooch were of great value, though the latter had been handed down through several generations. It was a point she did not feel inclined to mention, instead complying with the request.

The shorter man (Lucy decided to call him Crossbones) held a pistol on the kneeling men while the apparent leader (now called Blackbeard, in keeping with the pirate theme) went to check the coach. She realized this assessment of the scene was somewhat absurd, but if these were coach robbers, it was fair to assume they might be connected to the other hijackings. She did her best to remember their faces, clothing, and heights. Then she linked it to what she knew.

A chill ran through her. If these were indeed the same robbers, then they left no witnesses.

But something was wrong about the whole thing. This seemed more a robbery of opportunity, not a well-planned heist. They had little of value, having come from a ball.

Blackbeard's glance inside the cabin had been more cursory than a real search. He then turned back to approach the two kneeling men from behind with an intention his search had lacked.

Lucy glanced to her left, where Margaret was handing over her jewelry. The eye patch was on his left eye. Lucy's side. That might give her a second to act.

Blackbeard raised his pistol, and Lucy realized a second was all she had.

She saw Jim spring forward at Crossbones, even as the trigger was being pulled. She saw Dashwood throw himself forward to duck under any shot that might be about to hit him in the back. It was a canny move, especially from someone the others believed to be drunk. It might have worked had Blackbeard been unprepared, but he had already been aiming, and the drop forward was not enough alone to avoid the shot.

But the fate of Captain James Dashwood was not to be decided by a single action. The instant before the fatal shot, his salvation arrived in the form of a flying jar of preserves straight to the side of his would-be murderer's head. The glass cracked, and the lid flew off, thick liquid splashing and the shock of the impact throwing the bullet wild, well above Captain Dashwood.

Eye Patch turned his attention from Margaret to Lucy, swinging the pistol around. Lucy saw the barrel in the moonlight, so close that her eyes almost needed to cross to make it out clearly. There was no time to dodge, no chance of missing at this range. No time, really, to overthink things. At least she hoped the others would be safe.

She squeezed her eyes shut but still saw the flash of light, heard the deafening blast, and felt the burning force against her face.

CHAPTER 43

THE MOMENT MARGARET SAW A FLURRY OF MOVEMENT ACROSS THE clearing, Captain Dashwood's words came to her with conviction.

Raise hell.

As the highwayman in front of her swung his pistol toward Lucy, Margaret was already moving. Two arms wrapped around his knees. As the pistol fired, she heaved upward. Her cry of exertion went unheard as the pistol flared by her side. Had the movement been enough to save her sister?

She had no way of knowing. Still grasping his knees, Margaret rose to her full height, driving her shoulder into his stomach so that he was laid out over her like a sack of flour. She swung him down with the full force and fury of her frame and a roar that should have frightened off every goat and suitor in the district.

The earth was no more forgiving than she was.

When he made no further motion, she turned to her younger sister, now on the ground with her hands to her face, still very much alive. She pulled her up into her arms.

"Meg? Is that you?" Lucy coughed.

Margaret's ears were still ringing, and Lucy's must be much worse. The violent energy of the moment departed, and she felt unsteady, hugging her sister tightly, her eyes turning to the chaos behind her.

Jim and the smaller highwayman had fallen into a grapple on the ground, the younger driver greatly disadvantaged by the shot that had passed through his shoulder. Even so, he fought as fiercely as his rival, both ruthless and inelegant in their combat, struggling over a knife.

Dashwood had now rolled to his feet. The leader was a fearsome sight, with no way of knowing in the limited light what was blood and what was preserves. It clearly stung furiously, for the man was rubbing and thrashing at his face violently. Dashwood clenched his fist and swung hard at the man's jaw. He reeled but swung back, grappling for the captain. They both fell to the ground, but it was Dashwood who ended up beneath, the larger man pinning him down, hands gripping his throat.

The stiff collar of the captain's stock offered some protection, but the man was formidably strong. Margaret felt the urge to dash over, but her earlier surge seemed to have robbed her of strength. Before she could decide, she saw Dashwood grab something beside him. He swung his hand back up, driving the broken glass jar into the neck of his attacker. When the grip slackened but did not cease, he swung again. This time his attacker fell aside.

Even at this distance she could see the blood on Dashwood's hand, a glass shard cutting both ways.

Rather than join the grapple he staggered to the coach. She watched as with deliberate action he opened an external compartment, withdrew a rifle, aimed it, and fired just as the third highwayman was about to stab for Jim.

His aim was true, and the fallen man made neither sound nor motion.

It had been less than sixty seconds since Lucy had thrown the jar.

Lucy whimpered, and her sister held her tight. Margaret glanced about the clearing, assessing their allies and their enemies.

Three were wounded. Three were dead.

Dashwood lowered the rifle and caught her gaze.

As he did, she knew two things for certain. Captain James Dashwood was a man of action. And there was still more to be done this night.

CHAPTER 44

$\mathcal{T}$HE MOONLIT ROAD WAS NOT TO BE DENIED RACERS AFTER ALL.

Margaret sat beside Dashwood outside, her eyes scanning the road ahead for dangers as they sped, unknowingly conscripted into the messenger role once reserved for her sister.

The attempted robbers were left where they had lain, and the carriage raced with all the speed Dashwood could urge from his horses, with no opponent but time. Occasionally Margaret caught a grimace on his face as his hand, lightly wrapped but still bleeding, gripped the reins firmly.

Lucy and Jim were within the coach. Her face had been scalded by gunpowder, her hearing faint, but she'd understood enough to be given the task of keeping a cloth pressed firmly to Jim's shoulder to staunch the blood.

Margaret's ears were ringing, though the whipping of the wind around her was louder still. Despite the familiar roads, she'd lost sense of direction and distance, trusting that Dashwood knew the way.

Soon enough they closed on a house. They were at the residence of Dr. Matthews, a retired army surgeon whose wooden leg had been of great fascination to the Elliot sisters in childhood. With Lucy able to walk under her own power, they helped Jim out of the carriage, Margaret holding him as Dashwood banged on the door violently. Moments later there was movement upstairs. The door soon opened, Dr. Matthews in his nightgown, a crutch under one arm, a lantern in the other. No words were spoken. The old man knew at once what was before him and ushered in his late-night visitors. Dashwood helped the barely conscious Jim into a chamber, and Margaret was pointed to the kitchen. She led Lucy in and seated her at the table.

"Can you still hear?"

"I can," Lucy replied. "I believe I can see, though it is dim and blurry."

A young woman about their age entered carrying a bowl.

"Miss? I've got a cold cloth and water. May I?"

Lucy nodded. The woman touched the cloth gently to Lucy's burning skin and she exhaled in relief.

The girl introduced herself as the doctor's oldest daughter, Kate. While she tended to Lucy, she asked several questions about her sensation, her vision, and her hearing. Lucy followed the path of a candle flame up and down, left and right; listened to tapping spoons; and explained all that had happened. Seemingly satisfied, the girl advised that she continue to wet the cloth every minute and keep her face cool. Then she left to help her father.

Margaret watched her sister quietly. She had seen Lucy upset or overwhelmed before, but this was something entirely different. She realized how close she had come to losing her.

"I believe I am improving," Lucy spoke quietly. "Cold water is a relief, and having washed my eyes they remain sore but no longer weeping. As to my hearing, my ears still ring and your words are muted, but I can make them out well enough."

Margaret smiled. Her sister was certainly sounding herself.

"What of Jim?" Lucy asked.

"I cannot say. Captain Dashwood said the bullet went right through, which apparently is a good thing if you can believe it. Less chance of infection. I hope Captain Dashwood's wound is being tended to as well."

"James was hurt?" Lucy exclaimed.

"A vicious cut upon his hand. He must have been in dreadful pain driving the coach. But he made amazing speed. It was quite terrifying being up there helping. I did my best. He told me when we began that he hoped my eyes were as good as yours. An odd thing to say."

"In the heat of the moment, perhaps."

"Perhaps."

There was a pause, and Lucy tilted her head. "Margaret? What is wrong?"

"Wrong?"

"You are sobbing. I assure you I will be all right."

"It is a foolish thing. After all, I am the only one unharmed here. It is indulgent for me to feel so put-upon."

"Meg? What is the matter?"

Margaret gathered her thoughts. "I killed a man, Lucy." She shuddered as she spoke. "I picked him up and I threw him down and I killed him. And I know full well that he'd have done the same to you or me. Given that choice, I'd make the same one again a hundred times. But he's still dead. That is a thing that can never be undone."

Silence hung in the kitchen again.

Lucy stood, walked around the table, and hugged her sister.

There was soon a rise in activity in the house, and indeed in the whole town, as word spread of the robbery.

In the kitchen the Elliot sisters were joined by Captain Dashwood, his hand now tightly bandaged.

"The magistrate and the militia have been alerted to our incident," he explained with a polite but efficient tone. "Jim is being tended by Dr. Matthews. He believes there is a good chance of recovery."

"And yourself?" Lucy asked.

He glanced at his hand. "I suspect I shall have a rather striking scar, but the movement is undamaged. Lucy, I am told that you are equally fortunate to escape permanent harm?"

"My ears still ring. And I suspect my pillow shall be uncomfortable for some nights ahead, but I am, I feel, already somewhat improved."

"And you, Miss Elliot?" He turned to Margaret. "Are you all right?"

"I am without injury, Captain Dashwood."

"I am aware of that. I am asking if you are all right."

"Of that . . . I am uncertain," she replied softly. "No matter the necessity, I am not comfortable with the taking of a human life."

"Nor should one be, no matter the necessity." He paused a moment before continuing. "I am taking a group of men to the site of the attack. We will assess matters from there. I have arranged for a coach and an escort to return you to Atherton. Your parents will no doubt be anxious, and your return will be a greater salve than any messenger. Lucy, I believe you should check with Dr. Matthews before you leave. He may have advice on treatment. Can you find the way?"

She nodded and slowly walked from the room. Margaret observed how his eyes stayed on Lucy until she had disappeared from view, as if unwilling to lose sight of her again.

Then he turned to Margaret.

"Had you and your sister not acted as you did, Jim and I should most certainly be dead and most likely the two of you as well. That is of little consolation to the doubt and self-loathing you are feeling. I am familiar with that face. I remember the first time I saw it in my shaving mirror. I have killed men before. It is the job of a soldier. That you know. But death comes in many forms, some swift and painless, some long and gruesome. I tell you this because I do not wish to give you comfortable untruths. You will not forget this night. But it will not define you. It is a part of who you are, not the whole. You danced at a ball tonight. That is as true as any part that came after."

She nodded, taking in his words and matching his gaze. "If I may, Captain, there is one aspect that bothers me more than the others. I think, perhaps, you may be able to offer some perspective upon it."

"I shall try."

"It was very easy. It was a moment of urgency, of course. But it was neither a challenge in strength nor in action. It feels like . . . it should have been harder."

"That is, perhaps, the darkest truth one learns." He nodded grimly. "It is usually easy. When they don't see it coming. When your intent overcomes their expectation. The act is easy. The will is hard. Before and after. Do not fear the strength of your arm, Miss Elliot. Have faith in the strength of your character."

She looked down at her hands, and they spoke no more until Lucy returned, the doctor having checked and discharged her injuries.

The magistrate and men arrived shortly afterward, and there was only time for the most brief of goodbyes before Dashwood was on his way and the sisters on theirs.

Seated in their coach, on their way to Atherton, the weight of everything finally overwhelmed Lucy and it was she who fell asleep on the shoulder of her sister long before they reached home. Margaret cradled her softly, half asleep herself. How long ago it seemed that she had been happily dancing with Oliver.

CHAPTER 45

IT WAS CLOSE TO MIDDAY BEFORE LUCY TRULY AWOKE, THOUGH HER sleep had been a broken one, her face hot and prickly and her dreams sharp with robbers and pistols.

Mercifully the day was a cooler, cloudier one, for a blooming summer day should have irritated her further. A servant had left a bowl of water, and she washed her face with the cool cloth for some time before checking her reflection in the mirror. There was red in her features, some spots darker than others, but that was the extent of it, more obvious on her upper right side than her lower left.

"It is," she said to herself, "as well as one could hope to be after being nearly shot in the face."

She stood, steadying herself slightly. There was something about speaking of the incident out loud that made her feel momentarily faint. Or perhaps it was her balance, for there remained a ringing in her ears, though her hearing seemed well enough. She moved her weight left and right, and once she was confident she could stand and walk unaided, she rang her bell for help dressing for the day.

Descending to the dining room, she first encountered her father, who swiftly hugged her with an affection greater than either of them often expressed.

"Lucy, my dear. Are you all right?"

"It is akin to sunburn, Father. I am sure it may itch for a few days, but no worse."

"That is then a small charity to savor. It is a dreadful business, Lucy. Quite dreadful. Your mother wanted to be here when you arose but also wished to go to town to see what the news was. It is a cooler day, so her hay fever is lessened, while my cold is worse. Margaret went with her. She explained things last night. My poor girls. Dreadful business. Such a dark set of affairs for the whole district."

"A set of affairs?" Lucy asked, for she was quite sure the words alluded to more than merely their own encounter.

"Come join me for lunch. You must be hungry. I shall explain the news as I understand it all."

As she ate slowly, Lucy learned that the prior evening had seen a spate of crime across the district. Another coach returning from the ball had been the target of a pair of highwaymen who had taken several expensive pieces of jewelry and a gold watch before leaving the coachman and guests bound and gagged, only discovered in the early morning by a passing farmer.

Roads had not been the only targets. The manor of Lord Rathbone had been burgled, thieves taking assorted gold, silver, and money. Later in the night, perhaps unsatisfied with the prior haul, they tried their luck again at St. Martins Hall. If they had hoped the inhabitants were in bed, weary after a ball, they were sorely mistaken. Sir Walter and George were still up and heard a noise. Having armed themselves, they went to investigate, which ended in George being cut in the arm and both thieves shot dead.

It was possible more events were still being uncovered, hence the other Elliot women traveling into town for news. They had been accompanied by several servants, and Andrew Elliot had arranged with the staff for a night watch at Atherton to be posted for the time being.

"It is most upsetting to me, Lucy. This sort of thing doesn't happen here."

"It has been happening here for some months. The St. Martins' coach, for example."

"It was a figure of speech, Lucy." He smiled faintly. "But you are correct. I should not be surprised if the events were related."

She nodded in agreement. But related how? Such an escalation was unexpected.

It was another piece of the puzzle, but it was no longer an abstract problem having threatened her life and the lives of her family. Each time that day she caught her reflection, far from warning her away, the sight made her more determined to solve it than ever.

Both Lucy and Andrew Elliot were eager for news upon the return of their family members, but there was little more to be learned. It was good fortune that there had been no further report of incidents from the night before. None of the men had been identified, which suggested they were all from outside the district, a fact that was both reassuring and unsettling to the local residents. That the threat had not sprung from within was a relief, but it left the uncertainty that interlopers might be waiting in the shadows.

Margaret explained that Jim remained in the care of Dr. Matthews, that his condition was stable, and that he had thanked the Elliot sisters for their aid in the crisis. He was to be transported back to the care of his parents as soon as he was ready to travel, Captain Dashwood insisting on covering the expense and care.

Of the captain there was otherwise no news, for he had not been in town during the time the Elliots were visiting. He had been spoken of in tones of admiration and more than a hint of caution. It was of course the duty of a gentleman to protect those in his charge, but the seeming ease with which he had dispatched the highwaymen clearly lent an air of danger to a tale that might otherwise have been thrilling. That a gentleman might dispatch a highwayman might be passed off as a brave tale; that he dispatched *three* held a little too much suggestion that he was skilled and possibly experienced in such a role.

Aside from a knife wound, George St. Martin was also well. From the intruders at St. Martins they had recovered a gold watch and ring that had been taken from the waylaid coach earlier that evening. The other items, including those taken from Rathbone Manor, had not been found. Lord Rathbone had met with Sir Walter St. Martin, who agreed that any further deliveries of value to the district warranted additional protection. They would both travel to London to ensure such measures were taken.

All these dark affairs had quite taken the shine off what had, until that point, been a charming ball.

Lucy concluded it was most likely that the goods were buried somewhere in the surrounding woods. With all those who knew the locations now dead, it might be centuries before anyone ever saw them again.

She felt a weariness throughout the day that she could not escape. Her attention drifted from needlepoint, to the pianoforte, to sketches, to the pianoforte again, but always in the back of her mind were the crimes of the previous night. She did not, as her sister did, harbor any particular guilt or regret for the fate of her attackers—they had quite clearly intended to kill Jim and Captain Dashwood, but that fact in itself raised further questions that she could not answer.

Why such certainty toward execution when the other coach party was simply gagged and bound? Had they raised a fight then perhaps it might have made sense, but the men had complied and offered no challenge. Perhaps, if it was the work of the same group as prior robberies, they were aware of Dashwood being on their trail and wished to finish him off. But if they were the same group, why leave the other coach party unharmed when previous victims were never seen again? And why veer now into burglary, a much riskier affair? Their tactics and execution seemed utterly different; from skilled and professional to sloppy and reckless.

Lucy stopped playing her music mid-fret. An idea had come to her with such urgency she felt certain of it: It did not seem to be the work of the same criminals because it was not.

A fallen branch might stop a coach of ballgoers, but a messenger coach with guards would never have fallen for such a trick.

The robberies of the brandy and of the army payroll had left no trace. They had been skillful and subtle. These latest had been rough and brutal.

Now that she saw it from this perspective it all made sense. She wished urgently to speak with Captain Dashwood, but with evening approaching and the dangers of the past night still fresh, it was no time to be out on the road. Visiting others was out of the question.

So it was that she was forced to sit through the night, restless with a combination of lingering spring humidity, a prickling face, and the full moon shining through her window.

The next day the looming clouds opened into what her father referred to as spring showers, but the weather persisted all day long, confining them to the house and Lucy to her thoughts. The two consolations were that her face was slightly less red than the day before and that Molly had made up a family remedy of an almond and honey salve that, while at once oily and sticky, did seem to ease the discomfort of her skin before bed.

CHAPTER 46

Two days passed before the rain cleared and the ground dried enough that Lucy was able to argue for travel. She did not wish to explain her destination to her family, instead suggesting that she was sick of being trapped indoors and wanted to go for a ride. With her face now on the mend, and no further incidents of any kind for several days, her father consented, though with conditions to stick to the regularly used roads and return well before evening.

The Elliots had two horses for riding. Horatio loathed Lucy with a vengeance, and Daisy stubbornly tolerated her when necessary, a sentiment Lucy reflected. She seldom rode for pleasure, but given the past days' weather and the experience after the ball, perhaps it would do her good, she thought, to get out.

Lucy approached the white-and-yellow mare as the stableman prepared her.

Horse and human eyed each other, unconvinced.

"Listen," said Lucy, "I don't like you, and you don't like me. But you've been cooped up here all week too, and I bet you want a good gallop. This way we both get what we want."

Daisy snorted.

Lucy shrugged. "Close enough."

Thankfully, any equine animosity was forgotten once they were on the open road, with Lucy letting the horse find her own pace on what she had to admit was a fine early-summer day. The fields and trees sped by, and Lucy had only to nudge Daisy left or right at each intersection as she steered them toward Elsworth.

It was not speed as Lucy enjoyed it, for she found riding uncomfortable, coaches being far more civilized. But under the circumstances, she was glad for the creature, who seemed to be enjoying herself.

The manor was quiet as Lucy drew up to the front door. Dismounting, she led Daisy on foot toward the stables, and while she did not expect to see Jim there, she was surprised to see neither horses nor coach.

It seemed Captain Dashwood was out on an errand. Yet the day was still young, and she saw no reason why she might not wait for his return.

"Miss Elliot?"

She turned to see Thomas Marbrook sauntering toward her.

"The master suggested you might be around at some point. Here, I'll take her if you want."

She handed him the reins with a nod. "She has been inside for several days. I believe fresh grass would be a treat."

"Well, we have no end of that at this time of year. You'd best head to the cottage. My wife has something for you."

She wondered why she had been directed to the cottage rather than the manor, but if Dashwood was to be away some time it made more sense for her to find company there. As she walked she felt circulation return to her legs unevenly, shaking off pins and needles as she tapped lightly on the front door.

It was opened some moments later by Mrs. Marbrook.

"Oh, Miss Elliot. I am pleased to see you looking so well. I have been told you were injured?"

"A light burn. If you did not notice it, then I am well recovered."

"I see now. I passed it off as seeming a little flushed from the heat. What brings you this way?"

"I was hoping to see Captain Dashwood. Do you know what hour he plans to return?"

Mrs. Marbrook frowned. "You haven't heard?"

"Heard what?" Lucy asked, her heart skipping. "Is he ill? Was there another robbery? Some aggravation to his wound?"

"Nothing so dire. He was in fine health when he left. The same cannot be said of his father. He has returned home to see him."

"Returned home? For how long?"

"Indefinitely, I believe. He's had us pack the place up. He suggested he might be returning again in autumn."

"But . . . but . . ." Lucy tried in vain to voice her many thoughts.

"I know you two were fond of each other. He was sorry to go so suddenly. Here." She opened an old cookery book and withdrew an envelope from between the pages. It was sealed with wax but had no name upon it. "He said to give this to you, and only you, by hand. For you to read alone. Here, use the sitting room. I have to finish lunch."

Unsure of what else to do and desperate for answers, Lucy sat in a well-worn, comfortable chair in the sunshine, broke the seal open, and began to read.

To my dear Lucy,

I regret that I cannot deliver this letter to you in person and cannot provide an opportunity to discuss the last evening we saw each other. Events have unfolded rapidly, and there are several reasons preventing our meeting in person.

While it is true that my father is in ill health, it is not wholly the reason for my departure. He has been an invalid for some time, but under the circumstances it made for a useful and verifiable explanation as to my sudden need to leave. With the deaths of the criminals who attempted to rob our coach and the St. Martins, my superiors are convinced that those responsible for the earlier hijackings have been identified and eliminated. There is, I suspect, political pressure to bring the whole affair to a close.

I am unconvinced. I should not be surprised if you have come to similar conclusions. As it stands, I might have pressed harder to remain at Elsworth had it not been for the suspicions I have since formed.

I do not believe the events of the night we were assailed were coincidence. It appears that the men who robbed us intended from the outset to kill me, and had it not been for the intervention of you and your sister they would most assuredly have succeeded. I now believe the other coach robbery was a diversion and that I was the target. The only reason for this would be that someone suspected my true purpose here and arranged to have me killed in a manner that appeared to be random violence. However, I believe the robberies at St. Martins Hall and Rathbone Manor were not random. Both men are involved in different aspects of military matters, particularly the development of something called the Iron Adder, which Napoleon would pay a fortune to acquire. Our adversary in this is playing a long game of espionage with the robberies, such as the brandy; a diversion. The men who were killed that night were merely paid to act on behalf of another, one far more cunning and above the brutish work we encountered.

This brings me to the primary reason for my departure. If my cover has been penetrated and my quarry is still at large, then I am no longer safe at Elsworth. Were the risk only to myself I might abide it, but it endangers others. Jim knew of the dangers, but Mr. and Mrs. Marbrook do not. Closer to my heart, there is you, Lucy. Already this danger has nearly cost your life. It would not be a leap of a great order to assume an affection between us and that you would be a prime means of either harming me or securing my compliance. That is a risk I cannot take, though it robs me even of the chance to say these words to you face to face.

This mystery is not yet solved, but I regret that, for now, I must solve it from afar and bereft of your aid.

I know you well enough to know you will think over this mystery, and I shall offer what else I know. Longburn Mire is an abominable place. One might hide an army there as well as a body. I uncovered some trace of tracks that suggested it might be home to several, but no proof could I find, nor, I suspect, may ever be found. You are well to stay clear of it. However tempting you may find it, please do not expose yourself to further danger. I know you will puzzle this out, but keep these thoughts private lest a threat turn your way.

I wish I could tell you when or if I shall be able to return. I am a man driven by my duty and my loyalty to country. As a result, I am perhaps unobservant of the real connections to those around me. It was not until I realized I must separate myself from your company that I felt the strength of my affections.

You are a singular and remarkable woman. It has been my great pleasure to spend time with you, and it is my great wish that I might do so again someday.

I hope that I do not presume too much with these words. I wish all the best for you and your family. Look after your sister. Stay safe and stay strong.

I pray that the last request I am to make to you may not seem the cruelest of all, for if ill tidings come to pass, you may look back upon these words as a fond recollection of me. I ask that you do not allow this to be. Any letter kept is a letter that may be read, and our adversary has already shown a willingness to take a life.

I ask that you burn this letter once you have read it.

Had I known the ball would be our last opportunity to speak together in private I should have seized eagerly upon it without hesitation. But life is often akin to the Night

*Races, the road ahead too dark to see until the moment it is
up on you and the need for decision too swift.*
  I hope we shall ride together again someday.
                                      Yours, with dearest regards,
                                        James Dashwood

Lucy finished, paused, then read the letter twice more, once
quickly and once with deliberate slowness so that she might hold
it in her mind. When she was done, she took the letter through
to the kitchen, opened the stove, and threw it within. The paper
flared briefly, flashing bright before curling down into embers.

Lucy closed the stove. The words were hers alone now. What
she might do with them she could not yet say.

They were not all he had left her. The man, it seemed, had
tempered his pragmatism with sentimentality. Within the envelope she held was a small chain with a silver charm in the form of
a night owl. For flying through the night.

The Marbrooks had returned, but Lucy declined their invitation to lunch, instead retrieving Daisy from the hitching post.

On the ride home she let the animal gallop at her own pace.
The spring air stung her face, but Lucy didn't care. If she went
fast enough, the wind in her eyes and the blur of the fields made
it hard to think, and that was exactly what she needed right now.

CHAPTER 47

THE FOLLOWING DAYS WERE AS DISPIRITING FOR LUCY AS HAD BEEN the previous rainy ones, only more so, for whereas before she had some hope of progress, now she had only tedium. Spring showers had returned, more intermittent, but in sufficient frequency to prevent any outdoor excursions. Lucy entertained herself, if it could be called such, by sketching and conceptualizing future alterations to a coach, but even this soon became tiresome, her thoughts uninspired and hardly worthy of being called innovations. The interest was severely dampened by the knowledge that any opportunity to put theory into practice was now far from her reach. She could perhaps contrive some reason and subterfuge to visit Elsa at the ruins, but though she was confident she could recall the path, she had no guarantee they would even be there.

While the races still appealed, she felt that spectating had lost some luster now she had experienced racing firsthand. It was only in the absence of the thing that Lucy truly realized how much she had been invested. Her previous existence, one she had never lamented before, now felt lacking in purpose. The past few months had been altogether too much at once to leave her unaltered; the thrill of racing, of intention, of intrigue.

The thrill of romance.

She had never denied that her attraction to Captain Dashwood had been more than pragmatism and mutual interest. There had been the dangerous moment in the woods, yes, and certain moments where the image of him had caused her to blush, but those she had rationalized as light fancy. But upon reading his letter, the true weight of her feelings became apparent. To misread the emotions of others was one thing, but how could she have been so foolish as to mistake her own.

She wished she had been more forthcoming, and it was now too late to correct such an oversight. It would not be particularly difficult to discover how she might write to him, but what should she say? Clearly their investigation could not be mentioned, given the lengths to which he had requested the written trail be concealed. It would be imprudent to discuss the Night Races or Torres with him for the same reason. She might attempt to articulate her feelings, but even if she were to succeed what would be the merit in such an exposition? He had made it clear that his return was not safe for either of them. To become no more than two people exchanging affections? That might be a part of their connection, but it was far from the whole. It would feel hollow. And so the letter she occasionally began to compose would instead be erased and drawn over with carriage designs that looked no different from many others upon her desk.

Andrew and Alice Elliot did not speak to Lucy of her mood, though they were aware of it. There had been occasions in the past where she had slipped into periods of melancholy and time had been a sufficient remedy for it.

She might have turned to her sister for council, but here too she felt a guilt that prevented it. The swift departure of Captain Dashwood had put an indefinite hold not only upon Lucy's prospects but that of Margaret as well. How foolish she had been to suggest that her connection to Dashwood might pave the way for one between Margaret and Oliver St. Martin. Lucy had given them that hope, and now it had been taken away. She avoided her sister, for she knew the painful feeling of a snatched future, a feeling Lucy felt responsible for.

The only solace offered by the days drawing on was that her

face was back to its regular shade and her hearing seemed back to normal. The irritation gone, she slept well, too well, perhaps, for she went to bed early and rose late, quite out of sorts with her regular habits. But the fewer hours she spent awake, the fewer hours she had to fill.

It was on one such morning that she was struck by a pillow with such force as to rouse her from both her slumber and her doldrums

"Get up," Margaret said plainly. "We're walking to town."

Had it been a request, Lucy might have declined. But there was a declarative nature to it that broached no refusal.

Lucy arose, took a late breakfast, and soon found herself on the path toward town. Their objective was unspoken, for Margaret said nothing as they walked. Silence was seldom unpleasant to Lucy, but something in it compelled conversation, and she could resist that urge for only so long.

"I am sorry," Lucy said, "for any pain I have caused you."

Margaret seemed so taken aback by this that it took her a moment to formulate a reply.

"That you have caused me? Lucy, whatever are you talking about?"

"The connection between you and Oliver St. Martin that I suggested. Now that I am clearly not to be married, it is a happiness denied you. I should not have been so forward in attaching hope to something I had no certainty of. It was imprudent of me, and I apologize."

Again Margaret paused, seeming to untangle her sister's reasoning.

"Lucy, no such thought of blame has crossed my mind. The chances of a union between us are no less than they were a month ago. You did me no wrong by announcing your considerations. Besides which, the departure of Captain Dashwood is by no means your fault. I know his leaving has been hard on you, especially in conjunction with the horrid events of the St. Martins' ball. But if you feel that I harbor any resentment toward you, or that you should harbor any guilt, then you are quite mistaken on both accounts."

Lucy only blinked.

"Besides, the captain's absence may only be temporary. If his father's condition improves then there is no reason he'll not return, especially if he cares for you."

The words were meant in kindness, but Lucy soon found herself weeping so fiercely they were forced to sit upon a bench beneath a tree. It was as if all her frustrations and fears, from the moment she had laid eyes on Captain Dashwood, till the last embers of the letter had crumbled away, had now overflowed. They all finally broke through the dam of logic and order she had so tightly constructed and the torrent washed away any hope of concealment.

When she had at last regained some semblance of herself, she looked about briefly at their surroundings to ensure they were alone. And then she began to speak, omitting no truth of things. From the Night Races to Captain Dashwood, their first races together, his mission, their excursion to the ruins, the truth of his departure, and his final letter. Everything flowed from her until at last she finished, and a wave of exhaustion and relief caught up with her all at once.

Her sister said nothing but took her shaking hand and held it firmly. For some time they sat without words, the countryside's summer sounds their only company.

"You know," Margaret said eventually, "if Charlotte Wyndham had told me that story, I should not have believed a word of it."

Lucy chuckled at that, sniffing and wiping her nose awkwardly.

"I wish, Lucy, I could offer some words of wisdom. Some philosophy. But I'm not sure Hume covers this sort of thing." Margaret took a breath, then stood. "Come on. Let's get to town."

Lucy arose, and together they walked on.

Not a single problem had been solved. And yet, somehow, she felt immeasurably improved.

CHAPTER 48

I AM AFRAID, MISS MARGARET, THAT YOU ELLIOT WOMEN HAVE DEVELoped a habit of ruining dresses. I have sewed up the hems, but it shall never match the standard of a lady at a ball."

"That is quite well, Mrs. Calloway. I have no desire to wear it again. I'm sure you will find another to appreciate it."

"I quite understand that you should not want to wear something that would remind you of such a foul turn of events. How fortunate it was that Captain Dashwood and his man were there to defend you."

Margaret nodded but winced slightly at the comment. Beyond the damage sustained, the dress had stains upon it that were only visible to the older Elliot sister's eyes.

"I am not too sure we'll find a home for it in the district," continued Mrs. Calloway. "It is too elegant for the purposes of any lady I know who might fit it. It shall, however, find a home in London, I am sure. I plan to meet with some old friends of mine there on an excursion next week." The seamstress paused in thought for a moment.

"Forgive me if I am presumptuous, Miss Elliot. I am to meet with several other merchants and dressmakers with stock in excess of my own. If it was your wish to acquire some more garments for the coming season, I am sure I could facilitate a fitting."

"I am grateful for the offer, but I am not sure we can entertain the extravagance of a trip to London merely for my dress shopping."

"Therein lies my presumption. If it would not offend your sensibilities to travel with myself and Mr. McDonald, then we have more than enough room for an additional passenger."

"I should not be offended at all," Margaret replied. "I have cousins in the West End who would, I'm sure, accommodate me for the duration of any visit. How long do you intend to be away?"

"Four days. It is all we can afford to be away from the store, but with the latest ball season over, there is a small window that permits it."

"I shall send word to my cousin at once. Some time away should do me good I think."

Lucy's feelings upon learning about the trip were mixed. Mrs. Calloway had been so generous as to extend the offer to Lucy too, but she had politely declined. London was a busy and cluttered place of unfamiliar things. Given time she might acclimatize— and there were certainly things she should like to do—but given so narrow a time as four days she did not think she would benefit at all from a change of location.

She was, of course, reluctant to part company with her sister, with whom she had so recently reconnected, but she saw no reason that her own inclination should delay her sister's travel. Her only request was that, should Margaret get the chance, then she should acquire any used technical manuals for coaches that she could locate. Margaret had laughed and told her that for Lucy she was always on the lookout for such things.

Five days later the Elliots took their coach to town, and from there Margaret departed with Mrs. Calloway and Mr. McDonald in a wagon that, for what it lacked in elegance, it made up for in cargo capacity. Lucy watched them go, feeling a curious sense of optimism that she could not rightly justify. Perhaps it felt, just a little, that things were returning to normal.

The following day saw Lucy's humor considerably improved. She no longer bore the weight of secrecy upon her shoulders and, she smiled to herself, Margaret's shoulders were well suited for such support.

She arose at a healthy hour, took a walk around the grounds, and returned to complete a needlework project she had been working on with intermittent attention since autumn. This done she began to wonder again at the greater mystery of the abandoned coaches. Dashwood had asked her that she do no investigation but acknowledged that this did not preclude contemplation.

She found herself again in agreement with the theory that their coach robbers on the night of the ball had not been directly responsible for the previous disappearances, but nor were the events unrelated. It pointed to a larger affair afoot. If Dashwood was correct about the engineering plans for this Iron Adder being the target, then the robberies at Lord Rathbone's and the St. Martins' had likely been connected and actually searches for information or correspondence.

But surely neither man would be so careless as to secure such papers in a place where common thieves might locate them. It pointed to a separation. Perhaps the theft of the brandy had not been intentional but an accidental acquisition. The real target might have been valuable information on its way to Sir Walter St. Martin, only to be stymied by the man's predilection for pickling. That would explain burying the chest until some later date, since it was not the intended goal. That the bodies might be dumped in Longburn Mire still made sense and pointed to ruthlessness. Did that ruthlessness extend to their own men? It may not have been the intention, but the end result of the ball night was five dead robbers, a hefty cost for any plan. Had the thieves been sent in the expectation that they were expendable? It was not yet clear.

She hoped Dashwood was having more luck then her, but she

could not see how, as he was far away and in possession of little more knowledge than she was.

In the end her thoughts reached no clear conclusion, and yet, once again, she felt better for them, rather than bogged down. Yes, Captain Dashwood had been forced to leave, but there was no reason to think he would never return. How they might engage after the shadow of this investigation had passed was something to look forward to rather than lament.

With this in mind she felt lighter and spent the rest of the afternoon immersed in sketches, first of some coach ideas and then, feeling an odd inspiration, of Torres and his team. The results were quite lifelike renditions of waxworks that were unmistakably modeled on the racers.

Though she lacked the company of her sister, Lucy did not find the following days empty, taking long, leisurely walks of increasing distance as her legs became more familiar with them, finishing several other long-neglected art projects and even spending an afternoon out with her father.

Andrew Elliot had joined Lord Rathbone and several others on a pheasant shooting party. The pastime had never been one she was especially fond of, with the loud, intermittent noises usually setting her on edge. Her purpose in doing so this time was explicitly to challenge her fears. Twice since the incident of the St. Martins ball she had awoken from a nightmare drawn from that memory of her near-death experience. She had decided that the best way for her to process this was to face it head-on, thus asking if she might attend with her father that afternoon. He was surprised but did not refuse.

Lord Rathbone was in better spirits than he had been in some days, convinced that the increased security and patrols should keep the road safe should any traces of the gang of thieves try anything. There was something in his words that confirmed to Lucy that Dashwood had been correct, that information was at risk rather than goods. For her part, Lucy merely attended and listened. Out of practical interest, she tried firing one of the fowling guns, something one of the attendants was happy to show her. It was discovered that Lucy Elliot was an excellent shot, so long as the target was no more than ten feet away and not moving. Between this, the loud noise, and the aversion to the thought of killing a bird, she concluded that the life of a hunter was not for her.

Instead she engaged in various conversations along the line. A new regiment of militia was expected to replace the group that had left earlier that day. Renovations were beginning to take place at St. Martins Hall. The headless horseman had been sighted again, this time by a groundsman out late.

Lucy processed all this with polite curiosity, careful to wear her hat in the warm sun to avoid burning again so soon.

The sound of shots was as unpleasant as always, but no worse for her recent experiences. The afternoon was declared a success, Andrew Elliot proudly bringing home a modest pheasant and his wife and daughter politely silent on the fact that the bird had grown considerably by the time it had been roasted and served for dinner.

CHAPTER 49

THE FOLLOWING DAY SAW TWO UNEXPECTED EVENTS FOR LUCY. THE first was the arrival of a package from London, which she fully expected to be from her sister but instead turned out to be from Mrs. Calloway. The parcel had a small note attached, which Lucy read with interest.

> *Miss Elliot. As mentioned, a dress for hardier wear.*
> *A friend in the city completed it yesterday. I might have*
> *waited until my return to deliver it myself, but your sister*
> *insisted on sending it straightaway to surprise you. She*
> *wishes you well and hopes to see you again by week's end.*

Lucy was as surprised and pleased as might have been hoped and went to her room at once to try on the garment.

It was a curious affair, light canvas with a brown hue, plain but well tailored. There were no frills that might tear or rip and the seams were especially sturdy. Lucy felt as if she were wearing a dress made from aprons and it should certainly not see a ballroom or any civilized gathering, but as hardy clothing that would resist and disguise stains, it was quite ideal. It was comfortable enough and gave her arms a wide range of motion. It seemed that Mrs. Calloway and her connections had done an excellent job of fitting the exact specifications.

She was in the midst of examining the dress in her mirror when she heard the sound of a coach driving up to Atherton. For a moment her heart leaped, and she wondered if it were Captain

Dashwood, but she realized the sound was all wrong. How strange a thing was it that she might tell a man by the sound of his coach wheels?

Curious to discover the visitor, she decided that formally changing would be too complicated an affair and instead took a chance that the plain dress should not be too odd as to be inappropriate for visitors.

She need not have been concerned, for standing at the door, having been welcomed in by her mother, was a visitor who managed to be as familiar as could be yet wholly unexpected.

"Margaret?" Lucy exclaimed, worried that her early return might be the portent of ill news. However the smiling demeanor and unexpected hug from her sister quite put to rest any such concern.

"Lucy . . . whatever are you wearing? Oh, never mind, I have such news. Come through into the parlor."

She followed Margaret to discover she was not the only arrival. Oliver St. Martin stood with their father. The man was as taciturn as ever, but there was a mirror of the mood she had just seen in her sister, which led her at once to a series of suppositions.

"As all the family is in attendance," the tall man began, "I ask that I might address you all together."

"By all means." Andrew Elliot nodded, taking a seat in his favorite couch, Alice sitting beside him and Lucy on a chair.

"I have been in London this week on business," started Oliver. "It was there by good fortune I chanced upon Margaret lunching with her cousins. They invited me to join, and I did so. We have met twice since, in honest circumstances I assure you, and it led to some discussion. My recent speculation has been successful. I am at present in negotiations for the purchase of a small estate in Norfolk. It is not large, but the income is steady. As you know, I have no claim to St. Martins Hall. But with this purchase I may secure a future. It is a future I wish to share with Margaret. We decided to return early from London to seek the blessings of our families."

There was a momentary pause as Mr. Elliot turned to his eldest daughter. "And, Meg? Is this your wish?"

"It is, Father."

There was a brief glance between the two parents, conferring in swift silence, and then he nodded with a smile.

"Then I wholeheartedly give you my blessing."

Margaret smiled and happily took the hand of her husband to be, a man who in this moment looked happier than ever Lucy recalled seeing him.

Since she had first entered the parlor she had greatly suspected this to be the objective and this the outcome, and yet it all unfolded better than she might have imagined. She wiped a tear from her face, discovering the fabric of her dress to be coarser and more impermeable to water than she expected.

There were congratulations and handshakes and hugs, which even Lucy engaged in. Mrs. Elliot was already discussing plans as to when and where the day might occur. As to be expected, it was Oliver who kept the most level head and suggested that, prior to any plans, he wished to talk to his father and introduce Margaret as his betrothed.

"I hope it is not too disorderly with the renovations." Mrs. Elliot chuckled.

"Renovations?" Oliver asked.

"Yes. Surely you are aware of them?"

"I have been in London a week and should have been a week more. That is quite enough time for my brother to have had a flight of fancy on renovations. Well, it is their house. We shall have our own soon enough." He smiled again, squeezing Margaret's hand. "With your leave Mr. Elliot, we shall be on our way."

"We shall be back in time for dinner, I hope," Margaret added.

"I look forward to it." Andrew Elliot nodded and escorted them to the front door.

Margaret and Lucy exchanged one last hug, and each could see true happiness in the other.

As she watched the coach drive off (a Thornbrook modified for long travel), Lucy felt a lightness and optimism. If Margaret and Oliver could overcome their obstacles to marriage, then it was quite possible that she and James could do the same.

The happy news spread through the household, and Lucy spent an hour making a list of all the activities and preparations that would be needed for a successful wedding. Margaret would, of course, have the final decision on it all, but Lucy felt it only right to give her a firm basis to work from. It would be a summer wedding, and that lent itself to all manner of possibilities that were restricted in colder seasons.

The only dampener to the fine mood of the household was that the couple had perhaps decided to dine at the St. Martins' instead, for there was no sight of them as the mealtime approached.

"George probably decided to throw them a banquet," Lucy suggested to her mother.

"Well, I suppose there will be ample opportunity to host them all in the coming weeks. I might even show Sir Walter my preserves."

Lucy was glad to see her mother's good humor remained.

As the summer sun finally slid below the horizon, Lucy found herself in the parlor, tinkering with a model coach while her father read the newspaper. The model was not a perfect replica, but she was able to plan what alterations she might make if adapted to a full scale. In addition, she was pleased to discover a handy pouch in one of the dress folds that could hold a few small tools.

She looked up as she heard an exclamation from her father.

"I say, Lucy, here's a bit of news about your Captain Dashwood!"

"Really?" She looked up from her work in surprise. "Not ill news I hope?"

"A bit of a mixed bag, I should say. Shall I?"

"Please." She nodded.

"'John Dashwood passed away yesterday at the age of seventy-two, following several years of ill health. Dashwood gained much standing during the Revolutionary War, with his political advice well received. Though ultimately unsuccessful, his fellows praised his determination and honesty in the colonial affair. He is survived by his only son, Captain James Dashwood, who succeeds him as the eleventh Earl of Westchester.'"

"The Earl of Westchester?" Lucy remarked, a chill running through her despite the warm night.

At no point had Dashwood ever mentioned such a thing.

But someone had. When?

George St. Martin. The night of the ball she had overheard him in the corridor. With everything that happened later she had quite forgot about it.

It was as if a pin had been pulled in her thoughts and they whirred in a widening gyre. George had been referring to Captain Dashwood. She realized now that there had been sarcasm in his tone in using the title, something she was prone to missing. What had his exact words been? No trace of the stolen goods had been found, and they suspected the Earl of Westchester.

She had assumed they were talking about the missing brandy. But what if something else had been stolen? Stolen by Dashwood that very evening, during the one dance where everyone was present and his absence might be overlooked.

Why would George suspect Dashwood?

Because Dashwood suspected them. Because they knew he was on their trail.

Another pin came loose as the machinery of her mind sped on. So much made sense in this new light. Robbers waiting on a known path to feign robbery but intend murder. The thefts at Rathbone Manor when it was known he would be at the ball. The St. Martins' intruders, there to pass on stolen goods only to receive bullets as their reward.

George had to be involved. Was Sir Walter? Was Oliver? Lucy froze as the possibilities crossed her mind.

But Oliver had not been present at the shooting of the intruders. He had not been involved in the planning of the St. Martins ball, which now seemed to have been part of a larger plan. Until she saw evidence to the contrary, she would not place guilt upon the man Margaret loved.

The man she was to marry.

The man she had accompanied to St. Martins Hall.

And who had not returned.

"Lucy? Are you all right?" Her father saw her stricken expression and her drawn silence. "Surely it is not so great a surprise that his father died."

His voice broke her from her thoughts. Her sister was in danger. Thoughts alone would not help her. Action had to be taken.

Lucy rose sharply to her feet. "I need to get to St. Martins Hall at once."

"Whatever do you mean? It is dusk. Surely you do not need to go now."

"Yes, Father." She was already striding from the room. "Now!"

CHAPTER 50

As THE LAST RAYS OF SUNLIGHT WERE VANISHING OVER THE HORIZON, Lucy sped through the night. She had thrown on riding boots and gloves but no cloak. Thankfully the night was warm enough and the workshop dress made of thick material. The cold she would deal with later. Daisy, sensing an urgent mood, did not put up the fight she sometimes would. If anything, it seemed she was starting to like Lucy, as the woman let her run as fast as she wished.

As she rode, Lucy slotted more pieces into place. Longburn Mire was half on the St. Martins' lands, easily close to home. The brandy robbery was now explained. Either George or Sir Walter had simply met the rider earlier on the road. The driver would have suspected nothing up until the moment he was killed.

Could her neighbors be so ruthless? Perhaps. George was capable of callous and impulsive things.

She could not decide what their motive might be, but it made sense in terms of means and opportunity. They would know the coach routes and times and the number of men. Sir Walter was kept informed on such deliveries. Dashwood had suspected him and perhaps uncovered some clues.

All these thoughts raced through her mind as the road became harder and harder to see. The stars were out, but there was no moon, and the faint glow on the horizon was almost gone. She knew the road well enough to tell the turns, and Daisy could see well enough to stay on the path.

What she would do when she arrived at St. Martins Hall she

did not know. But she hurried anyway. Margaret's life might depend on her speed.

As she approached the grand home, Lucy had her first confirmation that something was amiss. With the daylight now gone, it should have been lit up, but she saw only a faint flicker of lights within. It was far too early for people to be in bed, especially with a guest and good news delivered. How exactly she might proceed came to the forefront of her thoughts. There was certainly danger, but she could not avoid it if she wished to aid her sister. Had the hall been fully lit she might have attempted to bluff, perhaps suggesting that Margaret needed to come home at once. Now she saw that was unlikely to be an option.

She tied Daisy to a tree branch, mostly out of sight of the main way. The mare, having had a good run, was pleased with the location and nibbled a patch of flowers.

Lucy walked slowly up the tree line. Her more muted dress would not show up well past twilight and with only a faint sliver of the moon still at least an hour away. In this deliberate fashion she made her way to the side of the building. The darkness within was curious, suggesting an absence of any staff or servants active, quite unheard of for a place such as St. Martins, which was notably larger than Atherton. But she had seen lights in some rooms upstairs, so the property was not altogether abandoned.

Stealth seemed her best option. She tested a side entrance and found it locked, then circled the building, finding no luck with any of the doors. It might not be empty, but the building was certainly well secured.

Standing in the darkness, a flash of memory came to her. The elves' entrance. Was the kitchen tradition also followed at St. Martins Hall? She stepped quietly around the walls once more, coming to what she believed to be the kitchen.

Fortune was with Lucy as she found a window not only open but large enough to let her slip inside. As she shuffled her way through, she felt a tension far worse than she had the previous time she had used such an ingress; the night before she had first heard the name of Captain Dashwood and her life had gradually been drawn into such unwanted disorder.

She scolded herself. Now was not the time for reminiscence. Not only was this not her home, but the stakes were much higher than mere discovery or embarrassment.

The kitchen was almost completely dark, and she stepped carefully until she found the door. She could not risk a light of her own, but a faint glimmer down the hall suggested that at least a few lamps had been lit for movement around the rooms. Closing her eyes, she constructed in her mind the layout of St. Martins Hall. It was a large building, and she had not been everywhere, but over the years she had seen enough of it that she could plot something of a course in her mind's eye.

Again it struck her as a betrayal that a family she had known most of her life might be involved in theft and murder. Perhaps she had never really known them at all.

The entrance hall was lit by a single lamp, which meant that she could see well enough but could equally be seen. She pondered briefly if it might be prudent to remove her boots, but the time it would take might not be worth the exchange, nor the lower speed should running be required. Holding her breath she listened, hearing nothing but her heartbeat and the creaking of cooling stone. At last she caught the faintest hint of a voice and cautiously made her way toward it, staying in cover as long as she could, then climbing the stairs as swiftly and quietly as she might.

The voices were coming from down the hall, a slip of light spilling from a room, and she positioned herself in an alcove, out of sight but able to make out the words.

"Once things are gathered, we head for the rendezvous point. They leave at eleven."

Her heart sank as she identified the voice as Sir Walter.

"We needn't bother clearing up our tracks now. By the time

the truth comes out we'll be long gone. Blasted timing. Why did he have to come home early?"

Lucy tensed. He had to mean Oliver, which meant that the younger brother had not been aware of the conspiracy. But also that he had discovered it upon returning to St. Martins. Where was he now?

"Is the coach packed?"

"Yes, sir," replied a voice she did not recognize.

"As soon as George gets back we leave. I don't want to see this place until we return after this is all over."

It was odd to hear Sir Walter talk in such terms. There was an anxious edge to his voice, events clearly not unfolding as smoothly as he had planned.

Yet there was another more pressing concern that came to her mind. George was returning. Which meant her way back was now compromised. Before she could decide what to do next, she heard footsteps. Even ducking into a side room would give her away. All she could do was press her back into the shadows and hope she remained unseen. She watched as George St. Martin passed straight by her, heading for the door to meet his father. The young man was dressed in travel clothes, quite unlike the bright costume he had worn at the ball when she had last seen him.

"About time," Sir Walter complained. "No more trouble?"

"Unfortunately there is." George sighed, reaching into his coat and drawing out a pistol, which he pointed directly at Lucy. "Come out now or I fire," he stated bluntly.

With no other choice, Lucy stepped out into the hallway.

"Lucy?" he exclaimed. "What the devil are you doing here?"

"Looking for my sister," she replied honestly.

"Of course you are." He sighed, as if it were more a frustration than a real problem. "Come with me. I'll explain on the way."

She nodded and began to walk down the hall as he indicated. "Are you going to put that gun away?" she asked, feigning confusion.

"No. I'm afraid not. I advise you not to run. I have no wish to do you any harm, but I will do if I must."

Lucy walked, contemplating how she might proceed. Playing innocent might be safer, but there was a collision of indignation and curiosity in her thoughts that drove her down a different path.

"Did that courtesy extend to the men you hired to rob our coach?"

There was a pause. Lucy wondered if he was contemplating shooting her there and then. Then he gave a wry smile, much more like the George she knew, though seen through a more sinister lens.

"Actually, they were under orders not to harm you or Margaret."

"But why did you need to kill Captain Dashwood?"

George laughed at her confusion. "I'm not surprised. The man keeps his secrets well. Your captain was not what he seemed. He was looking into us. He didn't realize we were looking into him. How did you know? About the coach robbers?"

"You know me. I solve puzzles. The missing coach. The robberies. Only when I turned up here tonight did all the pieces finally come into place. George, what on earth is going on? What is this all about?"

"What is it about? It will sound like such a petty thing, Lucy. It's about money."

"Money? Surely you cannot be in want of that."

"We shouldn't. But Father made losses in his business. Investments in various foreign spices and plantations, would you believe. When it went bad he tried to cover his losses. The blasted fool was in so deep we risked losing the hall. Can you conceive of it, Lucy? The St. Martins being forced to sell St. Martins Hall? He had no idea what to do. And no spine for it."

"But you had an idea, didn't you? You've always been spontaneous."

"I suppose so. Father knew the routes coaches took and how they'd be guarded. I found some men who weren't afraid to get their hands dirty. Two robberies went off without a hitch. The second was a challenge, but once we took out the guards and the drivers, we just left things quiet for a while. The clerk holding the strongbox thought he'd been rescued when he heard me so he opened the door."

"The brandy wasn't even a robbery, was it? You just met him in the woods."

"It took some convincing for Father to allow it. Dashwood was poking around by then, you see. We had to put him off the trail. Robbed our own coach. I thought that would be the end of it. The army payroll was enough to tide us over until . . ." He trailed off, clearly embittered.

Lucy finished the thought. "Until you married Charlotte Wyndham."

"It was such an easy solution." He bristled with frustration. "She would have given us enough money to settle things. But her stupid father was just as stupid as my stupid father. He'd followed his advice! I saw what that was, his family being ruined. I wasn't going to let the same thing happen to us!"

"So you came up with another plan. A ball, and robberies while people were vulnerable."

"It almost worked. But I underestimated Dashwood."

No, Lucy thought. *You underestimated the Elliot sisters.*

"Luckily for me he got called away. We were free to move ahead again. Everything was going to plan. And then my lanky brother shows up with your sister. He was meant to be away another week. It's frustrating, Lucy. You create a well-oiled machine, and then you keep hitting bumps in the road."

"Well, that's racing." She shrugged.

He appeared slightly confused by her comment, but his attention turned past her to the end of the hallway. She recognized the entrance to the cellar, where a man stood guard with a lantern.

"Another one?" the man asked curiously.

"It's one of those nights," George replied.

The man nodded, turning a key and unlocking the door.

George took a lantern from off the wall and gestured for Lucy to descend the steps. She did so, moving slowly downward, aware that her only chance was to humor George for as long as she could.

They reached another door, and he motioned for her to draw back the bar. Beyond it the stairwell opened into a large shadowy room, illuminated by a single candle. There were rows of shelves, which she realized were stacked with dozens of jars of preserves.

"Lucy?" came an exclamation from within.

She saw Margaret approach, but her sister stopped as she caught sight of George behind her and the pistol in his hand.

"Please, George." Margaret shuddered. "Don't hurt her."

"I have no intention of it. Do you really think me to be such a monster?"

"I no longer know what to think of you. Whatever villainy this is part of, I do not know how far you might debase yourself."

George seemed not to be offended by this. Whatever path he had chosen, he had done so wholeheartedly.

"Lucy. Please join your sister and my brother."

"You are no brother of mine," came a voice from the shadows.

As Lucy stepped forward, she caught sight of Oliver, seated on the floor, a bruise visible on his temple even in the dim light. It seemed he had not come here quietly.

"No brother of mine would so shame the St. Martin name," Oliver sneered.

"I am trying to save the St. Martin name!" his brother yelled back with a sudden fury. "While you and Father fritter away money with your bad investments, I'm doing the real work. If it were up to you, we'd already have been thrown out of this place."

"Family is more than a building, George. Honor is worth more than gold."

"Well, I suppose we'll find out when we receive our gold. Chain her up."

To her shock, Lucy realized that both Oliver and Margaret

each had a shackle around their ankle, chained to a sturdy link in the wall.

As the guard with the lantern stepped forward, George kept his pistol level.

"One of our ancestors used this room as a dungeon. It turns out it's more useful than a storeroom for preserves ever was."

Reluctantly Lucy held out her foot as the man locked the iron around her ankle.

"You'll have a slightly better deal," George continued. "Two water barrels. Several shelves of preserves of all kinds. It should last you long enough to be found."

"This is madness, George." Oliver shook his head sadly. "Whatever you are planning, you know the law of the land will not forgive this."

"Laws change, little brother. Next time we meet I hope you will have come to your senses."

With that he turned away, and the guard followed, leaving the three alone in the candlelit cellar.

"Lucy. I'm so glad you're safe." Margaret hugged her. "Why did you come here?"

Sitting on a small barrel, keeping her voice low, she explained everything. There was no point hiding anything from Oliver now, and she went into detail about the investigation, the robberies, and the truth about Captain Dashwood. She did not mention Torres or the Night Races, for their own privacy. Nor did she mention her feelings for Dashwood and their connection, as she felt they had little relevance to their current circumstances.

Once she had finished, Oliver sat stoically, processing it all.

"So that is it, then." He sighed grimly. "You have explained to me what my brother would not. I knew something underhanded was afoot, but I had no idea the depths of it. I thought perhaps some dubious speculation at worst. I wish we had stayed in London. Then I should not have led the three of us into this imprisonment."

"It is no fault of yours," Margaret countered. "It says at least something of your brother that he should leave us here rather than kill us mercilessly. Clearly he has that capacity in him. But then, so do I, I suppose."

Lucy threw her a glance, but she nodded softly in reply.

"I have told Oliver of my actions on the evening of the ball."

"I love you no less for defending the lives of those you care about." He put a hand on her shoulder. "There is a world between that and the heartless murder my brother has done. How can he ever expect forgiveness? All the wealth in the land will not buy off the laws of England."

The words he spoke struck Lucy more than the disappointment in his tone.

"Not the laws of England," she said quietly. "But there are other laws."

"Lucy!" Margaret gasped. "You cannot mean—"

"Treason." Oliver cursed. "They mean to sell out our nation to Napoleon."

"That is what George meant." Margaret was agitated enough to rise to her feet. "They plan to return once Britain is under the boot of France."

"And after tonight it will be too late. Whatever my brother means to do, it will happen tonight. They shall be across the channel by morning." Oliver pulled at his chain in frustration, but it was built to hold desperate souls and mere brute force would not break iron.

Lucy sat unspeaking. Planning. Looking around the room. Assessing their options.

The fate of the British Empire now lay with the wits of Lucy Elliot.

CHAPTER 51

THE THREE PRISONERS SAT IN SILENCE, THEN IN DARKNESS AS THE candle burned out. Margaret had placed another candle and flint near at hand for when she might need them. For all his callousness, George had not lied about their resources. There was food and water enough in the cellar, sacks for bedding, and candles for light. Yet, as there was no need for further illumination once the candle spluttered out, they decided to spare another.

Margaret sat silently, back against the wall, her hand in Oliver's.

Lucy faced problems head-on, taking them apart and reassembling them like a model until she found a solution that made sense.

After a time there was the muted sound far above of horses' hooves fading into the distance. Only once they had fully disappeared from hearing did Lucy speak.

"Margaret. Please light the candle."

There was a spark, and on the third try the candle caught, casting what seemed like a flare to their unaccustomed eyes.

From a pouch in her dress, Lucy drew the tools from where she had placed them earlier in the evening, when fine-tuning her model. She had not been searched, for there was no reason to suspect a young woman like her to be holding them.

She passed the tools among her companions.

"Our first obstacle is the shackles. I am no locksmith, but I do not imagine they will be of a complex design. Unless any of us has knowledge of such, I suggest we each try at once to improve our chances."

The three began to try working the locks, each with their own ability, Lucy mechanically minded, Oliver dexterous, and Margaret with brute strength. No obvious solution arose, but they persisted.

"Why did you wait?" Margaret asked softly.

"To make sure they didn't check on us one last time. They will be off on their way now, hopefully with all their men with them."

Margaret nodded and continued her focus, trying to level a pin out, but it was Oliver who had the first success, his shackle unbolting with a satisfying click. It took him several attempts to replicate this, but eventually all three were unchained and free to roam the cellar.

The door remained barred from the outside, and examination suggested that neither the timber nor the hinges would be a weak point to allow escape. The one positive was that there was no sound of a guard or any flicker of light suggesting a lantern outside. The shelves were all of light wood, and the numerous jars offered nothing more than an unlimited food supply for their immediate future.

But Lucy had not spent her time in the darkness focusing on a single path of escape. It was simply that her alternative would be difficult and dangerous.

"There is a small chute in the roof. It was probably added for ventilation during Sir Walter's bottling. It was how we were able to hear the coach leaving."

Margaret peered up at the stonework above them, noting a narrow gap in the high ceiling and a grate above it.

"It must be fifteen feet up," she remarked. "Do we build a ladder? Make a rope?"

"Nothing so dignified I'm afraid," Lucy replied.

"Whatever do you mean?"

"She means you have to lift me," said Oliver bluntly.

"Lift you?"

"I'm tall enough and thin enough to reach it and fit through

if I . . . if I stand on your shoulders. I know it might seem indecent but—"

"I don't care if it's indecent. I'm just not sure I can manage it.
But I'm willing to try."

As Lucy had predicted, it was as far from dignified as could
be imagined.

Lucy helped Oliver up and then braced her sister as best she
could while Margaret very carefully and slowly rose. They had
layered some of the sacks around them, but in truth they would
only be a small help if he fell. Margaret gripped his ankles until
she reached her full height and then locked herself in position as
it was his turn to straighten up.

As Oliver stretched, his hands grasping for the ceiling, Lucy
saw the determination on her sister's face. Strong as she was,
she was not at all accustomed to such a feat, and her face was
flushed as she drew small rapid breaths, trying to move as little
as possible.

"There is a grate with a trapdoor above," Oliver called down.

By good fortune the disuse of years had weakened the frames
rather than seized them up and a small application of force was
all that was required to break them open. From there he was able
to lever himself upward, awkward and stilted, his feet rising, relieving his weight from the shoulders of his betrothed. The grate
was not designed for human passage and Oliver was aware that a
slip from this height might be lethal to him and doom the others. But, in the face of adversity and discomfort, Oliver St. Martin
showed a tenacity and willpower that matched that of the Elliot
sisters, who watched him from below, helpless to aid him.

Over the course of a minute, inch by inch his waist and then
his feet disappeared into the darkness.

"I shall go around," he whispered.

"Be careful," Margaret called back quietly.

It seemed redundant, but Lucy suspected her sister had
needed to say something.

They heard nothing more as Oliver shifted away into the night.

There was a risk that a guard still remained, but they could do little but wait as the seconds ticked by. How long would it take him to enter the hall and make his way back to the basement? He certainly knew the path well enough, but as the seconds dragged on, they could not help but wonder if something had gone wrong. In the back of her mind, Lucy wondered if the plan failed, what might be the next plan of escape. None that came to mind were especially hopeful and were much more dangerous. Most involved fire.

Before she could delve further into this, there was a noise and the cellar door swung open. Oliver stood, holding a lantern in one hand.

"My apologies for the delay. They locked everything up. I had to break the window on the patio with a stray rock."

"We must hurry." Lucy was already moving past them. "They shall be on their way already, and we need help."

Together they ascended the stairs to the darkness of the house above.

"Well," Oliver said dryly, "at least the coach is still here."

"It's not going to be much use without horses," Lucy replied. Then added, "That was sarcasm, wasn't it?"

The three stood looking at the empty stable, uncertain how to proceed. It was clear they were the only souls remaining at St. Martins Hall, but concern for their own safety had now moved on to the greater threat.

"We'll never get to town in time on foot. We don't even know where they're heading," said Oliver.

"Lord Rathbone might," Lucy mused. "He's involved with army affairs."

"That's a long way on foot." Margaret sighed.

"I know a shortcut." Oliver reached for a pair of high boots. "Longburn Mire." He pointed out into the darkness.

"At night? That's madness," exclaimed Lucy.

"My brother and I have known the paths since childhood. Dangerous. But not madness."

"I'm going with you," Margaret insisted, casting off her shoes and reaching for another pair of boots. "We'll take a rope too."

"You two go." Lucy nodded. "Daisy should still be tied up down by the path. I'm going to try to get help."

"From where?"

"From a band of coach racers living in an abandoned castle. Be careful. Both of you."

With that she hurried off, bearing a lantern of her own, casting one glance back as the couple, not betrothed for more than a day, set off into the darkness of Longburn Mire.

CHAPTER 52

LUCY DESCENDED THE HILL CAREFULLY, THE GROUND FEELING COOL underfoot. Daisy seemed glad to see her. It was a warm night, but the mare was getting cooler, had drunk her fill, eaten every flower within reach, and was now inclined to leave. As luck would have it, Lucy was of the same opinion. As she mounted the horse, she hoped she could remember the path to a place she had been only once.

Though she now had a lantern, the faint crescent moon rising in the sky cast little extra illumination. Daisy was equally cautious, trotting down the path toward the gates.

Once out of the St. Martins Hall grounds Lucy caught sight of a light ahead. Eager for help, she urged Daisy on, but as she drew near, she caught sight of the same man who had been posted outside the basement door earlier; lantern in one hand, pistol in the other. She had failed to consider the danger until it was too late, her approach already announced by lamp and hooves.

Cursing her carelessness, Lucy remained calm, bringing Daisy to a stop.

"Mr. St. Martin said someone might escape. That you were clever."

Not so clever that she didn't fall straight into a trap. At least the others were now well on their way to help at Rathbone Manor.

"Off the horse."

On horseback she had a chance, even if she had to ride while shot, hoping Daisy would know the way home. If she dismounted now, any hope was lost. Lucy weighed her options, concluding that the man would show less mercy than George had.

Still she said, "No. I shall not."

"I will fire."

"I am well aware of that. I am not—"

She stopped sharply, her attention drawn to another sound in the still night. Horses' hooves. Rounding the corner, moving slowly, came a white horse and rider, bearing a lantern. Even from a distance she could see that the rider had no head.

So intent was her focus that her would-be assassin also turned and was equally surprised by the sight.

The headless rider stopped twenty feet from them, standing in silence.

Whatever his initial reaction, her assailant was clearly a hardened man who quickly recovered his wits.

"Whoever you are, leave out of it."

The horseman said nothing.

"I'm not scared of a silly costume." He waved his pistol in the direction the rider had come from. "Now go back the way you came or—"

The sentence was cut off by the retort of a pistol, and the man collapsed to the ground limply.

Lucy gripped her reins tight. Daisy, startled by the noise, reared slightly but was held in check by her rider. The phantom horse seemed unaffected, even as its rider lowered the pistol, still smoking. The action had been so swift that Lucy had not seen it drawn.

The presence of a calm horse seemed to ease Daisy, who still shuffled but made no motion to bolt.

Lucy watched as the rider drew closer, and with the proximity she recognized that it was no more than a clever costume, a black hood in contrast to a white outfit. At night, at distance, it would indeed seem to be a headless specter.

He raised a gloved hand and drew away the hood.

"Hello, Lucy," said Dashwood.

"I needed a way of doing reconnaissance in secret," Captain Dashwood explained as they rode, side by side, down the lane. "Your local legend of a headless horseman provided it. I could be seen and most people would dismiss me as a ghost story or not mention the sighting at all."

"Charlotte Wyndham saw you. She told me about it."

"The night she was returning from St. Martins Hall. I wanted to make sure her coach was going where expected."

"So you already suspected the St. Martins?"

"Among others. After their ball my suspicions were greatly heightened. But I knew I had to evade further attempts on my life or yours. I must apologize for the deception. It was well meant, but I regret any harm I may have done you."

"I must confess I am taking the news poorly. But it should not be the focus of our thoughts. Are you confident this is the way to the ruins?"

"I should be." Dashwood chuckled. "It's where I've been living."

Dashwood's arrival back at the camp was not a surprise, but the presence of Lucy at this hour immediately suggested something was amiss. The team hastily assembled around the campfire, and Lucy explained the events of the day and the treachery of George and Sir Walter.

"From my connections, I know that the plans for the weapon are being taken from London to Edinburgh for manufacture," Dashwood explained.

"If they get them to France, it might tip the balance of the war." Torres nodded grimly. "That is how they hope to regain their fortune. Napoleon's coffers are overflowing at the moment and he would gladly pay."

"Because of the other robberies, security on the coaches has been increased. But that security was all hired by Sir Walter," said Dashwood.

"And the robbers are already on his books," Hekili offered as he whittled a piece of wood, knife gripped tightly in his large hand.

"I must admit, it's a clever plan. Scare up the need for more men, then stack the ranks in your favor." Dashwood sighed. "Their team intends to meet with George and Sir Walter. From there they'll head for a ship somewhere on the coast. But it's a large coast."

"Walton," Torres stated, clear and calm. "North of the military camps. Leads to the headland. Mostly abandoned. Even the church fell into the sea a decade ago. A perfect spot for a smuggler's run."

No one asked what Torres knew of a smuggler's run.

"They'll want to be in and out fast," the Spaniard continued. "Hekili? Tides?"

The man mused for a moment, drawing on his years-old sea knowledge.

"Between midnight and two I'd say."

"The shipment leaves at eleven, you said, Lucy?" Elsa checked her pocket watch. "That was ten minutes ago."

"Señor Torres, you know the road they'll take?" Dashwood asked.

"I believe so."

"Well, then. They already have their men on board, which means there's no way we can stop them stealing those plans. So we'll just have to steal them back."

CHAPTER 53

SIR WALTER ST. MARTIN WONDERED IF HE WOULD BE PERMITTED TO keep his knighthood or whether he should ask for a French title. "Marquis St. Martin" sounded wrong. It did nothing to improve his mood. Sitting on the back of the covered army wagon, he anxiously watched the road as it fell out of the light of their lanterns. It was a side coastal thoroughfare, broad enough for two coaches to pass each other, but the army wagon was heavier and slower, so it followed behind his son's coach. For the moment Walter was glad for the separation. George's confidence had edged toward insolence in recent weeks.

He did not share his eldest son's confidence in the plan. It was already off target from his perspective, thrown into disorder by the appearance of Oliver and the Elliot sisters. They should have had several days before anyone suspected their involvement; more than enough time to be on the Continent and clear of British law. But beyond that, he felt the sting of reproach that had been in the eyes of his youngest son. He had never been close to Oliver and he had known well enough that this betrayal of nation would never be forgiven. But to experience that firsthand was something he had not anticipated. They might now be safely secured in the cellar, but that cold final look from his son followed them along the road. He only hoped he could outrun it once they were at sea.

The mercenary beside him wasn't anxious, merely bored and looking forward to his payday. The idle man toyed with a bayonet in his hand, taken earlier in the night from a young army man. There had been two guards not on Sir Walter's payroll and an army clerk as an official. They would be found floating in a river the next day at the earliest, too late to stop them. St. Martin and son had sunk far these past months. His only hope was the fortune that was to be their reward. Until then all he could do was wait.

"Do you hear hooves?" Sir Walter asked his companion.

"Of course I do. We're on a coach."

As a knight of the kingdom, Sir Walter was not used to such insubordination but then he supposed that title would not be with him long. Or perhaps with anyone.

"Not us, you fool. Behind us." Sir Walter peered into the night, but could make out no sign. Their lanterns only lit so far, not designed for broadcasting.

But he could hear it. He was sure he could hear it.

The longer he looked, the more sure he was that he could make out something. A dark shape that wove slightly from side to side. A shape getting closer. Or was it simply his imagination, his nerves on edge and his mind playing tricks on him as he stared into the abyss?

"I think you're right," the mercenary said, leaning forward.

The confirmation did nothing to ease Sir Walter's tension.

He saw it now. A small coach. A phaeton perhaps, black fabric flapping in the wind, a single dark horse drawing it forward.

It had no lights. Madness on a night like this. The distant light cast from the rear of the army coach could offer no more than a guide point, revealing nothing of the road. The driver would be all but blind.

And yet he was sure it was coming closer.

He drew his pistol and fired into the darkness, immediately regretting it. At this range there was no chance of hitting anything and reloading on a moving coach would be no easy feat. How far was it to the headland? It couldn't be more than half an hour now. Who could have followed them? What rider would be out in the dark like this? It made no sense. Yet again the plan was coming unraveled.

The mercenary beside him was of sterner disposition and had greater experience with coaches and crime. He lifted his rifle but did not fire blindly, instead waiting for a clearer shot. No matter how brave the driver was, boldness would not stop a bullet.

Sir Walter strained his eyes as the dark coach drew closer still. Fluttering cloth seemed to billow around it like smoke in the night. Like sails on land. It was unearthly.

Beside him the mercenary lifted his rifle to his shoulder once more, watching closely. The nearer the coach came, the better he could make out the detail. A single horse. A strange, stripped-down frame. A tall driver and a short messenger side by side, dressed in black.

It was only shapes. But shapes were all he needed.

He gripped the barrel, bracing himself, feeling the shake of the coach and readying the shot. He pulled the trigger, and the driver twitched as the bullet hit home.

Then continued as if nothing had happened.

Sir Walter and the mercenary exchanged glances; equally confused.

Suddenly their shadowy pursuer swerved, slowing as it left the road.

From a different angle they could make out the shape better, the odd dark sails and lantern light pouring from a narrow shutter, downward behind the vehicle.

Why on earth would you light the undercarriage behind your vehicle? asked a voice in the man's head.

"To follow!" he gasped.

He swept his eyes back to the main road where two horse-drawn coaches were now bearing down on them.

"We're under attack!" screamed Sir Walter. He began trying to load his pistol, but he was panicked and the coach speed made it near impossible.

The mercenary beside him was more clearheaded, but the task of reloading his musket was no easy one.

He glanced up at the coaches, now close enough to make out vague shapes and faces, though their lanterns were aimed forward, flashing in his vision.

One coach he was unfamiliar with; either driver or messenger. On the other sat Captain James Dashwood and Lucy Elliot. Dashwood he understood. The man had vexed him for months. That he should return at this critical moment was frustrating but almost inevitable. But Lucy? The girl to whom he had given jam?

"Capsicums," he corrected himself quietly, followed by "It doesn't matter!" very loud.

Things were falling apart. Lucy Elliot wasn't meant to be here. It meant she had escaped. If that was true, then others might already be on their trail.

Beside him the mercenary finished reloading his musket. This time he wasn't going to waste a shot at the coaches. He began to take aim at the closest horse to him.

A crossbow bolt struck him in the shoulder.

The mercenary winced but didn't fire, immediately turning to the woman in the long coat seated in the messenger position. Gritting his teeth, he raised the rifle toward her, ready to strike her down before she could reload.

Had he the time, he might have admired the technical prowess of Elsa Reinhardt and wished that he himself had a weapon that could reload so quickly.

But he did not have time. What he did have was a second crossbow bolt in his throat. He tumbled off the side of the army wagon, rolling into a ditch as the two coaches sped past him.

"Go faster!" Sir Walter yelled at the driver. He had abandoned trying to load his pistol, finding such complex fine action impossible.

To his very slight relief the wagon driver seemed to heed his command, speeding up enough that the gap between them and their pursuers seemed to widen. He didn't care whether it was the driver urging them on or the removal of one body reducing weight. All that mattered was that they were finally gaining ground.

Perhaps, just perhaps, they would escape after all.

There was a thump. Metal hitting wood heard, but not a bullet. Not a crossbow bolt either. It sounded too heavy.

Sir Walter looked at the thick metal bar and followed it up the rope, back to the chasing coach.

It took several seconds for him to process what had happened.

It was a harpoon. His coach had been harpooned.

Sir Walter St. Martin lost what remained of his mind.

CHAPTER 54

"WHAT ON EARTH IS HE DOING?" LUCY ASKED, HOPING FOR INSIGHT.

"I have no idea," Dashwood replied.

He threw a glance over to Torres who met his gaze and shrugged.

So far their plan was working, Ulcha providing cover with the sails, pushing her horses hard for a brief chase then veering off. The straw stuffed dummy had drawn the initial fire. Elsa had taken out one guard and Torres and Hekili had managed to link their coach and the wagon together to ensure it couldn't get away.

But now their prey was acting in an unpredictable manner. Sir Walter tugged and ripped at the canvas of the wagon in a frenzy, as if in a desperate attempt to destroy it. He seemed to be completely ignoring the harpoon.

Through the open roof of Torres's coach Hekili tied off the rope, the memento of his whaling days now put to good use. Though they had no means of drawing in the wagon, it prevented it getting farther away. Whenever they closed sufficient space Hekili would tie off another section, gradually closing the gap.

While the former whaler's actions were calm and methodical, Sir Walter continued his frenzy, with little rhyme or reason. There was a ripping sound and the covering of the wagon finally gave way, the wind peeling it off and sending it billowing. If it was a desperate attempt to halt his pursuers it had failed utterly, caught by a gust that drew it up and over both speeding vehicles.

No sooner had it passed overhead did those following realize it had not been his goal, and there had been a method to his madness after all.

"Is that . . ." Lucy trailed off in disbelief.

"Yes," Dashwood replied flatly. "That is a cannon."

The Iron Adder, the one-and-only prototype of the infantry cannon, gleamed in the lantern light, looking every bit as deadly as the name implied.

"I thought you said they only had the plans." Lucy stared at the vicious-looking weapon pointed back off the wagon.

"Obviously my information was out-of-date."

"Obviously. So . . . cannon rules."

"Cannon rules." He nodded grimly.

Sir Walter had not revealed the cannon without intent to use it, and he was already lifting a bag of powder, emptying the contents down the barrel.

"Dashwood!" called Torres. "Get alongside. I'll draw his fire."

"Draw his fire?" Elsa exclaimed loudly.

Torres drew back on his reins, the horses slowing slightly.

In response the army wagon began to move away only for the rope to go taut, wrenching the rear slightly upward. Sir Walter stumbled, but held on to the cannon and continued his frantic work.

Dashwood moved to the right, closing ground more swiftly.

Whether he would be fast enough remained to be seen.

Lucy could see the older man had little regard to the mess he was making all around him, ramming shot into the barrel, clearly intent on blowing away his pursuers altogether.

Close enough to try for a shot, Elsa raised her crossbow but switched her aim from Sir Walter at the last second. The mercenary messenger, now unhindered by the wagon covering, raised his rifle to fire at Torres and became the more immediate threat. Elsa's bolt missed but forced the man to crouch out of sight, delaying his impending shot.

Sir Walter was a closer target, but he was moving wildly, often behind the cannon, making him harder to hit. Elsa reloaded rapidly, ready to fire again, but was once more drawn to the messenger. This time her bolt hit home, hitting him in the chest and knocking him back, at least for the time being.

Beside the wagon, Dashwood urged the horses forward, slowly drawing level with them.

"I need to stop him firing that cannon," he called to Lucy.

"I agree."

"Keep her steady, then pull ahead."

Before she could protest, he had handed her the reins and climbed back onto the roof of their coach.

She was now driver and messenger in one.

Elsa fired again, this time hitting Sir Walter in the arm. The frenzied man barely seemed to notice.

"Dante?"

"Dashwood will make it."

"If he doesn't—"

"He will," he asserted. "But you might want to get down."

Lucy tried to keep the ride steady as they rode alongside the army coach. The horses were well trained, but her experience up to now had been purely observational.

A moment later, any chance of swapping back vanished. Dashwood leaped forward, flew through the air, and crashed onto the deck of the army wagon, sprawling but unharmed. Lucy's eyes darted back and forth, forward and to the side, knowing she could do little but stay in the chase.

In his manic focus Sir Walter was as oblivious to the boarder as he was to the bolt in his arm. All his attention seemed to focus on the singular task of firing the cannon. As he gripped the firing cord, Lucy was sure she heard a wild giggle.

Dashwood seized Sir Walter's ankles, tripping him forward.

As Sir Walter fell, his weight landed on the rear of the cannon, tilting its barrel upward a fraction. With an almighty hiss and roar, the Iron Adder fired for the first and last time.

A wall of grapeshot erupted from the barrel, shattering the roof of Torres's coach into a shower of splinters. The Spaniard, crouched as low as he could, gripped the reins tight, the horses panicking but not scattering. Elsa had already ducked, and Hekili was lying on the coach floor, each of them unharmed but for a few splinters.

Lucy gripped her reins, the army horses jerking but drawn back in line. She glanced to the side to survey the damage.

The rope no longer being tied to the roof that was no longer there, there was no more link between the wagons. With Torres's coach half destroyed and the scared horses, there was no way to maintain speed enough to keep up.

The army wagon slowly began to draw away.

Dashwood and Lucy were on their own.

CHAPTER 55

CAPTAIN DASHWOOD, EARS RINGING, LUNGS FULL OF SULFUR, crawled to his knees. He was not altogether a stranger to cannon fire but seldom this close and never on a moving vehicle. That he had already been low and flat had helped him avoid some of the concussion from the blast, but it was still disorienting.

Wiping his watering eyes, he caught sight of Sir Walter St. Martin. The man was unquestionably dead. The Iron Adder was designed to be lighter, more mobile and with less recoil than its predecessors. But it was also not expected that the person firing it would be leaning against the back of it at the time. The force of the impact had crushed the former knight's chest, killing him instantly. Glancing back, Dashwood hoped his compatriots had been luckier.

The smoke of the firing was clearing rapidly as the wagon sped onward and Dashwood was able to gather his bearings. Torres and his shattered coach were falling behind, but Dashwood could see that the driver and messenger were in one piece and there was enough of the coach left to hope for the same for Hekili. But he also recognized that they were swiftly moving out of sight. He turned about, assessing his situation.

In front of him the wagon driver was frantically trying to keep control of the horses, but they seemed to have had some army experience, for the cannon shot had not wholly driven them wild. Farther ahead, on the back of the other coach, he saw a rear guard reloading. Beside him, Lucy continued to move ahead, now gaining on the St. Martins' coach, her horses seemingly spurred on by the shock rather than scattered.

He took a breath of the now fresher air and took a step toward the driver, the only other person aboard. He did not at all expect the figure that lurched up to attack him. The guard who had been felled by Elsa's crossbow bolt had not pulled out the offending shard and was looking to vent his pain and fury on the nearest target. Dashwood had no time to draw his pistol before the man barreled into him, and they both fell onto the cluttered back of the wagon.

It was a frantic, artless brawl, the wagon bumping along the lane, floor scattered with bags, barrels, and the body of Sir Walter St. Martin. Finding himself pinned, Dashwood covered up to defend himself from a series of angry blows before finally managing to get his foot up and kick the man back. They both tumbled, and Dashwood landed painfully on a box of supplies. Gritting his teeth, he rose slowly, catching sight of his opponent doing the same. The wounded man seemed to be hefting an iron bar from the floor and Dashwood glanced about for a weapon, finding none.

Only when he faced off against the man did he realize it was no mere iron bar but Hekili's harpoon, wrenched from the wood, its jagged point now aimed toward Dashwood. This close, in the hand of a snarling man covered in blood, it looked like a murderously dangerous weapon.

Dashwood stepped back as the spear point was thrust at him. From this range he might be able to draw his pistol and fire, but the odds were not in his favor. Instead he moved about, trying to keep the cannon between the two of them. It was not a large cannon, but it would limit the method of attack slightly, which he hoped would be enough. He dodged a thrust, but it came too quick for him the grab the weapon to disarm the man. The second attack was a wild swing, which Dashwood ducked, the steel of the blade sparking over the iron of the cannon.

"Stop!" Dashwood yelled with all the urgency he could muster, but the man was beyond reason. He swung again and Dashwood dodged aside, the weapons of different eras clashing against each other. This time what Dashwood had feared came to pass. One spark landed on the floor of the coach bed, already sprinkled with debris and powder. It crackled once, and Dashwood knew instantly that the man with the harpoon was no longer his most immediate threat.

To the surprise of his attacker Dashwood turned his back and lurched for the front of the coach. With his foot he kicked the quick-release joint, detaching the horses from the wagon. With his hands he wrenched the reins from the unsuspecting driver. Then he took a step and leaped with all his might toward the back of one of the horses. He landed awkwardly but clung for dear life to the harnesses, the already panicked animals now released and powering ahead, out of control.

The wagon driver, with no means to steer, pulled on his brake lever to slow the speeding cart. He did not see that the sparking gunpowder behind him was rapidly spreading over the surface of the coach. It was only a few seconds later that the flame reached the half-spilled barrel.

Dashwood saw a flash, the night road around him lit up, and an instant later he felt the force of the blast. The wagon became a blossom of smoke and fire, erupting outward, illuminating all around. A hail of wood, fire, and iron ripped into the air and the only existing Iron Adder was thrown some distance before shattering the trunk of a tree on impact.

He gripped the rigging tightly, feeling the force and the heat, but thankfully far enough ahead that the shrapnel missed him and the animals. For now the horses had the sense to stay with the path, which was of good fortune, for they had now reached the coast and the road was narrowing. If the horses lost their nerve and took a wild turn to the right, they would dive off the cliff, to the rocks far below, and they would take Captain James Dashwood with them. Inch by inch he drew himself upward until he was at least clear of their galloping legs. Freed from the load of the wagon, the horses had gained ground with the St. Martins' coach now close.

He glanced to see his own horses beside, Lucy holding the reins and letting them run. They were near enough to lock eyes, but at these speeds there was little they could do for each other. Then he turned his eyes to the front as another mercenary emerged from the St. Martins' coach.

CHAPTER 56

LUCY'S STOMACH DROPPED AS SHE SAW THE MERCENARY AHEAD review the scene. Dashwood was a perfect target, still trying to right himself on the horse. The mercenary seemed to come to the same conclusion. He raised his rifle, bracing himself, lining up the shot. There had to be a way. Something she could do. Drawing back, she tied the reins off roughly, leaning over to one side. The hidden compartment opened, and she pulled out the coach rifle.

Intent on his prey, the mercenary had not seen her, but he had found his shot. There was no time for her to brace or aim and she fired blind, the recoil knocking her back on the seat.

Her shot went high above the mercenary but succeeded in drawing his attention. Caught by surprise, he shifted aim and swiftly fired at what he saw to be the more dangerous target. The frantic shot and the fact Lucy was on her side caused it to go low, hitting the coach with a clang of metal. Suddenly the running of the coach sounded different, her mind racing to identify it. To her dismay she saw the quick-release mechanism, impacted by the shot, as it gave way and executed its function, disconnecting the horses from Lucy's coach.

The mercenary grinned, knowing she had no chance of keeping pace now. With cool efficiency he began to reload, Dashwood once again in his sights.

Lucy ignored the reins, instantly dismissing executing the bold move that had saved Captain Dashwood. She had only two options. She could pull the brake and hope the momentum of the coach would bleed off before the road curve threw it off the cliff face. It was her best hope for survival, but it would guarantee that the other coach would escape.

She pulled the second lever instead.

The coil-spring boost rapidly expending itself and the coach beyond her control, Lucy turned and pulled herself up onto the roof. She felt the kick of momentum, the two coaches drawing directly alongside each other. There was no time to delay or overthink. She threw herself toward the roof of the fleeing coach.

With the coaches close and matching speed, the jump was easy enough. But only a few seconds after landing, the St. Martins' coach drew around a sharp corner and she was forced flat, gripping onto a spar. It was a most perilous position to find herself in, but remained preferable to the alternative. With neither horses nor driver, the coach that she and Dashwood had so diligently restored, customized, and raced, flew one last time, out over the edge of the road, flipping forward so that it was completely upside down when it impacted with the rocks below, showering into the ocean. No amount of salvage and repair would be enough for it to be roadworthy this time.

Lucy desperately tried to find purchase with her boots, her only relief being that the mercenary seemed too intent on his rear target to notice his new passenger. Straining herself, she drew up her feet flat, now facing back along the road.

She was amazed that Dashwood had managed to draw himself onto the back of his horse, holding tight without saddle or stirrups. She saw him fumble at his side, then draw a pistol, which swayed wildly. At this range, on a charging horse, he was unlikely to make such a shot. The mercenary was already lining him up, and with limited control of the horse Dashwood would be unable to avoid it. Another few seconds and he might be able to gauge the shot, but the mercenary would get there first.

The man raised the rifle to fire. Lucy reached over the roof and yanked his aim upward. So surprising was the movement that she found herself in sole possession of the rifle.

Even as he turned she pulled it alongside her, out of his reach. She herself, however, was still in range, and he lashed out, gripping the canvas fabric of her collar. She had no leverage in this position, and she felt that it would only be a few moments' work for him to drag her off and into the path of the oncoming horses.

But before he could do anything, a shot rang out. The odds, it seemed, had fallen in Dashwood's favor after all, and the mercenary fell back onto the road, the horses galloping over him.

The falling body was the last straw for the wagon horses, and they both came to a sharp halt, Dashwood lurching forward but managing not to be thrown. Lucy watched his shocked gaze as he melted into the darkness behind the speeding coach.

For a moment she was frozen, then a noise drew her attention. She swung around onto one knee, raising the rifle at the same moment as another mercenary drew a pistol, crouched in a similar fashion. They both froze, aware of the deadlock. Then Lucy heard a click, her eyes darting to the right. George St. Martin stood, leaning over the roof, another pistol aimed directly at her. Beyond him she caught sight of her horses, released and now speeding ahead into the darkness. At least they were safe. She herself was in far less secure circumstances.

"I should have known you wouldn't let it go." George laughed.

He was more in control than his father had been, but she recognized some of that wild energy. She had never equated George's carefree nature with callousness, but she saw it now. He was enjoying the adventure of the moment, barely concerned with the fact that his father had just died in a violent fashion.

"That certainly is an element of my character," she replied, still holding up the rifle.

"You've lost, Lucy. Put the gun down and you might get out of this alive."

He was lying. Even she could read that as plain as day. As soon as she lowered the rifle he would shoot her. She'd caused him more trouble than he could forgive.

But what other choice was there?

Even if she jumped, the road would likely kill her at this pace, let alone the rocks below. And if she let them go, it could mean the doom of everyone she held dear. She had one shot and two targets. Neither would solve her problem, and the other would shoot immediately.

There was no answer. There was no time.

She felt panic flare in her and immediately instinct kicked in.

Underwood, Thornbrook, Rawleigh, Pemberley Cross—

A thought flashed through her mind.

"Pemberley Cross," she said quietly.

"Pardon?" George asked with a smirk.

"Your coach," she replied. "It's a Pemberley Cross."

She lowered the rifle to her side.

And fired.

Lucy Elliot was a very good shot so long as the target was less than ten feet away and not moving.

The shot shattered through the link pin and the axle of the front right wheel. It immediately jammed and, already weakened, splintered away, the front right side of the coach driving directly into the ground.

Propelled by the force, the entire coach catapulted forward, just as the rival coach had done during her first race.

Lucy, at the rear of the coach, was as ready as she could be for such sudden force, kicking out with all the power her legs could muster. Suddenly she was flying, the salt air whipping past her, the dark sea far below. Her upward motion complete, she began to fall, still moving forward, but now down toward the water and rocks. Her dress billowed, catching the air as she went, slowing her ever so slightly. If she hit the rocks, it would make no difference at all. But her gambit had paid off.

With a jarring shock she hit the water. It was still cold in early summer, but the force had thrown her far enough to clear the sea edge.

Spluttering she turned, drawn to the only other light she could see, the twisted remains of the coach, upside down and driven by momentum as it overran the cliff face and plummeted to the rocks below. As this happened she thought she saw a figure drawn behind the remains of the coach, and she heard a panicked howl, as George St. Martin, caught in the reins, was dragged after it. There was a splintering of wood and metal. Then silence and darkness.

Lucy did her best to paddle, though she already felt the cold waters draining the life from her. The canvas of her dress had created several pockets of air, serving her better than any other of her garments might in such circumstances. But Mrs. Calloway had constructed it for durability, not floatation. Lucy kicked and failed and decided that, if she survived, learning to swim would be a good idea.

Floating in the darkness was disorienting, and she was unsure of which way she was facing. Even if she could kick off her boots and swim, she had no idea which way to go.

The dress was losing buoyancy faster now, the waterline rising. It was a shame. Had the dress been waterproofed it should have functioned much better. Waterproofed and sealed. Perhaps some kind of inflatable floatation device.

The water was up to her neck now, but at least the initial sting of the cold was gone, replaced with a dull chill. An inflatable system would have the benefit of greatly reduced storage at sea, but it would still need a means to inflate it, and a consistent body.

She tilted her head back, trying to keep water out of her nose. A loop structure would have strength but also allow someone to hold on to it where a ball would not. But an inflatable loop might have other purposes too.

She kicked frantically to gulp down a breath of air. There simply wasn't time to solve the problem at that moment. Not while she was drowning.

She kicked again, but this time the surface refused to appear. The canvas was weighing her down, the air pockets altogether gone.

She held her breath. There was no other option.

She continued to sink.

Underwood.

Thornbrook.

Rawleigh.

Pemberley Cross.

Norfolk.

She hoped Margaret and Oliver would be happy.

CHAPTER 57

LUCY COUGHED AND SPLUTTERED.

Something thumped her back, and she coughed once more, this time throwing up a mouthful of seawater that burned her throat; the salt and bile stinging.

She sucked in air voraciously, then coughed and choked again.

"Easy. Try to take shallow breaths," said a voice.

There was a fire. She could see the light of it for the first time. It was some distance away, down the rocks, the remains of the St. Martins' coach and lanterns now a blazing bonfire.

She rolled onto her back. The rocks were only slightly less uncomfortable than on her knees. As suggested she drew small breaths.

By the light of the fire she saw James Dashwood seated beside her, looking down at her, a mix of relief and concern on his face.

"You're not wearing a shirt," she thought out loud.

"I'm trying a new look."

"I like it."

Was that a blush on his cheek or just firelight?

She drew herself up, finding a spot on the rocks where she could sit with only mild discomfort.

"Are you cold?" she asked.

"Yes." He chuckled after a brief hesitation.

She reached an arm around his waist, turning to face him, wrapping her arms around him as he did the same for her, their heads resting on each other's shoulder.

She felt the heat of his body, of his breath against her neck. The cold, the damp, the rocks, all seemed to melt away.

They sat that way until help arrived.

It was entirely inappropriate but, given the circumstances, Lucy didn't mind in the slightest.

CHAPTER 58

ᒪUCY ALWAYS FELT OUT OF PLACE AT WEDDINGS.

It was not that she wasn't happy for those involved, but such a large group, with such high emotion, tended to make her uncomfortable. She was pleased to discover that, given a much closer connection to events, she was better able to process that emotion.

Margaret and Oliver looked as beautiful and handsome as could be, their clothes of a fine summer style, a testament to the experience of Mrs. Calloway and Mr. McDonald.

Lucy had seldom seen her sister happier, and there seemed, in the moment, to be a sense of completion about things. Everything, from the flowers to the seating, was precisely how Lucy had imagined it, in no small part thanks to her efforts in planning, and she could find no more fine-tuning to be done.

In the absence of further work to do, and while the pastor was speaking eloquent but familiar words, she found herself reflecting on the recent events that had led them here.

Torres, Elsa, and Hekili had been the first to arrive, following the light of the blazing wreck and glad to discover that their friends had escaped that fate. With the makeshift chain of reins that Dashwood had used to descend the cliff, they drew them upward, Lucy first, and offered a blanket and a coat. Torres's coach was, for the time being, mobile, a remarkable feat given the upper half of it was utterly disintegrated.

Ulcha arrived shortly after, leading a group of men on horseback, Lord Rathbone at the front. Margaret and Oliver had made it to Rathbone Manor, weary and filthy, but unharmed and bearing the urgent news. As swift as Lord Rathbone had been to gather men and ride, the fleeing traitors would have escaped if not for the pursuit of the Night Racers. On reaching the coastal road, Lord Rathbone had recognized the Irish messenger at once and followed her onward, catching up to the rescued pair and the ruined coaches.

There would, Rathbone explained, be politics to be done.

Officially, Sir Walter and George had died in a tragic coach accident. The truth of the matter was an open secret in the district, but it was not spoken of, for the dishonor and shame of the affair was something society preferred to remain unmentioned.

With his father and brother gone, Oliver St. Martin inherited the family estate, in addition to the accumulated debts. He resolved to sell the land, but his savings, and generous wedding gifts from Lord Rathbone and Captain Dashwood helped to settle finances into a manageable state. The next few years would be lean, but neither Oliver nor his new bride were given to excess. There were moments of melancholy when he thought of his lost family, but also moments of happiness when he thought of the one he had gained.

A copy of the cannon design had been retained in London, and there was talk of building more, though Dashwood reported wryly that the sole test firing had been of limited success. The war would not turn overnight, but it would turn, of that he remained confident.

The ongoing business in London had kept him engaged for some time. He exchanged letters with Lucy, sometimes as idle as the itinerary of his day, sometimes as precise as the application of aerodynamics under a coach carriage.

In between letters Lucy had been kept busy with the planning of the wedding. The focus and energy she dedicated to the task was such that she mused one morning that it was good fortune she was required to plan no more than one wedding at a time. That very afternoon a letter arrived inviting her to do just that.

It was, she'd appreciated, eloquent and to the point, such that no hidden meaning or ambiguity might be made of it.

> *My dear Lucy,*
> > *I request your hand in marriage.*
> > > > *Yours, Captain James Dashwood*

In so few words he'd demonstrated that he knew so much of Lucy Elliot that she did not doubt her reply for a moment.

> *My dear James,*
> > *I accept.*
> > > > > *Yours, Lucy Elliot*

That was still in the future, Lucy mused, coming back to herself, seated in the church. There was this wedding to complete first.

There was an exchange of vows, the blessing, the procession, and then the transition to St. Martins Hall, the meal, the dancing, all elements as orderly yet charming as could be wished for. Charlotte Wyndham invited her to visit in Kent, and Lucy agreed, resolving that it might offer an excellent opportunity to learn to swim.

When the evening had moved on, the celebration and the noise and the people becoming slightly uncomfortable, Lucy excused herself to be alone on the patio.

The summer air was warm and still. She stood for several minutes before she heard familiar steps. Where once she might have irked at having her privacy interrupted, now she felt comfort and, of course, that still novel flutter of excitement.

"I hope," said Dashwood, "that I am not too late for a dance."

"You might even have time for two. How was London?"

"Hot. Busy. Crowded."

"That has always been my impression."

"I shall be here at least the week. I thought we might go over the plans for the wedding."

"That would be nice."

The full moon rose slowly above the trees.

"I also received a letter from Dante." He laughed softly. "He says the brandy is excellent and hopes to share a bottle next time we visit. And he is eager for another race."

"Did you come by coach?"

"I did. I hope it is a match to your specifications."

"We shall have to see."

He held out his arm. "Will you ride with me, Lucy?"

She slipped her arm through his, placed her hand upon his, her head on his shoulder. "Yes, James. I'll ride with you."

Surrendering to contentment, she took a deep breath, taking in the scent of lavender and lemongrass, of oranges and opportunity.

She closed her eyes and pictured the road ahead.

ABOUT THE AUTHOR

R. M. Caldwell is based in Hamilton, New Zealand, and writes and directs theater, as well as being on the board of an independent theater.